THE LOST GIRLS

SARAH PAINTER

SISKIN PRESS LIMITED

This is a work of fiction. Names, characters, organisations, places, events, and incidents are either products of the author's imagination or are used fictitiously. Any resemblance to actual persons, living or dead, or actual events, is purely coincidental.

Published by Siskin Press Limited

Cover Design by Stuart Bache

PREFACE

This book is set mainly in Edinburgh and, as such, includes Scots words and dialect such as 'ken' for 'know', as well as the popular Scottish refreshment a 'half and half' (in Scots - 'a hauf and hauf') which comprises a half pint of beer with a dram of whisky on the side.

Although Edinburgh is magical to me, it is a very real place. I have mostly adhered to its current geography, so you can walk in Rose and Mal's footsteps, but have taken a couple of small liberties for the sake of the narrative. For example, I have set the story when the Royal Infirmary hospital was still at its original location near the Meadows.

ALSO BY SARAH PAINTER

The Language of Spells

The Secrets of Ghosts

The Garden of Magic

In The Light of What We See

Beneath The Water

The Night Raven

For my big brother, Matthew,
who always has my back.

PROLOGUE

Françoise had been at her new job for exactly six days and she still kept getting lost. The building of Hôpital Beaujon was a warren of corridors and unexpected staircases, and it always took her three times as long as it should to get from one place to another. She skidded into the emergency department, narrowly avoiding becoming a patient herself.

'Finally,' the administrative assistant said, with a sour little twist of her mouth. 'Cubicle twelve.'

It was always busy in the department so Françoise was not surprised to find she had a patient waiting, but she was a little disappointed. She had missed breakfast in the morning rush and was over an hour late for her lunch break. Maybe she would be able to take five minutes after this appointment to eat a pain au chocolat and drink a quick coffee.

The patient was a young girl. She had glossy black hair kept in a single long braid, wisps of fringe framing

1

her delicate features. Her skin was luminescent and her cheeks rose-pink. Her clear eyes telegraphed health and vitality, and Françoise looked around the cubicle automatically for the girl's companion or small charge. It didn't seem possible that this vision of beauty, with no outward signs of injury, could be her patient.

'I need help,' the girl said. Her French was perfect but there was something off about her accent. She was from the south, perhaps, although southerners were usually darker in skin tone.

'Of course,' Françoise said, pulling over a metal chair on castors and sitting down. 'What can I do for you?'

'You are Françoise Pascal?'

'It is of no matter,' Françoise said. She hadn't been a doctor very long but she'd already become accustomed to the delaying tactics of patients. This girl was probably embarrassed. Perhaps she had genital warts or thought she was pregnant. 'Why don't you tell me why you've come to the hospital today?'

'I have a pain,' the girl said. Her voice was pleasantly low. It sounded like a much older woman and Françoise felt herself leaning forwards, listening more closely.

'Where?' Françoise said, clicking the top of her pen and preparing to make notes.

'Here.' The girl placed her palm onto her chest, over her heart.

'Can you describe it?'

'A pain.'

'Stabbing, dull ache, throbbing, pinching—'

'A pain.'

2

'Any other symptoms? Shortness of breath? Muscle weakness?'

'No. Nothing like that.'

'Okay, well, I'll just take a look at you.' Françoise untangled her stethoscope from around her neck. 'If you could lift your top for me, I'll listen to your heart first.'

She turned to her notes and scribbled, giving the patient a moment to adjust her clothing.

'Françoise?'

'Yes?' She looked up. The girl had lifted her t-shirt, exposing a black bra and more porcelain skin. Françoise was used to bodies, of course, but this girl was mesmerising. It was hard to remain professional, and she felt flustered and idiotic.

She scooted the chair across the floor and put the stethoscope into her ears. She rubbed the disc to warm it up and placed it onto the girl's chest, keeping her gaze locked on the patient's shoulder. Every doctor learned tricks to put the patient at their ease, to demonstrate that however intimate or invasive the scenario, it was business as usual to the medical professional.

Françoise was having difficulty with the heartbeat, and moved the disc. She adjusted the ear buds, making sure they were firmly attached. She was so intent on her work and on appearing professional that she felt, rather than saw, the girl's hands wrap around her throat. She jerked back, shocked, and the stethoscope clattered to the floor.

She had received staff training in handling patient aggression, but it had concentrated on de-escalation and intervention before the patient acted out. Nothing had prepared her for this. The hands around her throat were not large but the grip was surprisingly strong. Françoise tried to break it with her own hands but she couldn't hook her fingers underneath to get any leverage. She made to say something in protest but all that came out was a squeak, the last escaping air from a burst balloon. She grabbed the girl's wrists instead and pulled. It made no difference. Her neck hurt and the pain radiated up and over her skull. The fingers were like metal bands. Françoise was panicking properly now. She wanted to take a breath. She needed to take a breath.

The girl looked horribly calm. She wasn't smiling and there was no spark of excitement in her eyes. She looked, instead, uninterested. Like she was ticking a task from a to-do list. Or carrying out an order. In an awful moment, Françoise realised that, even if she were able to speak, she wouldn't be able to reason with her attacker. She knew with utter certainty that the girl meant to kill her. Was going to kill her.

Françoise forced herself up, kicking the chair away and using her whole body to try and break the grip. The girl held her upright easily, as if she were a fraction of her size, rather than the same height and build. Françoise leaned backwards with all her weight, hoping to pull the girl over, maybe break her grip just enough to pull her hands away and get some air.

The pain she'd felt when the hands had begun squeezing had receded now. It was taken over by the screaming desperation in her mind and stabbing sensation across her chest as her lungs cried out for oxygen.

Her head pounded, then began to swim as if she'd

been punched hard in the temple. With terrifying speed, Françoise felt a kind of calm acceptance. There was a blank whiteness advancing from the right, pulling a curtain across her mind. In the part that was still functioning, she noted the symptoms of oxygen deprivation, listed the side effects and expected time of death. She knew that her windpipe had been compressed. The force of the grip was strong enough. She knew that she didn't have long and that she was actively experiencing brain damage. It was the kind of thing she could've written up for a medical journal if she had the time. There was never any time, though, the days bleeding together in one long helter-skelter ride. She was going faster and faster, and lights were blinking on and off.

Then the curtain swished fully and all was white. Pure blinding white.

CHAPTER ONE

Rose opened her eyes and the world rushed in. Sky. Pavement. Scottish Georgian architecture and a biting edge to the air. The dizziness and disorientation never lasted for long and, sure enough, she was already beginning to feel balanced. She was outside the refurbished 1960s psychology block on George Square, the large panes of glass and slabs of concrete achingly familiar. Her mind was foggy and her eyes stung as if she hadn't slept well, but the world was no longer spinning and the sense of essential wrongness was receding. She shook her head lightly, as if to clear it. She wasn't meant to be here. She had been somewhere else. She had been inside, she was almost sure. Or she had been watching people who were inside. Somewhere very clean and white and with a big curtain which swished on its track...

A group of students walked past her and into the building. Their laughter was too loud and it grated against her nerves, but it made something click. She was Rose MacLeod. She was a student. She had been asleep in bed, or maybe she had been watching a television drama, but then she had passed out and lost a chunk of time. That happened. She did the usual post-blackout check, digging into her pocket and checking the date and time on her mobile phone. The sunlight was as weak as usual but it still felt too bright, and she wished she had remembered her sunglasses. Of course, she couldn't actually remember leaving the house. One moment she had been in bed – she was almost sure she had been in bed – stretching out and feeling the covers slip and slide over her body, and the next she had simply arrived here, in this place.

She had her rucksack, thankfully, and her notepad and favourite mechanical pencil, and the hefty Introduction To Psychology by Gleitman et al. that they were expected to lug to every lecture. That was one thing she couldn't complain about – her blackouts were very efficient. She had no idea how she'd got from her bedroom to the university, or what had happened in the intervening ninety minutes, but she was dressed and had an adequately packed bag. As usual.

Given all of that, it was irrational to feel annoyed that she didn't have her sunglasses. *Bigger picture, Rose.* But that didn't help. The sun was still too bright and she was still irritated by her lack of eye-wear. It wasn't sensible; possibly it wasn't even sane, but she couldn't hold onto the terror she knew she ought to be feeling. It was eclipsed by her annoyance over not having her sunglasses. *Like that was the important detail.* She didn't know if it was some kind of coping mechanism, but perhaps it was true that you could get used to anything if it happened often enough. Or her blackouts were seizures that were steadily destroying her brain.

On that cheerful thought, she pulled up her sleeve to look at her latest tattoo. Even though her phone had already confirmed that she'd only lost an hour or so, she felt the need to check. Ever since the day she'd awoken without her phone or bag and discovered that a couple of weeks had gone by, she'd started having inkless tattoos done. Phones, clocks, even newspapers, felt far too mutable. The evidence of the world around her was slippery and her mind contained terrible blank spaces where memories ought to sit. Something etched onto her own skin, something she couldn't wake up without, seemed like a post to hang onto. A staff in the storm. The inkless tattoo had left a kind of wound which healed from dark red scar tissue, gradually fading to pink, to white over time. Then she'd had another one done. It wasn't much of a sense of control but it was better than nothing. Her fresh tattoo, done only a couple of days ago, stood out red and raw-looking, the edges of the rose raised and slightly sore when pressed. It confirmed that she hadn't been gone for long, that she hadn't missed much time and could trust the lit screen of her phone.

Astrid appeared from around the corner and Rose pulled down her sleeve, hiding the tattoo. Astrid was alone, headphones in and her walk distinctively bouncy and rhythmic. Astrid always looked like she belonged in a music video and this morning was no exception. Her blonde hair glowed in the sunlight and she wore a battered leather jacket over skin-tight jeans and spike-heeled Victorian boots which laced halfway up her calves.

As she approached a boy walking in the opposite direction veered off course and walked into a litter bin at full speed. He bent double with an audible 'oof' sound before falling to the side and ending up on the pavement. Surely he couldn't be drunk at this time in the morning, Rose thought. Although, he was a student. Perhaps breakfast drinking was all the rage. It wasn't as if she would know.

'Am I late?' Astrid popped her earbuds out and glanced at the door.

'No,' Rose smiled. She looked at Astrid and instantly felt fine about everything, even the way she had awoken on the street, fully dressed and ready for the day. She couldn't decide if it was worrying that she wasn't more freaked out. It was nice that her heart wasn't racing, pleasant not to feel panicked, but what if this new calm was a bad sign? What if calmly accepting losing chunks of time and consciousness was actually a sign of madness?

'God, I hate this,' Astrid said as they walked through the main entrance and towards lecture theatre A. 'This guy is so fucking boring.'

Rose nodded but didn't say anything. She never wanted to agree too wholeheartedly when Astrid complained in case she decided to leave university altogether. Then Rose would be completely alone. A terrible thought.

'It's just an hour,' Rose said. 'We can survive anything for an hour.'

Astrid was fiddling with her iPod, not listening. 'I'm so hung-over. I'm never going to get used to hangovers.'

Rose followed her into the theatre and up the stairs to sit in their usual places at the back. Astrid promptly put her head on the desk and closed her eyes. 'Don't let me drink ever, ever again.'

Rose hadn't been with Astrid the night before. She hardly ever went out with her and her enormous group of friends and admirers. Rose was more of a lectures-and-tea kind of friend. Probably the most boring, timid friend Astrid had ever had, in fact. She distracted herself from this depressing thought by opening her notebook and clicking her pencil.

'Too loud,' Astrid said, opening one eye.

'Sorry,' Rose whispered. 'I'll write quietly. Don't think I can stop him, though.'

Professor Lewis wasn't an especially shouty lecturer but he was certainly louder than a mechanical pencil.

He was waiting for the rustling and talking to settle, for students to stop unpacking their bags and opening books. He fiddled with his microphone, angling it towards his face and tapping the top to make sure it was working.

Rose glanced at Astrid, still struggling with the feeling that she had been somewhere else entirely just a few moments ago. All at once it occurred to her that she would be a less boring friend if she told Astrid about her blackouts and memory loss. She could explain that although she knew certain things, like her name and that she lived at number forty-two Bruntsfield Close with her mum and dad, and that Astrid was her best and only friend, there were huge gaps. She knew she was following a joint-honours degree in English Literature and Psychology at the University of Edinburgh and that she was in the first year, but at the same time she didn't quite believe it was true.

She could tell Astrid about the frustrating feeling, right at the edge of her mind, that she wasn't in the right life. That there was another one, a more real and vivid one, just beyond the grey of her student existence.

'Astrid,' she began, speaking quietly. 'Do you ever feel like there's something not real about this place?'

She hadn't meant to say that. Not exactly, but the words were out and now Astrid had lifted her head and was looking at her with a worried expression. She put a hand onto Rose's arm and she felt a little better. The desks were solid and real and the lighting was hurting her eyes and the sound of paper rustling filled her mind, pushing everything else out.

Astrid put her head back down and closed her eyes. 'Concentrate for me, okay?' she said, and Rose obediently looked to the front of the room.

Professor Lewis glanced up at the smart board and then turned to the assembled students, lifting his chin in a signal that the lecture was about to begin. A thin red line appeared on his neck, just above his collar. It was as if an invisible person had taken a red Sharpie and drawn on his skin and, for a second, Rose thought she was imagining it. Then the red line grew thicker, blood welling up along its length and spilling down over the front of the professor's checked blue and white shirt. He slumped to the floor, behind the desk and out of sight.

The sound of his body hitting the floor was a hollow thump, but it acted like a detonator, sending a ripple through the rows of students. Each row fell or screamed, blood flowing from person after person as if caught in some awful game of tag. Rose gripped the edge of the desk, bracing herself for impact, but whatever had rolled through the theatre was nothing more than a breath of air on her cheek. Her hands went to her neck and felt it whole, unmarked, uncut.

The air was filled with the scent of copper and the sounds of people crying, screaming, gasping and gargling. The boy sitting in front of Rose slid to the side, a dead weight that landed unnaturally on the empty seat to the right. Rose put her hand on Astrid's shoulder, panicking now. Astrid wasn't screaming or crying. That meant she must be okay. Like Rose. They were the only ones in the back row, whatever had happened had obviously run out of power before it hit them. They were okay. She felt bad for thinking anything like 'okay' in the circumstances, in the enormous room filled with the dead and dying.

'Astrid?' Her own voice sounded like it was coming from far away. She wasn't sure, actually, whether she'd spoken out loud at all. She shook Astrid's shoulder and that was when she saw it. The blood. It was seeping out from underneath Astrid's folded arms, spreading across the narrow desk. In a moment it would begin to drip onto the floor.

Rose opened her mouth to scream but then the world seemed to jump frames, as if she was watching a film, a film that surrounded her completely. The blood was gone. The sounds of terror were replaced with the sound of Professor Lewis clearing his throat and saying, 'Today we're going to look at cognitive bias.'

Astrid shifted a little, moving her face so that it rested more comfortably on her folded arms. Rose leaned closer, checking the desk, her hair and face. There was no blood. There was no screaming. No crying. Just the sound of scribbling pens on papers, the echoing voice of the professor and a faint electrical hum from the lights and computer equipment.

Rose leaned closer still, catching the scent of shampoo from Astrid's head. She looked perfect. Her skin almost glowed, like an angel in an old painting. Astrid shifted again, and then opened her eyes. They widened and she sat up, grumbling. 'Personal space, Rose. Remember the bubble.'

Rose opened her mouth to say 'everyone was dead a moment ago' but, thankfully, she managed to force the words back down. 'Sorry,' she said, instead. 'I thought I saw a bug on your shoulder. But I didn't. There isn't one. You're fine.'

'And you're weird,' Astrid said. She closed her eyes. 'More than usual, I mean.'

When Mal Fergusson was seven, his father taught him

how to spot a demon. 'Look at their eyes,' he said. 'They're dead inside and if you look, really look, you'll see it.'

Seven-year-old Mal had accepted this as truth but, when he got a little older, he began asking questions. Did demon eyes look different? Were they a particular colour? And what about the rest of their bodies? Were they unnaturally pale or tall, or did they have long fingernails or teeth?

'They look like us,' his father had replied. 'Like us, only wrong. The hair will stand up on the back of your neck.' He touched Mal's neck, and that brief contact had cemented the moment in Mal's mind.

Since his father's instruction when meeting one of these creatures was to stab it through the heart with a silver knife, Mal rather thought that there should be more of a test than 'makes my hair go prickly' but he didn't say anything. That would've been insubordination and his father didn't respond well to any hint of disrespect.

Once he was hunting regularly, Mal soon realised that his father's advice had been correct. No matter how flimsy it sounded as a tool for diagnosis, there was something undeniable about demons. You just knew. In fact, Mal found it almost impossible to believe that civilians couldn't tell. His questions changed from 'How can you tell it's a demon?' to 'How can you not?' How could they be so blind? 'They don't want to see,' his father had said. 'And I don't blame them.'

Walking across the Meadows with some rare sunshine lighting up Arthur's Seat and pretty students sitting on the grass with giant plastic cups of iced coffee, Mal conceded that his dad had had a point. If he could press a rewind button on his life and make it so he had never been trained, had never found out what it felt like to stare into a demon's eyes and see pure evil staring right back, he would hit it so hard and so fast.

But there was no such button. Proof, as if Mal needed it, was waiting for him in the Royal Infirmary. It had been five years since his big brother entered the place, and at least four since Mal had felt the slightest hope that he would ever leave it. Mal didn't let himself miss a visit, although he switched the days in case anybody unfriendly was watching his movements. He didn't think that Euan was a high priority for any of the nasties he and his family had bumped up against, but that was the problem with his line of work; it made you paranoid.

The familiar antiseptic smell of the hospital filled his nose and he felt his shoulders tense in readiness. It never got any easier. Never became routine. Euan wasn't asleep. You didn't need to be medically trained to see that. The gentle wheeze of the respirator and the muted beep of the life signs machine were enough of a clue, even if you were likely to mistake the unnatural stillness of the figure in the bed. Mal knew that he ought to sign the paperwork and let them turn the machines off and, before every visit, he told himself that he would, but once he got there he just couldn't do it. He was a coward.

The nurses were always so friendly, so kind. They didn't give any hint of judgement. Not about the fact that he only visited once a month, or that he hadn't given them the ability to free up a bed in the ward. Now Emily, one of the regulars, ran through Euan's care plan, as if it made difference. 'He had a wee pressure sore on his right leg, but we've got it under control,' she said.

Mal asked, as he always did, 'Is he in any pain?'

'No, dear. He's well dosed.' She patted his hand and Mal felt like a fraud. He didn't deserve her sympathy. He ought to do the right thing and let Euan go.

In the beginning, before the words 'nothing more we can do' and 'keep him comfortable', Mal had stayed in the hospital, refusing to leave. Then, he'd visited every day. Then every other day, and, after the realisation that Euan wasn't about to open his eyes and ask for breakfast, every week. After missing a couple of visits, Mal had officially allowed himself to switch to monthly trips. He'd told himself that Euan didn't know any different; that, as the doctor had carefully explained in her refined Edinburgh accent, his higher brain functions were gone, his essential Euan-ness had left the building.

Still, the guilt endured. What if he knew? What if, despite the medical science which said otherwise, he was trapped in there somehow? In the old days, people used to call bodies 'soul cases'. What if Euan's was still that? A case for his soul, keeping it safe and happy? What if he switched off the machine and destroyed that haven, dooming Euan's soul to some unknown torment?

All of this was made rather more difficult by the fact that Mal wasn't even sure there was such a thing as the soul. His father had believed that the soul was the fundamental difference between demons and humans, and that their lack of one was what made demons evil. However, Mal couldn't help noticing that demons didn't exactly have a monopoly on doing bad things.

Today, Euan was neatly shaved as usual. It didn't matter how many times Mal told them that his brother had never been clean-shaven in his life, it seemed to be a policy and, as such, inviolable.

Mal greeted him with a louder-than-necessary 'hello' and a squeeze of the arm. He thought the shape underneath the cotton pyjama top was thinner than last time, although he couldn't be sure.

He pulled the visitor's chair closer to the bed and then spent an inordinate amount of time adjusting its position, taking off his jacket and sitting down. Once he was in place, he knew, there was nothing to do. He had bought a paper in the WHSmith downstairs, and now began reading from it, feeling self-conscious as always. Euan wouldn't have read this paper when he was awake; why should he care now?

Still, he persevered. In the beginning, he'd read that speaking out loud to coma patients was important, that you should never assume they couldn't hear you, as medical science couldn't be certain what was getting through or when a person might regain a level of consciousness. The doctors didn't talk about levels of consciousness anymore. They gently reiterated that Euan's condition was unlikely to improve, and, if pushed, they would admit that 'unlikely' was only a way of covering their arses. The more proper term was 'never'. They would slip a pamphlet across the table or pat him on the shoulder while murmuring that it might be time for him to consider his brother's options. More euphemism. Euan had no options. It was bed or death. What Mal would never admit to the doctor – could hardly admit to himself – was this: he lived in hope. Not only did you read about people waking up from thirty-year-long comas with no apparent ill effects (very, very occasionally, but still), but medical science was continually improving and developing. Added to this was the nagging feeling that one day, somehow, Mal would stumble across some piece of spellwork that would bring his brother back. He wasn't supposed to ask questions, but sometimes Pringle would ask him to retrieve or deliver an item that was clearly not mundane. An amulet that exuded power, or a stone that shone with a colour he had never seen before and made his eyes hurt to look at for too long. Surely, eventually, he would come into contact with something powerful enough to heal Euan.

After the hour had ticked by on the clock and Mal felt like he could reasonably leave, he folded the paper and put it on the bedside table, took the chair back to its original place and kissed Euan on the forehead. It was a parental gesture. Not that his father had ever kissed him – on the forehead or anywhere else – but Mal liked to think that Euan felt the affection of the touch. Maybe it infused his dreams with a mother figure or a more caring, gentle father. One who had taken him to football matches and the cinema, rather than for knife-throwing practice.

Outside the hospital, Mal stood for a moment, breathing the cool city air. There was something about visiting the hospital that made him feel very alive. It added to his guilt, but he couldn't help it. He took a moment, performing the adjustment from one world to the other, and then set off towards the Grassmarket. He had work to do.

CHAPTER TWO

Eve flipped backwards, her knees securely hooked over the bar. She let her body hang, feeling the blood rush to her head. The tent upside down was a familiar sight, comforting. The sawdust on the ground so far below gave her no fear whatsoever. She had been working the trapeze for a year. No, for years. She couldn't remember not doing it. She swung around and over, putting her legs out straight on the top loop and doing a brief, mid-air handstand before letting gravity and momentum swing her around. She sat on the bar, the spinning in her mind like an old friend. She spent so much time on the ropes that she felt more off balance when she was on the ground.

She took a breath and swung herself upside down again, using her legs to make the trapeze move, building up momentum until she was carving wide pendulum arcs. The air rushed past her body and vertiginous views swooped with her, the beige canvas coming closer at the extreme edges of her swing. Then, in the space between one blink and the next, the canvas changed from beige to deep red. No, she thought. Not again. As the walls swung past and her head spun, she lunged for the platform and hooked the safety line. She waited, pulse pounding, until her vision cleared and her ears stopped ringing. The blood was rushing in her ears and she felt sick. The walls were billowing red silk and she wasn't wearing her warm-up costume of black Lycra. Instead, she had a silvery costume covered with pale pink and blue sequins in a harlequin pattern. She forced her arms and hands to work, to climb down the ladder. She felt possessed with the need to get onto the ground, to lie down before she fell.

As soon as her feet touched the sawdust she knew the arena wasn't empty. A black shape unfolded from the shadows. It was a figure, moving quickly, arms outstretched and a silver shape held rigid and pointing. A second later, she fell backwards. Something had hit her in the chest. It was a solid blow like from a tree branch, but instead of a bruising pain, she felt a burning whiteness in the centre of her chest. Looking down, she didn't see white smoke or flames or even a massive wound, but a bloody red stain spreading out from a hole. And then there was nothing.

Rose was in the dining room in her house. The curtains were drawn, and billowing as if the window was open and there was a stiff breeze. The walls were moving in the same way, as if they were made of material too, and it gave her motion sickness. Her mother was standing in the corner, her back to Rose. She was wearing a coat as if she was just about to go outside.

Rose was frightened. She didn't know why, but she was frightened that her mother would turn around. She felt as if she was in trouble for something, that she was about to get told off. A feeling like that, but magnified by several thousand. She dug her nails into her palms. She was dreaming. She knew this wasn't real. She was asleep and all she had to do was wake up. She gouged her nails deeper, willing the pain to form a bridge back to reality.

Slowly, her mother began to turn. She rotated slowly and smoothly, not like a person but like an object spun by an invisible hand. Rose knew she was going to scream before her mother turned fully to face her. She knew, in that dream logic way, that the figure wasn't really her mother and that what she was going to see would be very bad. But the foreknowledge didn't help her, didn't stop the horrible shock. The figure was her mother but it didn't have a face. Instead, there was a greyish puffy substance like uncooked dough.

Rose's mouth filled with saliva and she tasted vomit. Her mother raised her hands slowly, as if asking to be hugged. Then her dough face began to bubble and pop, as if the heat had been turned up. The substance began to slide away from her neck; it was doubling in size, growing and slipping all at once.

Rose couldn't close her eyes. No matter how much

she didn't want to see her mother's skull appearing beneath the goo, she was dreaming and no one is allowed to close their eyes in a dream. Instead, she screamed and the dream changed.

She felt herself tip backwards and, suddenly, she was falling. She could smell sawdust and feel air rushing past her body. She woke up before she hit the ground, her heart thudding and sweat cooling on her skin.

Daylight was shining through a gap in her bedroom curtains and her phone said it was morning, the day after she had gone to sleep. That was a relief. She checked her tattoo, just to be sure, and got out of bed to shower and dress. Her hands shook as she squeezed shampoo into her palm and she felt dizzy with the leftover adrenaline.

She only had one lecture that day – cognitive psychology at eleven. She forced herself to go through the motions. She listened to the lecturer and took notes, pushing down the panic of the previous day and the sick taste of fear left from her bad dream. She considered, for what felt like the hundredth time, that perhaps she ought to see a doctor about her strange symptoms. Or perhaps it was stress. That was what happened to students, it was well known. There were posters up around the university screaming about mental health. She had been hitting the books too hard. Perhaps she needed to go to one of the yoga classes at the union.

What would really help, the only thing that she felt would help, would be seeing Astrid. When the lecture was over, she packed her bag and went to find her friend. Astrid worked every Tuesday in the ticket booth for the

Edinburgh ghost tours, right at the entrance to Greyfriar's Kirk.

The weak spring sun shone on the Grecian-inspired McEwan Hall, and brightly-dressed students flocked across the paved slabs of the newly-developed Bristo Square. The light transformed the city's buildings, making them beautiful with the blue sky as a contrast to the grey stone.

Outside the green-painted front of the art shop, an entwined couple barged her off the pavement onto the road. She turned around to say something cutting to their retreating backs, but the sight of their tilted heads, their bodies forming both a question and an answer, made her throat close up.

Ignoring a gaggle of tourists visiting Greyfriar's Bobby, Rose waved at the statue of the little dog and turned into the Kirkyard. The Gothic architecture and wrought-iron gate of Greyfriar's Kirk looked almost cheerful with its backdrop of pale blue sky.

Astrid was slumped in the little wooden booth, her head resting on her folded arms. All Rose could see was a waterfall of corkscrew curls and her elbows.

'It's a miracle you haven't been fired.' Rose poked one of the elbows.

Astrid sat up, blinking slowly. She stretched her arms above her head and yawned. 'Late one last night. It was epic. You should've come with.'

'Let me in.' Rose knocked on the wall. 'It's freezing.'

Astrid scooted back and unlocked the door.

Inside, Rose was enveloped in the good smell of planed wood and linseed oil. It was like a shed designed by a goth gardener, with an odd pointed roof and a hatch in the front to serve customers. Pins were shoved through customer receipts and notes directly into the tongue-and-groove walls, and a travel kettle was balanced on top of a stack of old catalogues.

Astrid shoved a fake eyeball at Rose. 'Squidgy face part?'

'No, thanks. I'm good.'

'Only fifty pence,' Astrid said, examining the rubber. 'They're not selling though.'

'I wonder why.'

At that moment a shuffling figure appeared on the main path. 'Your best pal's arrived.'

'Christ on a bike.' Astrid rolled her eyes extravagantly.

'Gotta give him props for perseverance,' Rose said. 'Consistency is very underrated.'

The figure arrived at the booth. He had grey hair, slightly too long and plastered to his scalp with grease. The tramlines left by a comb made Rose's stomach turn over.

'What time is the tour?'

Astrid snapped her gum. 'You know fine well, Robbie.'

'Does it go underground?' The man licked cracked lips. 'I'm particularly interested in Mary King's Close. If it doesn't go to Mary King's Close then I'm not interested.'

Astrid pointed to the poster lying on the counter between them. It said 'Mary King's Close tour: Experience the forgotten city.'

The man glanced at the paper and then fixed his unnerving stare back at Astrid. 'I need to know if it goes underground. I only—'

'You've taken the tour before. You know exactly—'

'No I haven't.'

'Fine.' Astrid gave a quick sigh. 'Do you want a ticket or not? Tour starts at seven prompt.'

'Are you doing it?'

'Sure am,' Astrid said. She snapped her gum again and gave Robbie a wide smile.

He put a crumpled ten pound note on the counter and Astrid replaced it with a small rectangle of red paper.

They watched in silence as Robbie retreated back through the graveyard. Rose didn't know how Astrid coped with the job – she seemed to have a revolving set of stalkerish fans. When she looked at Astrid, though, her friend was watching Robbie leave with a curious expression of satisfaction on her face.

After a moment, Astrid turned to Rose. 'So. To what do I owe the pleasure?'

'You missed cognitive psych again.'

'Crap. He didn't notice, did he?'

'No, but—'

Astrid relaxed back on her stool, resting against the wall of the booth. 'Don't do that to me.'

'What about the essays? The exam?'

Astrid waved one hand. 'It'll be all right.'

'How?' Rose frowned. 'Seriously. I'm worried about you.'

Astrid laughed, then shot a hand up to cover her mouth.

Rose tried not to be hurt, but in that moment Astrid looked like a stranger. With her blonde curls and flawless white skin, and her wide, toothy grin, she looked like every scary pretty girl Rose had been teased by at school. Something tilted and a tiny voice at the back of Rose's mind said, 'That's not your memory. You don't remember going to school.'

'I'm sorry.' Astrid made a visible effort to compose herself. 'You're right. I need to be more careful.'

She pulled out a packet of chewing gum and offered it to Rose. The smell of cherry menthol cut across Rose's sudden confusion. And then something else occurred to her – the sweet, medicinal scent had been in her nightmare last night, overlaid by the cloying pine of sawdust. Had Astrid been in her dream? Rose's heart was hammering.

'You okay?'

'Just tired,' Rose said. 'I had a bad dream last night.'

Astrid popped a fresh piece of gum into her mouth. 'Tell all.'

'No way.' Rose shook her head. 'I'm not one of those boring people who foist their subconscious onto others.'

'But I'm interested. Really.'

'What time does your shift end?'

Astrid slumped back onto the counter. 'Fine. Don't tell me.'

Rose thought about going home alone and going to sleep. Fractured images, her mother's face melting, blood spreading across the floor of the lecture theatre. She kept her face carefully controlled. Maybe Astrid was right. Maybe alcohol was the answer. 'I was thinking we could go out. To the pub, maybe.'

Astrid sat up again, her face very suddenly wide awake. 'I beg your pardon?'

Rose shrugged. 'I just thought it would be nice. Time I tried some new experiences.'

'What have you done with the real Rose MacLeod?' Astrid was smiling, but it didn't look right. Strained. Rose felt her stomach swoop, just as it had in her dream. In an instant nothing looked right and Rose was falling through air, the scent of sawdust thick in her nostrils, choking her. Astrid's smile had turned to a frown and Rose realised that she had taken too long to answer. She was being weird, and if she was weird she might lose Astrid forever. She forced a smile of her own. 'You're always on at me to go out. I don't see what the fuss is about.' She pushed the bad dream to the back of her mind. She wasn't about to tell Astrid that her nightmares had been so horrific recently that she was willing to endure anything to put off going to sleep.

'We could go for a quick drink,' Astrid said cautiously.

'Great.' Rose worked hard at appearing casual, normal. 'I'll see you later.' Then she remembered. 'Oh, hang on. You're doing a tour.'

Astrid frowned. 'No I'm not.' Then her face cleared. 'Oh, I just told Robbie that so he'd buy a ticket. It's Thomas tonight.'

'He's going to be disappointed.'

29

'Fuck it. Crazy bastard has been on my tour twenty three times and every time he swears blind it's his first.'

Across the city, Mal pushed away from the wall where he'd been leaning for the past twenty minutes. The afternoon sun was hidden behind layers of grey cloud shrouding the city in early darkness, and the wind felt as if it was blowing directly from Siberia. His shoulder was frozen through like a joint of meat in a giant fridge. He pushed that particular image away and stamped his feet to get some feeling back into them.

He'd followed his target from The Royal Mile, down to the west end of Princes Street and into the New Town. He had dodged shoppers and office workers, keeping the target in sight until they hit a less affluent part of the west end. Eventually, the mark slowed at a small row of shops – a kitchen-goods emporium that looked like it had made a big mistake in its location, a second-hand store selling vintage tat and collectibles of dubious value, and a kebab shop with luminous yellow and orange signage.

The target ducked into the second-hand store, where Mal couldn't follow. It was a small shop with nowhere to conveniently loiter without drawing attention. He knew the place, and knew that behind the grimy front door there was a cluttered room with all viewing angles covered from behind the counter with a series of mirrors. The owner was a dirty-haired misanthrope who, on Mal's previous visit, had thrown him out for not buying anything after fifteen minutes of browsing.

The target emerged just as Mal was resettling himself against the wall. Thankfully, he continued into the smaller, residential streets behind the shops, the crowds finally thinning out. He was keeping a normal pace and seemed unconcerned, but Mal followed him for a few minutes longer, making sure he was alone. He'd jumped a demon once only to realise that there were four more in the vicinity. That had been a close run and not something he wanted to repeat. He was older now, and far wiser. He'd made it to thirty, an age he never thought he'd see, and that was down to his strength, combat skills, and hyper-vigilance. The target turned down a side street and Mal increased his pace a little. He walked past the turning, glancing casually as he did so. The target was closer than he expected, so he continued across the junction before doubling back to the side street.

The target had disappeared.

Mal loped down the street, cursing silently. The target must've entered one of the houses – tall town houses with several flats in each. He had no way of knowing which, although he'd guess it would be nearby. There hadn't been time for the target to get far down the street. Mal carried on walking, keeping his pace regular and his posture seemingly relaxed. Body language was ninety per cent of successful close surveillance. And the other ten per cent was pure luck, he thought, seeing a front door that was ajar. He walked on a little further before stopping and pulling a piece of paper out of his pocket, pretending to consult it. He was just a regular guy, checking a friend's address before visiting. He turned back, preparing to check out the house more thoroughly, when he caught a movement surprisingly close and dodged just in time to escape a blow to the head.

Mal had his knife out and his balance back in time to block another attack, the target close enough for him to headbutt and then place a knee into the soft part of his lower belly. The good thing about demons was that they had the same anatomy as humans, the same weak spots. Mal brought his knife up in an arc, slicing the man-shape vertically through the chest, then stepped behind him, looping an arm around his shoulders to pull him close, a parody of an embrace. He drew the knife across the demon's neck quickly and deeply and then stepped away, letting the body fall to the ground.

There were lights in the windows of the houses and Mal didn't know whether anybody had called the police. In a residential area like this, it was a fair bet that they had. If he thought he'd been unobserved, he usually cleaned up after himself, moving the body, burning it in the woods and power-washing the ground. It felt like the right thing to do, rather than leaving the unpleasant task for some other poor bastard. He couldn't risk hanging about now though, so he dipped down and quickly frisked the body, trying to avoid kneeling in the pooling blood. The demon was wearing super-skinny jeans and it was obvious there was something in the right hip pocket. It was tightly wedged, so Mal helped matters by slicing through the fabric. The object was a small, smooth stone, dull black and with a bronze-coloured pin stuck to the back, making it into an ugly brooch.

To most folk it wouldn't look like precious bounty,

but Mal had ceased to be surprised by the things Pringle and his other clients asked him to procure. That was the thing with powerful objects – they so rarely looked the way you'd expect. He pocketed the brooch and moved away from the mess of gore. Not for the first time, he wished that demons would obligingly turn into dust or burn up of their own accord when vanquished. That would be civic-minded of the things.

He headed back into town, to his favourite bar. It was dark and unpretentious and filled with the kind of hardcore drinkers who kept to themselves. He ducked into the cramped bathroom, the first turning before the bar area, and washed the blood from his hands. He avoided his face in the mirror.

His clothes didn't seem badly stained. Nothing was showing up on the black, anyway, and he congratulated himself on his forethought. If he'd driven the knife into the guy from the front, up underneath his ribs, then he would have fallen onto Mal and bled all over him. From behind was much cleaner.

The girl behind the bar was new. She smiled toothily at him. 'What can I get for you?'

He surprised himself by ordering a half and half and, moments later, depressed himself with the realisation that it was the drink of choice of the sad clientele. He drank it anyway, and flipped open his old Nokia to call the client. Once upon a time, he'd been a man on a mission. He'd been his father's son, fighting the righteous fight. Now, his father was dead and he was working for the man. The man with the money. Any man or woman with the cash, or, at a push, any demon. He preferred to kill the supernatural, but he wasn't above working for them. He realised that his beer had already gone, and knocked back the remains of his whisky. The phone lay in his hand like a dead thing. He rolled his shoulders and reminded himself that he didn't feel anything, but he still couldn't make himself press the call button.

Tomorrow, he decided. He would call Pringle in the morning. He ordered another round and made automatic small talk with the barmaid, letting the sounds of the bar wash over him. Tonight, he was celebrating another successful job. Another payment into his account. Although what those payments were ever going to amount to, he didn't know. Suddenly he felt like shit. He could feel his mood sliding downwards so he made himself move from the bar stool with its comforting proximity to alcohol, and go out into the street. The cool night air helped to sober him up. Not that he was drunk. He didn't get drunk. He got numb on occasion, a little bit Pink Floyd his brother called it. The big geek.

Despite most *definitely* not being drunk, his feet weren't behaving themselves, and they found every crack in the pavement. Once, they even found a short flight of steps leading into a closed shop, and he went down on one knee for a few seconds. How many 'hauf and a haufs' had he had? Enough to make several wholes, he guessed, although he couldn't remember.

A group of girls with short dresses and high heels staggered past, their voices piercing and their good humour brittle and ready to break. He didn't need the sight to know they'd be vomiting later, but knew he didn't exactly have the high moral ground. The sky above the curve of coloured buildings on Cockburn Street was dark, a couple of stars struggling to twinkle through the light pollution. He made it to the Royal Mile and across the bridge, patting Bobby on the head before dropping down into the Grassmarket. The tall buildings seemed to be leaning down over him, like disappointed parents.

It was quieter here. The stag and hen parties wouldn't really be out in force until the weekend, and the shoppers and after-work quick-drink crowd had long ago gone home. He was just thinking that it was a good thing he wasn't the kind of person who had to be worried about spookily quiet, dark, narrow streets when something very heavy hit him in the back of the head and he went down. All was darkness. No stars.

Mal felt the pain in his head before anything else, but that was quickly followed by its equally strong friends in his back, ribs and arms. He badly wanted to open his eyes, but he could feel that his arms were pinned behind him and that he was seated, interrogation-style. He had the sinking feeling that with the opening of his eyes would begin a new set of horrors, and was in no particular hurry to bring them forth. He was thinking things through, of course, but his planning and assessment was strangely calm and that was somehow worse. He would've thought that the horrible numbness of recent months ought to be banished by a situation like this. He ought to be frightened. If not terrified, then at least mildly alarmed, but there was nothing. I might die, he thought, trying to goad himself into wakeful anxiety. Fine, the thought came back. That would be fine.

After a few moments and still alive, he focused on his situation. It was quiet. He hoped he was alone, perhaps tied up and left somewhere, but it was also possible that an array of bad people were lined up in front of him, just waiting for him to be conscious enough to respond satisfactorily to a beating. Or torture. He'd had some of that before and wasn't anxious to revisit the experience. The thought was enough to clear away the fug of nothingness and he felt a spark of irritation. He wasn't supposed to have to deal with this kind of shit any more. That was part of the fucking point of being a gun for hire. Everything was supposed to be neat and businesslike, with none of the messy old vendettas and grudge matches and taking sides.

There wasn't a lot of light in the room or cave or wherever he was. Unless he was blindfolded. He cracked an eyelid, half expecting the soft brush of material against his lashes. Nope, nothing.

He risked opening his eyes a little further and, when nothing either jumped into focus or hit him in the face, he took a proper look. The lighting was dim, just a trickle coming in through a gap in the curtains. Heavyweight curtains, floor-length. Fancy.

His insides contracted with relief when Pringle walked in. He was wearing the same clothes as usual – a pale pink, fine knit jumper with a tiny embroidered leaping stag in the upper right corner, and beige chinos. His expression was mild and inexpressive, and everything from his light brown hair and blue eyes to his smoothly shaved skin and unremarkable features was designed to be instantly forgettable. Mal had tried, once, to recreate an image of Pringle in his mind when not actually looking at him, and it had been impossible.

'What the fuck?' Mal was aiming for bored irritation, but he was worried that fear had bled into his voice.

He heard a sound and realised that there was at least one person stood behind him. Mal told himself not to tense up. If he was going to get hit, it would be better if he stayed relaxed. Your body absorbed the blow better, minimised the damage. That was the theory, anyway.

'I'm sorry about this,' Pringle said. 'But there's been a mix-up.'

Relief flooded through Mal's body. 'I'd say so.'

'You targeted the wrong being.'

He took a second to process the words then said, stupidly, 'What?'

'My friend is rather upset, and so this,' Pringle waved his hand around the room, encompassing Mal tied to the chair, the goon behind him, the array of wicked-looking silverware on the side table, 'is required. For the look of things. You understand?'

'I didn't get the wrong one. I never get the wrong one.' That was why he had no trouble getting the work. He had a nose for the supernatural. He could hone in on a demon or a shape-shifter or a lupine or even a bloody piskie without breaking a sweat. It was a rare trait in a human, according to his father. He ignored the habitual prick of his conscience. He was well-practised at ignoring the little reminders of his dad and was very careful not to think about what his dad would say if he knew about his son's chosen profession.

'I'm afraid you rather did.' Pringle shook his head regretfully.

'I didn't kill a human. There was no mistake.' Mal hoped that was true. Killing an innocent bystander. A human being. That would be a new low, even for him.

'Not human, but not the target. You were supposed to retrieve an object, yes?'

'I did,' Mal said. 'It's in my pocket. Or it was before I got clubbed.'

Pringle inclined his head and Mal felt a hand pushing into the pocket of his jeans. 'My jacket pocket,' he said hurriedly, before the investigation turned more personal than was necessary. Again, the relief flowed through him as the disembodied hand produced the brooch he'd taken from the demon corpse and delivered it to Pringle.

'This isn't the object,' Pringle said. 'It's interesting, though.' The brooch disappeared.

'Honest mistake,' Mal said, a spark of panic igniting. He took a conscious slow breath and looked into Pringle's eyes. 'I've never let you down before. Give me another chance and I'll make it right. Sort it.'

'Absolutely you will,' Pringle said. He attempted a smile, and the thing that lived inside Mr Pringle became briefly visible. It wasn't pretty. Then he nodded to the unseen figure behind Mal and turned to leave.

'Wait,' Mal began, but whatever he had been going to say was cut off by the sound of his neck snapping violently to the side with the first blow.

Mal was dropped outside his flat in Bruntsfield. Pringle was a class act like that. The full service beating. He staggered on the pavement, his legs not quite holding him up. He put a hand on the wall to steady himself and felt a sharp pain in his chest. He waited until the car had gone before going inside, even though they clearly knew where he lived.

Inside, he was hit by the smell of old milk. He'd left some out on the counter in the kitchen after making a mug of tea, and the place was filled with the sour odour. The birds were furious with him, they flew around dive-bombing his head and shoulders. One landed on his head and began pecking through his hair, its tiny claws gripping his scalp painfully like a reproach.

'Easy,' Mal said, reaching out a finger to stroke the head of a chaffinch which had landed on his forearm and was attempting to eat his cuff. The bird twisted its tiny head and tweeted indignantly before flying to the top of the bookcase.

A brightly coloured bird of paradise with iridescent green and yellow wings which tapered to a deep indigo at the tips regarded him balefully from the IKEA table which served as his desk, dining area and tool bench. 'I'm sorry, Monty.' He spread his arms wide. 'I got held up.'

Monty let out a screech that could've stripped the paint off a Ford Focus at twelve paces.

Mal gave up and concentrated on cleaning the kitchen instead. He looked away as the chunks of sour milk slopped into the sink and tried not to think about how close he'd come to disaster.

His new brief contained new information. It wasn't fair that he hadn't been given these details previously, but fairness wasn't a big part of his world so he didn't sweat it. You don't miss what you never had.

He shook out a handful of seed and went back into the living room to feed the birds. They didn't need to eat and most of them didn't bother, but a couple – like Monty – seemed to enjoy the nostalgia trip. Mal had brought the birds home after he disposed of their owner. They were charmed creatures, technically dead, and could probably have survived alone indefinitely, but Mal found he couldn't just shut the door. Entombing them in the fetid basement he had found them in didn't seem right. Monty hopped along the table and pecked at his hand, getting more skin than seed. 'I said I'm sorry,' Mal said, not even caring that he was talking to a bird. He'd read an article once that said people with pets were better adjusted than those without.

There wasn't anything left to eat apart from crackers and a softening apple, so he fixed a plate of those and opened a beer. Then he settled into the top-brand leather recliner he'd rescued from a target's house and clicked on the television. He ate his dinner and drank his beer and tried his best to ignore the pain in his ribs. That bastard had cracked at least one. He tried not to think about how it was going to hurt like a mother every time he coughed for the next three months. He made a mental note – no coughing. Got it.

He occupied himself in this manner, watching a

crime drama and eating his meagre supper and drinking a second beer and swallowing a few painkillers before falling asleep in his chair. It wasn't much of a homecoming, but – the thought drifted in as he lost consciousness – he was still alive. He felt the brush of feathers against his cheek, and he slept.

CHAPTER THREE

The grey morning light hit the plastic-coated armchairs in the day room. It reflected off the speckled ceiling tiles, the crisp packets that sat in a sad pile on the low central table, and the pool of yellow vomit that was spreading slowly across the industrial carpeting. Aislinn closed her eyes and remained very still. She didn't want to see the orderlies as they hauled Big Paul off to his room, or Big Paul's twisted features, miserable and desperate. Most of all, though, she didn't want to catch one of the nurses' eyes and be asked to 'be a poppet and help clean up'.

Even with her eyes shut, however, Aislinn couldn't stop the mind pictures. She could see the scene just as clearly as if she were watching. She put her hands over her ears but it didn't shut out Big Paul's wailing, the grunts of the male orderlies as they struggled to heft him out of the room, the squeak of the swing door and, underneath it all, Wee Al's stream of profanity.

After it was over, she put her hands back into her lap. Covering her ears might be considered a sign of distress and she didn't want the nurses to calm her down. Aislinn felt a hand creep into her own and stifled the urge to pull it away. The hand was small and slightly damp and Aislinn gave it a gentle squeeze. The hand squeezed back and Aislinn gave up the darkness and opened her eyes. It was Mary, one of the old dears of the institution. There were a few who'd been put away when they were just girls and they didn't know any other life. Whether they'd been nuts to start with or the institutions had sent them that way was debatable.

'He's not very well today,' Mary said, nodding towards the swinging door through which Big Paul had so recently exited.

'No,' Aislinn agreed. She wanted to disentangle her hand, but she didn't want to offend Mary. She was a nice enough nutter. Older than God, too.

Mary's legs dangled off the edge of her chair, her feet inches off the ground. With her green Alice band, messy white hair and pop socks, she looked like an incredibly wrinkled child. 'I'm not very well.' Her mouth turned down at the corners. 'I've got a pain.'

'Oh dear,' Aislinn said vaguely. She inched her hand away but Mary tightened her grip, leaning forward in an alarming way. Her face was suddenly inches from Aislinn, the sour-milk smell of her breath blasting into her face, the yellow gunk in the corners of her rheumy eyes unpleasantly close. 'I'm possessed,' Mary whispered. 'By Beelzebub.' A gob of spittle shot out of her mouth.

Aislinn pulled her hand smartly away and got up.

'Fuck. Shit. Bollocks.' Wee Al's litany was still going. He rocked back and forth, tapping his hands on his knees after every sixth back and forth. Business as usual, in other words. 'Fuck. Shit. Satan,' he said now.

Aislinn didn't look at him and she didn't look back at Mary, who had started to cry. Big sobbing gasps like a toddler denied an ice cream.

'It's nearly Countdown,' one of the orderlies said brightly as Aislinn walked past. 'You like Countdown.'

Aislinn didn't bristle at the condescending tone. Truth was, she no longer even registered it. Besides, she appreciated the woman's kindness – it was true, she did like Countdown – but she was done. Totally fucking done. She had counted the ceiling tiles in every room in the hospital, she had taught herself to play chess, learned to read and write in French – although she'd never tried speaking it, and spent more time than she cared to count in therapy. Personal therapy. Group therapy. Art therapy. Movement therapy. As Aislinn walked to her room, she counted her steps. One of her little habits. And when she got to her door she joined her hands and lightly tapped her fingertips together, one by one from the pinky to thumb. It was a trick she'd learned from a girl called Becky, who'd stayed in Mackinnon two years ago. It was true, there was nothing like a mental hospital to make you mad.

Feeling calmer, she pushed open the door and let her room embrace her. This was the closest thing she had to a sanctuary. Not the actual room, which she shared with another girl, and not even the bed itself, but what it represented. After lights out, when the hospital quietened down and the routine of therapy and visitors disappeared and the residents were stashed in their rooms, sedated for the most part to ensure a good night's sleep, Aislinn transformed her bed into a magic carpet. She closed her eyes and went travelling. She went to the jungles of Borneo and talked to the orangutans, she put on a sharp business suit and travelled first class to London to meet with government officials on secret missions, she sang on the West End stage and made grown men weep with the beauty of her voice, and, sometimes, she shrank down to a child again. A blonde child this time, rosy cheeked and perfect in every way. And she had dinner with her imaginary family – a mum, a dad, an annoying little brother and a faithful family dog that sat under the table begging for scraps and farting vociferously.

Now she lay on the hard mattress and stared at the ceiling. She calmed her breathing and concentrated on leaving her body, floating away. Her breathing slowed and her vision blurred and, when the buzzer that signalled tea time sounded, she felt a stab of self-congratulation. Another hour successfully passed. Another hour down.

Tea was a three-course meal. It invariably began with soup. Thick, gelatinous, grey soup. Mushroom, cream of chicken, leek and potato... There wasn't much to choose between them. Suffice to say, if you dropped a spoonful onto the tabletop, it formed an unbreakable bond with the Formica. They could market this stuff to

NASA, she thought. Then she said it out loud. She had a horrible feeling that she'd said the same thing yesterday and the day before that. The worst thing was, she couldn't remember. It didn't matter how many tablets she tucked into her cheek and spat out after the nurse's back was turned; her brain was softening. Soon it would drip out of her ears and bond with the tabletop alongside the soup.

After the soup and the beef casserole with a single scoop of mashed potato and boiled cabbage came dessert. This being Aislinn's last day on the planet, she would've liked something sumptuous and decadent. A pecan and caramel roulade or New York cheesecake like she'd seen advertised in the free supermarket magazines. She would even have been happy with an individual chocolate mousse – they were bought in, at least, and had the advantage of being contaminant-free. At least, until you peeled off the plastic lid. Everything else in this place was infected. Infected by the smell of disinfectant and despair.

You're being maudlin. Aislinn used her most stern voice in her head. Her other voice replied, I'm eighteen years old, I live in a loony bin and I'm killing myself tonight, if this isn't the time for being maudlin I don't know what is. She heard a weird snorting sound and a second later realised that it was her. A kind of laugh. What was that called? Gallows humour.

Tonight, however, the dessert was a square of yellow sponge cake, topped with jam and shredded coconut with a single scoop of vanilla ice-cream. It wasn't the worst dessert the hospital served, she counselled herself. And, really, did she really care that much? What was a crappy bit of sponge cake when weighed against the tower of shittiness life had put in her way?

To her left, Bulimic Andrew toyed with his cabbage, and to her right, a new girl sat hunched in on herself, staring at her plate of food as if it had personally offended her. Last week, Aislinn would've welcomed the new girl. She would've tried to make conversation, shown that she was an ally, a possible friend. Today, she didn't bother. She wouldn't be here in the morning, so there was no point.

Andrew's chair scraped back and he heaved his bulk upwards. 'Andrew, please sit down. Meal time isn't over.' It was one of the nurses. Correction: it was the new nurse. The guy.

The new male nurse and the creepy way he looked at Aislinn. He was another reason for checking out tonight. Another reason at the bottom of a short, but compelling list. She stabbed the rock-hard ice cream with her spoon and began to lever out a chunk. First off, she was crazy, which was pretty rubbish luck. Secondly, her mother had shuffled off this mortal coil when Aislinn was ten. Shuffled off the mortal coil was one way of putting it: stepped off a kitchen stool with a rope around her neck was another. Not having a father – or not one she knew about – led to reason number three. Her adoptive parents, AKA her aunt and uncle. Aunt 'just call me Heather' and Uptight Uncle Ray. Heather and Ray might not have been bad people; Aislinn found it very difficult to tell. All she knew was that they had sectioned her, taken away her freedom, her rights as a person. It wasn't the stuff of dreams.

A few streets and half a world away, Mal woke up in his chair, his neck on fire from sleeping awkwardly. He stretched his arms up without thinking, gasping as his ribs reminded him that they had taken a kicking. He had slept the sleep of the dead for over twelve hours. He switched on his phone and it immediately buzzed with a notification. Pringle had sent him a message.

He tapped the file and an image filled the cracked screen of his phone. It had been taken covertly, at an awkward angle, but it showed two young women sitting at a table in a cafe, their heads bent together like they were sharing a secret. The blonde girl was facing the camera, with her head dipped down, a small smile visible on her lips, but the target was side-on and blurred. She had obviously been moving when the shot was taken and her face was an indistinct smear. Mal noted the long black braid down the middle of her back and the delicate bones of her wrists. He would be able to recognise her, he thought, blurred picture or not.

Demons usually took human form. He had slain ones which looked like big weightlifting guys, and small, skinny dudes like his most recent kill. There hadn't been many women, though. Euan's theory was that demons had been humans at one time, but had been so evil they had turned somehow. That tied in with their father's teachings on the soul: if a human was bad enough they would eventually lose their soul and become demonic.

'That's why they're usually men,' Euan had said. 'Men are more violent. Most murderers are men, and all the despots and dictators.'

Playing devil's advocate, Mal had argued with him. 'What if they didn't become demonic through their actions – what if they were forced into it? Like their bodies were invaded and taken over by the demonic spirit.'

'Hijacked, like?'

'Exactly. What if we're killing the human as well as the demon that is inhabiting their body?'

Euan was cleaning his knife collection and he just shrugged. 'Doesn't matter. It's not like we have a choice.'

Mal tried to remember his brother's voice more clearly. He remembered him saying those words, but could no longer hear them. Still, he clung to the sentiment. And if this particular demon happened to look like a young woman, that wasn't his fault. He had no choice.

Mal lurked by the exit to the lecture hall on George Square. He didn't like it, but there was no other word which summed up his activity. As young, healthy, innocent students poured past him on the pavement, he felt the blackness of his own soul grow darker by comparison. At one time he had been so sure that he was on the side of goodness, of right. His father's mission had been a clear path. Now, as Mal saw his target appear from the entrance, looking exactly like a girl and nothing else, he had never felt so uncertain. Not taking his eyes from the girl, he pulled his phone from his pocket and called his contact on Pringle's crew.

'She doesn't look like a demon.'

'We never said demon.'

Mal's stomach lurched. 'Why does your boss want a mundane?' That was less confrontational than saying 'I'm not hurting a human.' Less likely to get him a one-way ticket to the bottom of the river.

'She's not that, either. Think of her as an object. A nice shiny bit of jewellery that Pringle would like retrieved.'

'It belongs to him?'

'Of course. This is his city. He owns everything in it, including you.'

'Right.' Pringle's rival, Mary King, would probably argue with that statement, but Mal wasn't about to kick things off.

'Your family knows the cost of thinking otherwise. Sorry. Knew the cost, past tense.'

Mal knew it was a calculated blow and he didn't respond, but he couldn't help reacting inside. The pain was swift and low and it left him temporarily dizzy.

'You'll finish your job.'

It wasn't a question so Mal didn't bother to answer. He just hung up and followed the target as she walked toward the university library. She was wearing a denim jacket and had a fabric rucksack over one shoulder. Her single plait reached to her waist, and when she turned he saw a neat profile and smooth pale skin.

Euan would have been horrified. That his target was an object disguised as a woman was neither here nor there. The fact that he was carrying out tasks for Pringle would have been more than enough. At one time he and Euan had fantasised about ending Pringle. The theory was that without the demonic head of the beast, the Sluagh would fall. They had no will of their own, after all. Problem was, even if they could have grown strong enough to take out Pringle, they would have needed to eradicate Mary King at the same time. Otherwise she would have simply stepped into his shoes. They couldn't win.

He wanted a drink. He wanted several drinks, in point of fact. Enough alcohol so that he could forget everything he knew about the life. Sometimes he thought he would give anything, maybe even his life, to not have the knowledge. Yes, there would be losses; he would no longer see trails of magic painted in the sky when the sun set on winter nights, and his undead pet birds would suddenly be as invisible to him as they were to most mundanes, but he would live in glorious ignorance. No more demons. No more killing.

Instead, he increased his pace until he passed the target, then stopped suddenly, holding his phone as if he were making a call. The target bumped into him and he turned to apologise. She held her hands up and shook her head, saying, 'No problem.' He looked deep into her eyes for a moment, willing himself to see something evil or, at least, non-human.

'Sorry,' he said again.

She walked past him and into the library. He had planted his tracker but he had a bigger problem. Was he really about to capture a human girl and hand her over to one of the worst monsters in the city?

CHAPTER FOUR

Aislinn had survived her very last day in the Carlton Secure Psychiatric Unit and now, finally, it was time. She lay on her narrow bed and listened for the sounds of her roommate falling asleep. She had gone through the bedtime routine with a feeling of delicious sentimentality. The last time she would brush her teeth, the last time she would refuse bedtime milk, the last time she would undress and put on her flannel pyjamas, the last time she would docilely take her sleeping tablet, and the last time she would tuck it into her cheek to spit out the moment the orderly had left the room.

As soon as her roommate was breathing the deep and even breath of the heavily sedated, Aislinn rose silently. She knelt on the floor, the nylon carpeting cutting into her knees, and slid her hand underneath her bedside cabinet. Her fingers brushed cardboard and then caught. She pulled out the folded emetic basin and gazed lovingly at the collection of little white pills inside. Some were furry and some had stuck to the cardboard, but they were all beautiful to her. Individually, they meant a night of sleep, ten or twelve hours of oblivion. Collectively, they meant escape.

She gathered the pills in her hand, scraping up the dissolved bits and wiping them onto the more intact tablets. She took a sip of water to wet her mouth and then tried to think of some suitable last thoughts. Which was ridiculous, since the tablets wouldn't work instantly. The most important thing was not to throw up. If she threw up it wouldn't work and the doctors would know what she'd done and she would be on suicide watch and it would mean a huge break before she was free to try again.

Footsteps, going quickly in the corridor. She leapt into bed and pulled the covers up, shoving the folded cardboard underneath her pillow and closing her eyes just as the door opened.

Her heart was hammering and she couldn't breathe deeply and evenly. In fact, she couldn't breathe at all.

'You'll not wake her up, now.' The voice was Nurse Jackson's. She was a broad woman with grey bobbed hair and a thin line of a mouth. 'Aislinn has to be sedated at night.' Her voice was sour, unhappy. If Aislinn hadn't been struggling to stop her heart from flying out of her chest, she would've enjoyed it.

'Not a problem.'

Aislinn struggled not to twitch at the new voice. It was a completely new voice. Male, well-spoken, with a light west coast accent. She wanted to see the man with the voice. And the act of actively wanting something surprised her. She had felt numb for so long.

'I'll need a wheelchair, though,' the voice said. It was quiet but commanding.

'Right.' Nurse Jackson sounded flustered. 'I still don't understand why she has to be transferred now. This is very unusual.' Her voice trailed away and Aislinn realised something: the man had authority over Nurse Jackson. A new doctor? A consultant? But why would they be bothering with her in the night? A stab of fear shot through her stomach. What if they knew? Somehow they knew what she'd been planning and had come to take her to a more secure hospital.

She could hear Jackson muttering as her footsteps carried her away.

The door creaked as it opened wider. Aislinn was desperate to open her eyes, but she kept them lightly closed.

'I know you're awake,' the man said. 'If you're going to give me trouble, could you let me know now so that I can sedate you.'

She opened her eyes and saw the shadowy shape of a man looming over the bed. She would've cried out, but the man held a hypodermic needle and she didn't want to give him any reason to use it.

'I mean you no harm,' he said.

That was a weird thing for a nurse to say. She opened her mouth to speak, and her throat made a dry clicking sound. She swallowed. 'You don't work here.'

'I'm a friend, I promise.'

She could hardly see the man's face – he had his

back to the door, blocking the light from the corridor. Still, he was younger than she expected. Too young to be a consultant or a senior doctor.

'I don't understand.' She wanted to believe his words, but they made no sense.

'I need you to be sedated,' he said. 'It will avoid questions. Can you fake it?'

She nodded. Okay. He was not an orderly or a nurse. He was... what? A psycho who broke into psychiatric units and kidnapped random girls? That didn't sound good.

'This isn't a hospital transfer but I swear you are safe. I need to get you out, though, and if you resist I will have to use this.' He held up the needle before slipping it into his jacket pocket. Aislinn stared at him, fumbling for a decision. She had the impression of broad shoulders, black clothes, and the face of an angel. If angels were tense-looking, handsome men with grey eyes.

The sound of the door at the end of the corridor and footsteps stopped her from speaking. She closed her eyes and forced her body to relax. She sincerely doubted that this guy was going to be allowed to wheel her out of the hospital in the middle of the night. And if he did, she was going to make a run for it the first chance she had. And if that didn't work, and he chopped up her body into little chunks... *You were going to top yourself anyway*. Although that plan seemed utterly remote to her, now, as if it had been dreamed up by a different girl entirely. Even the tiniest possibility of getting out of the hospital was enough to reignite her will to survive.

'Do you need help?' Nurse Jackson's voice was

surprisingly loud and Aislinn realised how softly the man had spoken.

'No, I've got her.' The man leaned closer. He spoke in a louder voice, now, using the professional tone that made him sound like every healthcare professional Aislinn had ever met. 'Aislinn, I'm going to lift you into this chair. We're going for a little ride. Okay?'

Aislinn let her eyes flutter half open. She made a sleepy murmur and shut her eyes again. When the man slid one arm behind her shoulder and sat her up, she kept her body floppy.

'Come on, dear.' Nurse Jackson shoved an arm underneath Aislinn's armpit and hoisted her upwards.

Aislinn let her head loll forwards and made a couple of unintelligible moaning sounds. It was a virtuoso performance, she thought. Once in the wheelchair she dropped her head to one side and commenced fake sleep-breathing.

'She's really out,' Nurse Jackson said doubtfully. 'Perhaps we should check her blood pressure.'

'She's in safe hands,' the man said.

Aislinn could imagine Nurse Jackson's expression and had to bite the inside of her cheek to stop herself smiling. The chair was moving backwards. The motion made her feel sick so she risked cracking her eyelids open. Nurse Jackson was walking ahead, aiming for the security doors. She punched a code and held the door open. Inside the first set of doors a kind of antechamber. Aislinn remembered being signed in there three years ago but hadn't seen it since.

'I'm not happy about this,' Nurse Jackson said. 'I

want that on record. And I will be speaking to your supervisor in the morning.'

'That's your prerogative, hen,' Aislinn heard the man say. He sounded completely relaxed. Bored, almost.

'Buzz them out.' This was to the night security guard, who tapped on a keypad until a loud buzzing noise sounded. Then he got up and, with maddening slowness, manually unlocked the double doors.

'You've got a minute and then the outer door locks. If you're too slow, push the button by the camera and I'll buzz you again.' The night shift guard was obviously feeling chatty. Probably he didn't get much of a chance to show off his excellent security skills.

And then Aislinn was moving again. The doors closed behind them, and after a stretch of identical beige corridor they arrived at the second door. It had a camera mounted above the top corner and a numerical keypad with a small flashing green light.

The buzzing was still going and the man spun the chair around, opened the door and backed through. Aislinn watched the corridor disappear as the door swung shut, locking with a snap.

This was the time to run. Part of her knew that, but the vast majority of her body and mind was processing the weirdness of the last few minutes and the shock of the cold air. Cold, moving, outside air. The pavement outside the hospital was quiet. Yellow lines ran next to the kerb and cars moved past on the road, tyres splashing through puddles. 'It's been raining,' she said. She wanted to take the words and stuff them back into her mouth the moment she had spoken. She sounded like a halfwit.

'Can you walk?'

The man was in front of her, and in the orange glow of the streetlight she got her first proper look at him. He was much younger than she'd thought. There was no way he'd pass for a consultant or even a senior doctor. He was wearing a black jacket over a black shirt and jeans. He had a light dusting of stubble and looked like bad news. Suddenly the unreality of the situation clarified. There was no way this man had convinced Nurse Jackson that he was official hospital staff. 'How did you do that?' She waved in the direction of the secure unit.

'Can I explain in the car? We're probably on CCTV out here.'

'Okay.' She got out of the chair and followed him to the kerb, where a rusting black sedan was parked on the double yellows.

Her instinct for self-preservation appeared to be on the fritz. Or maybe I really am mental, she thought. After all, only an insane person would get into an ancient black BMW with a complete stranger.

He opened the passenger door for her and then crossed in front to the driver's side. She hesitated. Was this suicide? Did she want it to be?

A muffled buzzing sound came from inside the building.

'Fuck,' the man said succinctly.

They were coming. Nurse Jackson and the orderlies and the security guard. Aislinn could picture them rushing down the beige corridors. She dived into the passenger seat and pulled the door shut. They were already motoring away as the outside door opened, and

Aislinn got only the briefest glimpse of Nurse Jackson's solid figure before the car turned a corner.

The traffic slowed for a set of lights, and as they stopped a car pulled alongside. Aislinn stared at the shadowy face of the woman driving. Her jaw was moving rhythmically and Aislinn automatically thought 'amphetamine' before realising that the woman was probably chewing gum. That she was in the outside world. Where the normals lived. Where the normals did whatever they wanted, whenever they wanted. No clocks. No schedule. No pills. No cabbage. A bubble of wild happiness burst up through her body. That wasn't good. That was definitely a mental reaction. You should be terrified, she reminded herself.

'I'm sorry about this. I really am,' the man said, his voice gentle.

That didn't sound promising. In order to stop the panic rising, Aislinn decided she would pretend he hadn't spoken. They were getting closer to the centre of the city and shops lined the streets. Many of them were still lit up, a host of colourful displays that seemed brighter and more interesting than anything she remembered from her life before the hospital. If she thought about shops then, all she could conjure was a dour-faced woman in the shoe shop, measuring with a little metal contraption and clicking her teeth. 'Wide feet.' That and the old-fashioned charm of the school uniform outfitters with its shelves of shirts and ties, and hanging rails of blazers.

'What time is it?'

He glanced at the clock on the dashboard. 'Just gone nine.'

It wasn't really late. Not in the real world.

After a moment, Aislinn said, 'I'm being very calm.'

His mouth twitched. 'I'd noticed.'

'So. Who are you?'

'I'm Mal.' He looked across at her just long enough for her to begin to worry about a car crash.

'Mal? As in Malcolm?'

'If you like.'

Aislinn smiled. She appreciated the art of question avoidance. It was one of her own specialities.

Mal smiled too. That was alarming. When he smiled he looked more dangerous.

She went back to looking out of the window. The car pulled off the main road, and within seconds they were in another world. Tall buildings crowded on either side and lights were few and far between. Mal took a sharp left through a narrow gap between houses and they were on a back street, a dead-end road lined with garages, padlocks gleaming on their doors, faced by the backs of the tall building blocks. Some windows were lit, and in one a woman was clearly visible, taking off her shirt. Another was a kitchen window, where an old man stirred a pot on a stove.

Mal pulled into a space between two garages and killed the engine. He twisted in his seat but Aislinn couldn't see his expression in the dark. 'I'm asking you to trust me a little further. I can't talk freely until we get inside.'

Well, that was probably line one of the psycho's

handbook. Lies to tell to control your victim. Aislinn's fingers tightened on the door handle. She wondered how far she could run before he caught her. She wondered if the people in the lighted windows would call the police if she screamed.

'I know about the things you see, and I can help you.'

She held herself still. 'I don't know what you're talking about.'

'Fair enough.' He got out of the car and opened the door for her. 'Coming?'

She realised that she had already decided to follow him. She'd come this far and, besides, she had nowhere else to go.

His flat turned out to be on the top floor. She was wheezing by the time they got to the last flight of stairs, and she wondered just how unfit she was. Three years of minimal activity. A lot of sitting and staring at walls and keeping herself still and calm. She collapsed into the flat, hoping for a sofa or armchair. Instead, she found books. Piles and piles of books. There were papers and journals, too. Scattered Biros and pencils, foil takeaway cartons and used mugs were marooned on the sea of literature.

Mal lurched across a teetering tower of paperbacks to reach the window and yanked the curtains shut. He flipped a switch and the wall lights came to life, bathing the squalor in warm orange light.

'Cosy,' Aislinn said. She knew she ought to be more frightened. Ought to run from this room and call for help. Instead she sank onto the nearest seat, exhaustion overwhelming her senses.

Mal left the girl sitting on his sofa. Her knees were together and her feet splayed, making her look even younger than she was. Her dirty blonde hair hung around her face, which was blotchy from crying. He put the kettle on and added a couple of spoons of sugar to her mug. She was in shock. Poor kid. He pushed aside the guilt and focused on the job.

'Here.' He passed the mug to the girl. She was sat in exactly the same position he'd left her in. Then Monty fluttered through the room and she flinched, spilling tea onto the floor.

'Sorry.' She made to get up, looking terrified, but Mal couldn't tell if it was the bird or the accident with the tea that upset her most.

'It's fine,' he said, keeping his voice low and gentle. 'It doesn't matter. The carpet is filthy anyway, you can hardly make it worse.'

She froze, half-standing, her eyes wide and frightened.

'Sit down, drink your tea. Can I get you something to eat?'

After another moment of inactivity, she slowly lowered herself back to a sitting position.

'And don't mind the birds. They're just pets.' He tried a small, self-deprecating smile. 'For company.'

Monty flew behind her head and she flinched again.

'I can put them in the bedroom if they're bothering you,' Mal said.

Finally, she shook her head.

The tea sloshed dangerously in the cup and Mal nodded towards it. 'There's lots of sugar in there, give you a bit of energy.' He sat down opposite her, careful to move slowly and smoothly, no sudden gestures. His ribs were still sore and the activity of the evening hadn't helped but he managed not to wince. 'I know you're frightened and I'm sorry. All I can do is promise you that I am not going to hurt you. I need your help with something and then you will be free to go. If you want me to, I can drop you near the hospital. I can't take you to the door – I'm sure you understand – but nearby. The next street along. Or, if you want to go somewhere else, I will either take you or buy your ticket.' He laughed a little self-consciously. 'I'm not exactly rich, so I can't promise a flight to Barbados, but I will do whatever I can to get you to wherever you want to go. I can promise you that.'

'You're going to let me go?'

The tremble in her voice broke his heart. 'I swear it.'

Aislinn lifted her chin and looked at him for the first time since they'd arrived. He could see the struggle on her face; she wanted to believe him but her instincts were telling her otherwise. There was nothing he could do to convince her, nothing to ease the burden of fear and anxiety. He was a monster. No matter that he wasn't going to hurt her, no matter that he was telling the truth and would do everything possible to release her as quickly as possible, he was still putting her through hell.

'Okay,' she said after a moment. 'But why do you need my help? What can I do?'

'You see things,' he said.

'No.' She shook her head. 'I don't.'

'They said you were ill,' he said. 'They said you were hallucinating. What did they diagnose? Schizophrenia?'

She nodded. 'First. Then bipolar.'

'Then you started lying. Self-preservation.'

She swallowed. 'It was too late.'

He nodded. 'I know. Once you're in the system, it's not always easy to get out.'

'They were trying to help,' she said. 'But the medicine made me feel weird. They play tricks with your mind and then you don't know what's real. Or what's supposed to be real.'

He nodded his understanding. 'It's hard to say the right things in those circumstances. You were sectioned three years ago, right?'

Her expression closed down again. 'How do you know these things?'

'I need someone who can see things clearly, see things that most humans aren't able to see. People with the sight are often institutionalised, diagnosed as mentally ill.'

She shook her head. 'I am ill. The things I see. They aren't real.'

'I'm sorry,' he said. 'They are. I know because I see them too.'

Her chin lifted at that, and he ploughed on. 'My birds, here.' He whistled with his arm out and Monty obliged by landing for a moment, ruffling his feathers and splaying out his beautiful tail. 'Yes,' Mal said to the bird. 'You are very handsome.' To Aislinn he said, 'They are charmed creatures. Everyday folk can't even see them, but you can. I was trained to see them, but I have to work hard to remember that they are there – it's like my brain wants to forget. I'm not naturally talented like you. You're more powerful—'

She laughed then, a sudden burst of sound that was halfway to a snort. A release of air that left her shoulders a little higher but her hand gripping the mug of hot tea shaking. 'I'm weak. Weak-minded. That's why I'm in hospital. That's why I came with you. I do as I'm told. I see things even though I know they aren't real. I tell myself they're not real but I still see them. If I was stronger I would be able to get a hold of myself—' She broke off, taking a huge breath.

Mal wanted to lean forward, but he didn't want to frighten her. He forced himself to remain still, just shaking his head carefully. 'You're not weak. You're not ill. Some people are born with this ability. It's not your fault.'

Her face went blank. She took a long sip of her tea, though, and he decided to claim that as a win.

'I have a blow-up mattress for you to sleep on,' he said. 'In here. I would give you my room, but the birds would get confused. I'll shut them in with me so you won't be disturbed.'

She glanced at the front door.

'It's locked,' he said. 'And the phone is disconnected. I'm going to lock the door to the living room, too, so you'd best make use of the facilities before I say goodnight.'

She nodded.

'It's just one night,' he said. Then added, for honesty's sake, 'I hope.'

'And you want me to do what? See something?'

'There's a girl. She looks about your age.' Pringle's crew might have assured him that the target was an object, not a human, but Mal wasn't about to take their word on it. His own senses were pretty damn sharp, but the stakes were too high.

'You want me to look at a girl? That's all?' Aislinn had relaxed enough for a bit of animation to enter her voice, and he had the smallest flash of the girl she must've been before being drugged and terrified and locked away. He couldn't let her go, he couldn't erase her tragic past, but he could be honest with her. 'I want you to tell me if she's human.'

To his surprise it was almost midday when he opened his eyes. With Aislinn in the flat, and still aching from his encounter with Pringle's crew, Mal hadn't expected to sleep. He lay still for a moment, listening for sounds of life in the rest of the flat. Either the girl, Aislinn, was sleeping soundly or she'd climbed out of the window. The birds were awake and flying around the room, but Mal hardly noticed. He was intent on the day's task. He was hoping to find the girl quickly so that he could release Aislinn as soon as possible. As if making little distinctions like that, small efforts to minimise the girl's suffering, made any difference as to the nature of his work. He was still a bad man. He was still using an innocent, pulling her into his world.

He knocked on the closed door to the living room. 'Aislinn, are you dressed?' He waited a moment. There was no sound from inside. 'I'm coming in,' he said, unlocking the door. She was sitting on the sofa. Naturally enough, she was wearing the same clothes she'd had on last night – pale blue flannel pyjamas. 'I'm going to need you to get changed,' he said, indicating the clothes he'd bought, folded on the table.

She nodded, blank-eyed.

'Unless you wanted to shower first?'

She shook her head, and he wondered if she was going to speak to him today. The brief animation of last night had gone, replaced with a zoned-out calm that he found vaguely alarming. She made no move to get up, and he looked around the room, hoping for inspiration. 'Did you want to watch some television? Have something to eat?'

She looked at him then. 'Mornings are circle therapy and chores. No television until after two, unless you have special privileges.'

He swallowed. Just how wrecked was her mind? He leaned against the table, trying to shorten his bulk, make himself loom a little less. 'You're not in hospital today. You can watch television now if you want. Or take a shower. Or have a nap. Read the paper.'

Her gaze flicked to the door. 'But not go for a walk? Not leave?'

'No,' he said gently.

Her shoulders hunched a little, making her look even younger. 'I'm fine, then. Thank you.' Carefully polite. Like she was refusing a cucumber sandwich at a tea party. Not that Mal had any experience of tea parties.

70

Which was probably why he was doing such a spectacularly bad job of putting the girl at ease.

'Okay,' he said. He opened the door wide and then went into his small kitchen to make coffee. Part of his preparation for this operation had included buying some breakfast supplies, so he was able to make two plates of toast and put them on the table. Luxury kidnapping. 'Help yourself if you want,' he said. He put a jar of crystallised honey and a butter knife on the table.

'You shouldn't leave that lying around,' Aislinn said, showing animation for the first time. 'Dangerous.'

'You're not going to stab me with a butter knife,' he said, more confidently than he felt. 'We're going to eat breakfast and make conversation like the good friends we are.'

She crossed to the table and nibbled at a piece of toast. They didn't chat, but Mal felt absurdly relieved that she'd eaten something. The poor kid was probably going through withdrawal from her meds, and he didn't want her collapsing on him.

Later, he persuaded her to go into his bathroom and change into the new clothes. He'd guessed on sizing, based on her height and the expectation that she would be on the high side of average body mass. Lots of the drugs used in the treatment of mental illness induced weight gain. Aislinn, however, had the figure of an undernourished child. The tracksuit bottoms ('yoga trousers' they'd been called in the shop) were stretchy enough to stay up, at least, but the t-shirt and hoodie drowned her slight frame. Still, at least it wasn't pyjamas. Better yet, the trainers fitted, and Aislinn seemed calm and ready to face leaving the flat.

Mal checked the app which showed the location of the GPS tracker he had planted on the girl. Object. He reminded himself to call his target 'object'. Otherwise it would be difficult to extract her and pass her onto Pringle. It. Not her.

'She's—' He stopped. Tried again. 'The target is in The Long Drop. In town.'

Aislinn didn't show any sign of having understood him. He ploughed on anyway. 'We're going to see her, you're going to tell me what you see, and then we're done.'

'Then you let me go.' She spoke in a flat tone, neither disbelieving nor hopeful. She was a good student repeating the lesson. Mal knew there was nothing he could do to reassure her or to lessen the stress. The kindest thing he could do was get this over with.

'When we're outside, you have to behave,' he said. 'No calling attention to us, no shouting for help, no nonsense.'

She tilted her chin to look at him, eyes wide and white. 'I won't.'

'Good. If you do as I ask, this will be over really quickly and then you will be free to go.'

She nodded. 'You said. You promised.'

'Okay, then.' He unlocked the front door and, still expecting her to bolt or start yelling or something similarly unhelpful, led her by the arm down the stairs and out onto the street. It was deserted and nobody witnessed him putting Aislinn into the front seat, putting on her seat belt and securing her wrists with a plastic zip tie. 'Sorry,' he said, covering her bound wrists with a spare coat. 'It's just a precaution. I'll take them off when we get there.'

Aislinn didn't answer. She seemed almost-catatonic again and he hoped it wasn't pure fear. He squashed his guilt down as far as it would go, knowing he couldn't afford it. He just had to get this job over and done with. It was that simple and that difficult. Like every fucking thing.

CHAPTER FIVE

Rose sat in the corner of The Last Drop and took several deep breaths while Astrid went to the bar. A group of students at another table had called out to Astrid and she'd stopped for a chat, her laugh carrying through the room and seeming to bounce off the wood panelling and the low beams of the ceiling, filling the space. Within seconds of walking in, it had seemed as if all eyes were on Astrid. Even the old locals turned and smiled appreciatively, and the woman serving behind the bar was leaning forwards, her red lips parted, as if wanting to get physically closer to her. Rose was happy not to draw any attention, but it also made her feel even more insubstantial than usual. If she went to the bar and tried to order, she felt the red-lipped server would simply look right through her.

Astrid returned to the table with three glasses. Rose hadn't known what to drink, couldn't remember if she drank alcohol or had even tried the stuff. She was certain she had never been into a pub, and definitely not this one, but something about it felt very familiar; the low ceiling and the wooden beams, the slight sagging of the window frames where the building had settled over the decades.

'Drink up,' Astrid said, taking a slug of her whisky. She looked around with an expression of satisfaction. 'Finally.'

'I'm not sure. Maybe just a coke to start with.'

'No chance. You bailed on me the other night and now you need to make it up to me. You promised a drink.'

'Coke is a drink,' Rose said quietly.

'Just try it,' Astrid said. 'You owe me.'

Rose took a sip of the clear liquid, expecting lemonade with perhaps a hint of something exotic. It tasted chemical and wrong and made her mouth go dry. She pulled a face and put the glass down.

'It gets better with practice,' Astrid said. 'I can get you some wine if you'd prefer.'

Rose opened her mouth to say 'I don't know' but shut it again, not wanting to seem any odder than she already did.

'Come on.' Astrid touched the glass.

With horror, Rose realised that Astrid wasn't going to leave her to quietly ignore her drink. She lifted it and took another sip, readying herself for the disgusting taste. Astrid was right, though – it wasn't quite as terrible the second time. She took another, bigger sip, and then another.

'Good job,' Astrid said. She knocked back the rest of her first whisky and started on her second.

An office type in a shirt and suit trousers came over and offered to buy them a round. Astrid barely glanced at the man, but she replied, 'She'll have a vodka tonic and I'll have a double malt. Laphroaig.'

'Isn't that leading him on?' Rose asked as the guy obediently headed to the bar.

'I think he can look after himself,' Astrid said. 'Besides, I accepted his offer at face value. Not my fault if he had subtext that isn't going to get anywhere near my shirt buttons.'

'Why did I decide to come here?' Rose hadn't meant to say it out loud. She took another sip of the horrible drink for comfort.

'Live a little,' Astrid said, drumming her fingers on the table and looking around the place as if she expected something that wasn't there.

'They don't have cake,' Rose said, trying to lift the heavy weight which was sitting on her shoulders. 'I don't call that living.'

Astrid turned her attention back to Rose. 'Tragic. You are a tragic waste of youth, you know that?'

Rose hated it when Astrid got like this, all spiky and impatient. She tried to think of something to say that would appease her, maybe snap her out of her strange mood, but nothing came to mind. She sipped at her drink, feeling a curious warm, buzzing sensation through her body. She touched a finger to her mouth and her lips felt strangely numb. 'Vodka is strong,' she said.

'Well, that's a triple,' Astrid said, with fake cheeriness.

That couldn't be right. A triple was a lot. She had asked Astrid to get her something weak. She fought to focus on her friend.

'I really want to hear about your dreams,' Astrid said. She was staring into Rose's eyes in a way that would normally make Rose feel very uncomfortable. 'Tell me.'

Rose shook her head. 'I don't want to talk about them.'

Astrid leaned forward and Rose felt the buzzing in her body increase. 'Tell. Me.'

The door opened and a man the size of a truck walked in, derailing her thought processes. He had short dark hair that looked army-issue and a beat-up canvas jacket in a murky colour. He looked out of place indoors, as if he should be hiking halfway up a mountain, or perhaps lying in a sniper trench in some far-off land. Rose's instincts were telling her to hide underneath the table until the man went away again, but she shoved down the impulse. Hiding under tables was not normal behaviour, and she didn't want to annoy Astrid while she was already so grumpy.

Rose looked away from the man, focused on her drink instead and thought about taking a sip. When she looked back, she could see that he wasn't alone. A girl with dark blonde hair that looked in need of a good wash was stood just behind him. She had been half eclipsed by his bulk, but as he moved to the left more of the girl appeared, revealing that the other side of her hair was just as matted and greasy-looking.

'Are you even listening to me?' Astrid said, tapping Rose on the arm sharply.

The girl with the tangled hair reached out an arm and pointed at Rose. 'She's so beautiful.'

Astrid looked from the pointed finger to Rose and back again. Rose was about to laugh, but Astrid looked panicked, and that sight was weird enough to kill the laugh in her throat.

The girl took a hesitant step forwards just as Astrid got to her feet, her chair clattering to the floor in her haste.

The girl's face was glowing with happiness. An insane kind of happiness. She had light grey eyes and skin tone that looked like she'd been living in a cave.

'So pretty.' She was slurring her words and Rose wondered if she was drunk.

'Come on.' Astrid tugged Rose's arm. She hauled her out of her seat with surprising strength and pushed her towards the back of the pub. 'Go, go, go.'

The crazy girl lurched towards their table then was abruptly pulled back. The man had hold of her arm, but she seemed oblivious to him. She didn't look away from Rose, and Rose found she couldn't stop staring back at the girl. The man's lips were moving, but Rose couldn't hear what he was saying. She had an urge to get closer, to listen.

'Rose!' Astrid was towing her in the opposite direction. 'Now!'

Rose obeyed, turning to see the door to the toilets. They went through the door, Astrid still moving fast. It swung shut behind them, almost clipping Rose on the arm, but instead of turning left and into the door marked with 'Grrrls' or even the one labelled 'Dudes', Astrid barrelled through the one marked 'Private'. She was muttering under her breath 'please, please, please', and when the short corridor opened into a storage area with a fire exit door she said 'thank fuck.'

The fear in Astrid's tone sharpened Rose's own. 'What's going on? Why are we—'

The door exploded behind them and Rose stopped asking questions and concentrated on running.

Astrid had already pushed down the metal bar on the fire exit door and was holding it open.

Outside it was dark and they were in a narrow alley. Astrid looked wild. Rose didn't recognise her. Her eyes were wide with fear and adrenaline.

'Okay,' Astrid said. 'Rose. You've got to close your eyes and get us out of here.'

Rose fought the sudden urge to laugh. 'What?'

'Close your eyes.'

'I don't understand.' Rose's tongue felt thick in her mouth, and although her head was clearer from the adrenaline there was a buzzing in her ears.

'Yes, you do. Deep down. Just do it.' Astrid took her hands. Her palms were cool and dry. 'I trust you. Do it.'

There was a bang as the fire door swung open and hit the wall. The man appeared in the alley looking utterly crazed. His mouth was open and he reached for her. Everything was happening in slow motion and Rose's hearing had gone funny, like she was at the bottom of a swimming pool. She gripped Astrid's hands and closed her eyes. Heat went through her body in one blindingly painful flash. And then, for one awful second, there was absolutely nothing.

Mal stood frozen for a moment, staring at the suddenly-empty, definitely-demon-free space. He tried to feel good, as if he'd vanquished the girl-shaped foes simply through the power of bundling after them in a busy Edinburgh bar, but it wouldn't stick even for a second. They'd escaped.

Shit.

He sniffed the air, hoping for a hint, but all he got was a nostril full of cordite, the burnt-match smell that seemed to go hand in hand with demonkind.

How had they done that? No demon had ever simply disappeared. They were corporeal. Dispatching them was messy work. He checked the alley, walking up and down, but there was nothing for two girls to hide behind and no fire escapes for them to have climbed, superhero-style.

Back inside, the bar chatter had returned to normal volume. People sat clustered at the small wooden tables, the surfaces crowded with glasses and bottles. Laughter punctuated the air. Mal squeezed through the happy hour punters until he found Aislinn. At least she hadn't disappeared in a puff of smoke.

'Pretty?' Aislinn said, her expression confused. Then, very clearly, 'Where's the pretty girl?'

'Gone.' Mal said shortly, still angry with himself. Anybody would think this was his first day at the rodeo. He tried not to imagine what Euan would have said if he'd told him that he'd lost a demon like that. Or his father. There was, at least, an upside to being an orphan.

'No,' Aislinn shook her head vehemently. 'No. No. No.' Her voice rose and a couple of punters turned to look.

Mal made a 'don't mind her,' face to the onlookers and took Aislinn's arm. 'Come on, let's get you home.'

'No.' Aislinn was still shaking her head, whipping it from side to side, making her look quite insane. Which was fair enough, really. Mal squeezed her arm in what he hoped was a reassuring manner. 'It's okay, calm down. She's gone. It's all over.'

Aislinn danced to the side. She smiled, though, looking suddenly beatific. That should've been his warning, but he was still too caught up in his own failure and confusion and he didn't react quickly enough. Aislinn's arm came up from her side and that was when he realised that she had a piece of broken green glass concealed in her hand. She slashed it expertly down one arm, dividing the tissue from the inside of her elbow to her wrist.

'Oh, Christ.' Mal grabbed for her hand, shook the glass out from it before she could do any more damage. Aislinn twisted in his grip and, because he didn't want to hurt her, she managed to break free. She grabbed a glass from the nearest table and smashed it. Tiny flecks flew into the air and one stung Mal's cheek. There was blood running freely from her slashed arm, splattering onto the floor, but Aislinn was intent on cutting her other wrist. 'Please, don't,' Mal said, shrugging off his jacket. People were up and shouting. Someone screamed. Mal was aware of someone else with their phone out, calling nine-nine-nine, giving the name of the bar in a steady voice.

Aislinn dropped the glass and reached out for Mal, stumbling. He caught her before she fell and lowered her to the floor. He tried to wrap his jacket around the arm that looked the worst, tried to apply pressure, to lift the limb. It was slippy with blood. Aislinn touched his cheek, her eyes dimming in her pale face. He wanted to jerk away but he didn't. He wasn't a good man, he knew that, but he didn't move away.

Aislinn smiled at him, right into his eyes. 'I like your pet,' she said.

'I'm sorry,' he was surprised to hear himself say. 'I didn't mean for this to happen.'

She went, then. Her expression slackened and the light went from her eyes. Mal heard sirens and climbed to his feet, letting the girl slump onto the floor. She was just a body now, it didn't matter, and he had to put some distance between himself and this latest cock-up. He left the bar without anybody trying to stop him. His blood-soaked jacket was a wet bundle in his arms, heavier than expected.

CHAPTER SIX

When Rose opened her eyes it took a few seconds for them to adjust to the lack of light. She was in a tunnel. A dim electric bulb encased in a metal cage cast a sickly glow onto the walls. Walls that looked oddly bumpy in texture. After a moment, the texture resolved into something so horrible that her brain simply refused to process the image for a further few seconds.

It was a bit like when she woke from one of her blackouts, except that she was more frightened than she had ever been before and she wasn't alone. Astrid was still in front of her, still gripping her hands, which hurt as if they'd been burned. There was water on the floor. As much as Rose tried to focus on that fact, she could no longer ignore the reality of the bumpy walls; they were lined with bones. Stacked on top of each other with thigh bones facing end-out, the pattern broken in places with a row of skulls.

'Oh my God.' Rose's voice was thin and she cleared her throat. 'What. The. Hell.'

Astrid let go of Rose and wiped her hands on her jeans. 'Excellent.'

'Not excellent.' Rose looked around, feeling the last shreds of her self-control ebb away. 'Not excellent at all. What is this place? How did we—'

'I think we should move.'

'Okay,' Rose said automatically.

'Like, right now.' Astrid put a hand on Rose's arm. 'It's kind of crowded in here.'

Rose felt the heat disappear and goosebumps spread across her skin.

Astrid began walking and Rose followed. Her brain was still refusing to process that they'd just apparently jumped from one place in the world to another, and was snagged on the bones lining the walls, as that was, sadly, the more manageable part of the scenario. The passage opened out into a squarish area, which had more passages leading off from it. Behind a low wall, there was an illuminated space about six feet across. Inside that stood an artificial hill with a miniature stone building.

'These were stone quarries originally,' Astrid said. She glanced back at Rose. 'We're underneath Paris.'

'Paris. Right. Gotcha.' By this time, Rose's brain had simply switched off. It had short-circuited, and she decided to just go with whatever this was until it came back online.

Astrid chose a passage without any hesitation and Rose followed. After a few more twists and turns, they passed through a circular space with a giant pillar in the middle made of yet more bones and skulls, then went along a long corridor with a low arched ceiling that seemed to go on for a very long time. The air began to get a little fresher and – although Rose thought she might've been imagining it – warmer.

Just when she was beginning to think they were irrevocably lost, the corridor ended at a spiral staircase. She followed Astrid up the steps, trying to remember to breathe and not to touch the walls, which were stone and not bone but somehow the colour and texture of bone. She wasn't sure she was ever going to stop seeing those neat piles of dead humanity.

She heard voices just before the final curve of the staircase, and then they were in a cramped room with a desk and a bored-looking woman who was idly flicking through a magazine. On her left, about halfway up the wall, was a clear-fronted case containing a defibrillator.

The woman saw her looking and said, 'For the fat tourists.' Rose heard and understood, while simultaneously recognising that she had spoken in French. *Pour les touristes obèses.*

A green door with the word 'sortie' was half-open and Rose tasted fresh air.

After the gloom of the catacombs, the spring sunshine was almost painful. The scent wafting from a bakery fought with the smell of car exhaust, dog shit and tree resin. As they walked along the pavement, a waft of blocked drain joined the party, as if to underscore reality with a fat black marker pen. 'I get it, I get it,' Rose muttered. In her mind, she added, 'Not dreaming.'

Astrid was moving along at a clip, her stride

purposeful and her eyes scanning upwards as if checking for something. 'What are we going to do?' Rose pushed down on her panic. No money. No passport. No suitcase of clothes or barterable goods. Not even her bloody hairbrush.

'Okay, metro's this way,' Astrid said. 'We need to find somewhere to stay.'

Rose found her feet were stuck to the ground. 'We're in Paris.'

Astrid stopped and backed up a couple of steps. 'Yes,' she said, almost gently. 'Rose. We have to keep moving. I'm sorry.'

Rose managed to force her legs into motion and she concentrated on following Astrid. They arrived at a metro station. The curly writing on the art nouveau sign made it, finally, inescapable. They were in Paris.

Of all the questions she had, Rose settled on the least disturbing. 'Why are we running?'

Astrid gave her a funny look. 'I don't think that man wanted to shake us by the hand.'

'No,' Rose said. 'I mean, why don't we just hold hands and teleport or whatever the hell that was?'

Astrid paused, pushing a stray curl out of her eyes. 'You think you can do that again?'

Rose looked inside herself, searching for some new area of her brain marked 'this is how you transport people magically from one place to the other.' It wasn't there. She squeezed her eyes shut in frustration. 'I don't know.'

'Do you remember being in Vassilikos? The turtles

on the beach and the sunset so red it was like the sky was bleeding?'

'No.' Rose was off balance, falling. 'I've never been anywhere. Was that with you?'

'Then probably not,' Astrid said. Her expression was a curious mix of disappointment and relief. 'I think what happened back there was a result of the extreme stress of the situation. You bypassed the filter. Thank Christ.'

'If you don't stop talking like this and start making sense, I'm going to freak out. Seriously and totally freak out. I'm going to sit here on this Parisian-bloody-pavement and have myself a meltdown.'

Astrid squinted at Rose. 'Are you saying that because you think you should, or are you really finding this that difficult? I mean, you're the girl who blacks out regularly and can't remember where or why. You're the girl who can't remember a single thing about her childhood.'

Rose stepped back, her insides suddenly liquid. 'How do you know that?'

'Sweetie. There is so much I want to tell you but I can't yet. You won't believe me, or you will believe me and your head will explode.' Astrid said this seriously, as if she meant it literally. Perhaps she did.

The cold feeling was back in Rose's stomach. 'Don't we need money?' She settled on practicality. 'For the metro?'

Astrid clicked her fingers. 'Damn. Yes. Stay here.'

Rose stayed. She watched Astrid march off a little way down the street. Once she was about thirty paces away, her gait changed. She became relaxed, absorbed. She began looking into shop windows. After a few minutes, Rose considered following her. Perhaps she was meant to?

A woman paused next to Astrid and, for a moment, Rose couldn't see her anymore. The woman was leaning towards the glass, peering at something inside. Then Astrid popped out from behind her and began walking at a casual pace back to Rose. She didn't pause or speak, just touched Rose's arm as she went past.

Rose followed her down the steps, feeling the change in air as they went underground. Astrid bought tickets using French that sounded fluent and assured, and they got onto the next available train.

The carriage was only half full and they got a seat easily. The strains of an accordion wafted over the air, reminding Rose that she was most definitely in France.

'Look.' Astrid leaned in close and spoke quietly. 'I've got enough cash for us to get a hotel room. For one night, at least. We can rest.'

'And take a shower,' Rose said. 'I'm disgusting.'

The woman sitting opposite visibly blanched. She had a creamy brown tan and a wrap dress that sat on her knee. Her hair was styled and she had neat earrings and a leather handbag.

Rose leaned in closer still and whispered in Astrid's ear. 'Did you steal it?'

Astrid went thin-lipped. She nodded once.

Rose sat back. Her head felt fuzzy. The air in the carriage was soupy. It felt unbelievably warm after the brisk temperature of a traditional Edinburgh spring.

The train stopped at a station and a couple of people

got up and exited. The accordionist got off the previous carriage and stepped through the sliding doors of theirs. He stood in the middle and began playing. Bored Parisians stared out of the window or at their own feet. Nobody made eye contact.

Rose tried to do the same, but her gaze kept being drawn back to the musician. He looked well fed and he wore a grey jumper that looked like it was made from a fine yarn, like cashmere. Busking in Paris was obviously quite lucrative. Unless cashmere was a basic human right in France. Like wine and decent bread.

Astrid was staring out of the window, seemingly lost in her own thoughts. Rose wanted to say that there was something wrong with the busker, that she had a bad feeling and it was getting worse. But then, nothing was right about this situation. It would be weird if she didn't feel odd.

The train surfaced and the view of brick tunnel walls was replaced with above-ground Paris. Streets, trees, tall buildings that looked old but in a different way to the ones in Edinburgh. The landscape looked familiar. It didn't seem possible that they were in Paris, though, despite the unmistakeably Gallic sound of the accordion and the graffiti on the railway siding that said 'Je suis Charlie'. Then, as if the city was answering back, underlining its Paris-ness just for Rose's benefit, the Eiffel Tower blinked into view.

Rose turned to Astrid to point it out and caught sight of the accordionist staring at them both. Properly, unpleasantly staring. She poked Astrid.

Astrid glanced up, then in one movement rose to her

feet and threw something into the man's face. Rose couldn't see what it was, her mind was playing tricks and it had looked as if Astrid had thrown nothing but thin air, but that couldn't be right. It must have been substantial. He stumbled back, his arms flailing, the weight of the accordion held by the wide straps he had looped around his shoulders. He grabbed at a seat back, which skewed his course so that instead of ending up on his back in the aisle of the carriage, he lay half on one of the seats as a horrified housewifely-looking woman on the other side tried to shrink away so that no part of her body came into contact with him.

The train was slowing and Astrid pulled Rose to the doors. She kept looking at the man even while she pushed Rose onto the platform. Rose stumbled, falling to the ground and scraping her knees. The pain and the panic took over and she felt her grip on consciousness fly loose. She was falling and she expected everything to go black. She was passing out, some part of her knew that, either from the shock of the fall or the terror which had, finally, taken over every part of her being. Instead of blackness, though, there was a flash of white.

CHAPTER SEVEN

Rose must have fallen asleep again. She wiped her face, hoping she hadn't drooled. She didn't remember having dinner or going to bed or getting up that morning, but she must have done those things because now she was sitting in the Costa Coffee on George Street. Another blackout. Another chunk of lost time. The light through the plate glass had that insubstantial night-is-falling look to it and the place was packed with people; students and shoppers and a few in suits. Astrid was sitting opposite with an enormous mug of hot chocolate. She was spooning whipped cream into her mouth with a determination Rose recognised from many other such cafe visits. The familiarity was soothing and she felt her heart rate slow.

She quickly checked herself. She was wearing a purple corduroy skirt, thick tights, a Fair Isle patterned jumper and her long brown boots. She turned slightly and found her coat over the back of her chair and her bag to her side. This was not normal. People didn't dress themselves in weather-appropriate gear when they fell unconscious.

Astrid paused. 'What?'

'Have you ever fainted?' Rose was surprised at how natural her voice sounded. She wasn't screaming or crying. But then, blackouts were nothing new and, as always, she couldn't hold onto a sense of panic. She felt rested, like she'd been asleep, but also wired and jumpy like she'd just had a boatload of coffee. Maybe she had.

'Everyone has fainted at least once,' Astrid said airily. 'Or passed out, at least. Haven't you seen the amount we all drink?' She put a hand onto Rose's arm. 'Why? Do you not feel well?'

'I think I've been losing time,' Rose began.

'That happens when you sleep. It's normal for humans,' Astrid said.

'Very funny.' Rose dipped a spoon into her own hot chocolate. It was creamy and rich, the sweetness catching at the back of her throat. 'I'm serious. I think something might be wrong with me.'

Astrid put down her own mug and regarded Rose for a long moment. 'I think you need a breather.'

'I don't think that's—'

'Time out. A holiday. Let's go somewhere. Italy's nice.'

'We've got uni. Lectures. Essays. Exams.'

'You're just listing things now.'

'Lists are good,' Rose said. 'Lists are sane. Lists are sensible. I need more lists in my life right now.'

'You need a plan,' Astrid said.

'Yes, plans too. Plans, lists. Maybe a graph or two. Or a diagram.'

'If you say the word 'spreadsheet' I'm leaving,' Astrid said, smiling a little. 'We should go somewhere hot and lie on a beach.' She stretched her arms above her head. 'I can't remember what it feels like to be warm all the way through.'

Rose was distracted. 'I thought you liked Edinburgh. You said the climate suited you.'

'It does,' Astrid said. 'But I fancy a change. The cold has got a little old.'

Rose still wanted to tell Astrid about her blackouts but the moment seemed to have passed. She thought, instead, that she might try to fill in some blanks. 'Where are you from again?'

Astrid eyed her. 'Northumberland. You know that.'

'Yeah, yeah. That's right. I forgot.'

'And I've got a mum and a dad and a younger brother and two dogs. Black labs.' Astrid nudged her. 'Your turn.'

'I'm from Edinburgh. I live in Edinburgh. I go to university in Edinburgh.'

'Family,' Astrid prompted.

'I live in Bruntsfield with my mum and dad. It's cheaper than digs. I don't have any siblings or pets. My mum is a—' And there was the blank. It reared up so quickly that Rose felt dizzy, felt like she might fall into it. She didn't know what her mum did. She knew there was an office in the house but she had no idea what either of her parents did in there. In that moment, she couldn't even picture her parents. There was just a space where they should be. Figures shaped like paper dolls that were completely black and featureless.

Astrid put a hand on her arm and Rose felt instantly better. The image of her mum and dad came back. Her mum had brown hair in a bob. There were a few streaks of silvery grey that she said she couldn't be bothered to dye. She had kind blue eyes and wore soft cotton fair-trade clothes in shades of aubergine and ochre. Her dad was really tall and skinny. He wore checked shirts tucked into cord chinos and brown loafers with a tassel which Rose hated and had begged him on more than one occasion to burn.

Astrid pushed Rose's cup towards her. 'Drink up. We need to go shopping.'

'Okay,' Rose said, obeying. She liked shopping with Astrid. It involved looking at things, mostly, rather than buying anything, but it was soothing. Astrid had definite opinions about everything and Rose could just go along for the ride, nodding and saying 'uh-huh' every so often. It was relaxing.

At that moment a woman walked past. She had a port wine mark on her cheek and the stain reminded Rose of blood, splattered over skin, the thick smell of iron. She doubled over, suddenly sick.

'What is it?' Astrid was by her side, her hand on her back.

'I'm fine,' Rose said. 'Just a stomach cramp.' There had been blood. She had seen blood in the lecture theatre, a hallucination or waking dream. The professor with his throat slit and the blood pouring over his checked shirt, soaking it in seconds. Another image, sharp and clear, snapped into her mind. Paris. On the metro.

'Did we go to Paris?'

Astrid tilted her head to one side. Didn't answer.

'On, like, a mini-break?' Rose was trying to make her question sound normal but as soon as the words were out, she knew they were ridiculous. University students didn't go on mini-breaks. They went travelling. During the summer holidays or on gap years. She rubbed her hands down her skirt, worried that they were still sticky with blood. Then she remembered her tattoo and pulled up her sleeve to check. The rose was faded. The skin had healed so that the pink ridges had flattened into silvery lines.

Astrid was watching her carefully. 'We've never been to Paris.'

She was lying, Rose thought, with a sudden burst of clarity. Then she realised that was ridiculous and shook her head to clear the thought.

Astrid reached out and touched Rose's arm. 'Are you sure you're all right? You look a bit spacey.'

A familiar calm swept through Rose. She felt sleepy and content, and as if all was well with the world. With her world. They would go shopping together. It would be fun. 'I'm fine,' she said. 'Just sleepy.'

Astrid moved back, but kept her hand on Rose's arm. The pressure was gentle but insistent, and Rose felt the contact like a lifeline. Something to hold onto.

Astrid was smiling properly now. There was a touch of something else around her eyes. Relief? 'You're always tired,' she said.

Underneath the blanket of calm, Rose was still thinking. *Paris. Walls made of bones. A man with murder in his eyes.*

Mal checked into a cheap hotel in Craigmillar and fortified the room by shifting the furniture and hanging protection charms above the door and window. He wanted to keep moving and use his flat as little as possible, at least until this job was over. It was too easy for Pringle to find him at home and he could do without another kicking. He would prefer to put off explaining his latest failure for as long as possible. Ideally, until he had turned it into a success.

He lay on the bed with his arms folded behind his head and watched television. At least, he pretended to watch television. Usually, he watched for a few minutes and his exhausted – or slightly drunk – brain gave up to oblivion, but tonight his mind wouldn't stop playing reruns. The girl, Aislinn, with blood running down her forearms, dripping heavily on to the floor. The light in her eyes moments before, the smile of pure joy.

He hadn't killed her, he told himself. She'd done that herself. She was a few twigs short of a bushel. That was probably always going to be her end, one day or another. Better she'd had a taste of freedom from that antiseptic place of misery first. He told himself these things over and over again, but he knew they were lies.

Finally, he sat up and clicked off *The Bourne Identity*. He got dressed quickly and went to a bar down the street, one that opened late and served decent booze. He would get drunk, really, really drunk, and then he'd be able to sleep. Well, pass out, but who cared. He could've drunk in his room, of course, but he always tried not to do that. It smacked of failure and desperation, alcoholism and misery. Whereas, he told himself as he pushed open the door to the dank little watering hole, drinking amongst miserable strangers was a positive life choice. Practically fucking healthy.

The guy behind the bar had long hair cut into a style that had last been fashionable in the nineteen eighties and had looked good never. He had a rabbity face and pale eyes that looked like they didn't see enough sunlight. Or, Mal assessed as he ordered single malt and a pint of beer, like they'd shrivel up in the light of day. According to his father, vampires existed. They were a kind of demon, but not worth bothering with. Pathetic creatures with none of the superhuman strength or sex appeal of the movies. Vampires did feed on blood, but very rarely. Mostly they ate nothing. They were dead and, it turned out, that really took the edge off a person's appetite.

A couple of drinks later and Mal was expecting the bar – and the world – to be looking a little brighter. Instead, his mood had bottomed out. He looked around the room to see if there was anyone worth fighting. Instead, he saw Robbie, an informant with an addiction to the supernatural. For a charm or two, Robbie would spill his grandmother's guts. Of course, Mal wasn't exactly sitting pretty on the moral high ground, a thought which did nothing to improve his mood.

Robbie hadn't clocked Mal. He was too busy

concentrating on his drink and had his back to the room. When Mal slid into the seat next to Robbie, he wasn't moving quite as smoothly as usual and rocked the table with his knee, but the little shit still looked gratifyingly alarmed.

'Mal. Long time no—'

'Got anything for me?' Mal said.

'What you looking for?' Robbie licked his lips.

'A girl. One who isn't really a girl, ken?' He didn't know he was going to say the words until they were out there, but they felt true. He needed to be busy. Otherwise he'd stay in this bar, drinking and fighting, until he died. There was a pit beneath him that had opened up the day Euan got hurt, and he knew he could just slide in, easy as falling asleep.

Robbie shrugged. Just a little gesture, but it made Mal want to grab the back of his head and smack it repeatedly into the table. Something in his expression must've translated, as Robbie hurriedly straightened up. 'I'm sorry, man. I don't know what you want me to say. There's stuff going on, there's always stuff, but—'

'I've got two missing girls. They disappeared in a puff of smoke.' Mal turned his hands palm up. 'Minus the smoke.'

Robbie nodded, opening his mouth to speak.

Mal raised a hand. 'If you say there are always missing girls, I will do something impolite.'

'Not missing. Can't help you with lost girls.' Robbie licked his lips again. Obscene. 'Dead girls, though—'

Mal put down his glass. 'Tell me.'

'There's always dead girls,' Robbie said automatically, and then looked panicked. 'I mean—' He stopped speaking, the brief moment of panic already clearly replaced by avarice. 'What's it worth?'

'The usual,' Mal said. 'If it's good information.'

'There was a lassie, Laura Moffat. Killed where she worked and polis are stumped.' Robbie paused for emphasis. 'And gossip says she's no the first.'

Mal was about to say that didn't sound unusual, but Robbie barrelled on. 'It's unusual 'cause they weren't, you know, violated or nothing.'

'Mundane girls?' Mal was trying to work out why Robbie thought this was his kind of job.

He shook his head. 'Mebbe not. And if it was *them*, there's gotta be some kind of power thing. You know what their kind are like.' He managed to affect a superior expression when referring to demonic kind.

Mal nodded. 'Any scrap of mojo and they want to hoover it up like it's coke and it's nineteen eighty-eight. Where?'

'Laura was in Peebles. Hit before that was France. Hospital in Paris.'

'What makes you think they're the same guy?'

'Just passing on the blether,' Robbie said. 'Man who telt me about the wee French girl said it was strangulation. Nasty way to go.'

'Your contact have any thoughts on the killer?'

Robbie shook his head. 'Only that he had to be pretty feckin' strong. It was a bare-hand job, not with a wire or rope.'

'So he didn't see it happen? That's speculation?'

'Aye.' Robbie had his hand out for payment.

Mal closed his eyes, wondering what the hell he thought he was doing. He was wasting time with the likes of Robbie just to avoid being alone with his thoughts. He had to get his house in order.

The next day, Mal was still in pain from his kicking at the hands (and feet) of Pringle's crew and he had a headache pulsing behind his eyes. He was strong from training and, thanks to a few basic charms, his healing was accelerated, but he still hurt. His dad used to say 'hurting is good, it reminds us that we're human.' He meant it in a practical sense of not pushing your physical limits, keeping yourself safe in the field, but Mal preferred to think of it in more philosophical terms. Although these days that was less comforting. He didn't hurt so much anymore, not emotionally.

Of course the one thing guaranteed to make him feel something was a trip to the hospital to see Euan, but he had woken with something else on his mind. A sense of purpose that he hadn't felt in a long time. As he shaved his bruised face, taking more care than usual, he thought about the lost girls.

Maybe he could look into the death of Laura Moffat, check to see if it was his kind of case. And if it was, he could do a bit of old-fashioned monster-hunting. He was too late to save Laura, too late to save Aislinn, but if he killed whatever got Laura he'd be balancing the scales a bit. Inch a little closer to the brother Euan had known. *Mebbe.*

He risked a trip back to his flat to pack. He showered

and drank a mug of very strong coffee with a handful of painkillers, then sat in his favourite chair with Monty perched on his knee and rang his friendly official contact. DS Robert Ingles used Mal when he needed to know things that he couldn't officially find out, and in return Ingles would let his fingers dance over the police database on occasion while narrating his findings out loud. 'I want to know about Laura Moffat. She lived in—'

'Peebles. I know. I remember her,' DS Ingles said, sounding grim. 'Don't tell me that's one of yours.'

Mal stamped down on his irritation at the sergeant's tone. It wasn't like Mal made these things happen. 'I don't know,' he said. 'Could be. What do you know?'

'Poor wee girl was just eighteen. In college, worked part-time at her local.'

'And that was the place?'

'As long as you're going to share,' he said. 'What's this all about?'

'Probably a wild goose chase,' Mal lied.

'You'll have to buy me lunch, then,' Ingles said. It was a well-worn line and both men knew it was never going to happen. They weren't pals, weren't even colleagues. Mal wrote down the Moffat family's address and the name of the bar.

'Who found her?'

'Owner of the pub when he went to open up next morning. Keith Roberts.'

'She'd been left to lock up on her own?'

'No. There was a senior member of staff, Jim Penny-cuick, but he was in the cellar changing the barrel when he apparently decided to take a nap. Didn't wake up until the proprietor started screaming the next day.'

'A nap?'

'He's rather fond of the product, as they say.'

'I assume he was—'

'Cleared? Aye.' The DS gave a short laugh. 'Thought we were onto a winner there, but no.'

'How so?'

'He didn't fit.' Ingles sounded distracted, as if someone was trying to get his attention in the office. 'Gotta go,' he said, and finished the call.

It wasn't much to go on. And Ingles had told him nothing which suggested something supernatural had happened, but Mal wanted to be busy. And, a small part of him admitted, he was keen to delay looking for his disappearing girl. She was clearly not human, or had some kind of power that wasn't entirely of the mundane world, but she looked human. He remembered the way her eyes had widened in fear and his jaw clenched. It wasn't going to be easy to hand her over to Pringle. It wasn't going to feel good, and it opened up all the messy questions about his current situation he would prefer not to answer.

It was freezing in the car and Mal was glad he had worn his jacket. He got the heater going after a few muttered swear words. There was thick grey cloud shrouding the city and the verge alongside the city bypass was encrusted in a hard frost. It looked dirty in the dark light, but as he pulled away from Edinburgh and into Midlothian, the sun appeared, turning the frost picturesque. He drove to Peebles, through affluent villages and friendly foothills sprinkled in snow. He parked on the wide main street of the town, near the mercat cross. It was a grand affair, set on top of a hexagonal stone structure, with three fish carved into one side.

Peebles had a well-to-do air, with a fine-looking hotel on the high street and individual shops with brightly painted fronts. He walked down Northgate and turned into a smaller side street to the pub. The Traquair Inn had a whitewashed front and a planter with heather by the door. It also did an all-day breakfast. Sitting at the bar, Mal ordered a bacon roll. It was a small area, clean and bright for a pub, and there were a couple of tables occupied by people enjoying fry-ups. The smell of grease was overlaid with last night's beer and a top note of lemon air freshener.

He waited until he'd finished his breakfast before asking questions. The food was good, and he didn't want to get thrown out before he'd eaten. The guy behind the bar was in his late forties to mid-fifties, with a moderate paunch. He looked well-tended, like he had a loving wife and played golf on Sundays. It was a fair bet this was Keith, owner and manager.

'That was great,' Mal said when the guy took his plate. 'Can I get an orange juice?'

He waited a beat while the man located a carton from one of the fridges. 'Is this your place?'

'Aye,' Keith said, pouring out the juice.

'I'm actually writing a story and was hoping I could ask you a couple of questions about Laura Moffat.'

'Journalist?' Keith looked more interested than

offended and Mal expected the next question to be 'how much are you going to pay?'

Mal shook his head. 'I'm writing a book.'

Keith glanced around the pub, as if checking for people listening. 'I don't want any bad publicity. It's not good for the trade.'

'I totally understand,' Mal said, not believing him for a second. People loved a grisly story. He made to slip off the stool. 'Thanks for the breakfast, anyway.'

'Hang on,' Keith said. 'You're not going to drop this, are you? You'll be asking around?'

Mal spread his hands. 'I'm sorry, it's my job to do the research. I don't want to be inaccurate—'

'Aye, that's what I'm worried about. I don't want you speaking to one of the nutjobs. They'll sell you a pile of shit and call it gold.'

'I just want the truth. Police haven't solved it and the family deserve some closure.'

His eyes narrowed. 'You know her folks?'

Mal thought about lying for a split second, but a place like this it was risky. Too small. He shook his head.

'She doesn't really have any. Didn't have, I mean. Orphan with a brother up north somewhere, but I don't think they were in touch. He came to the funeral but no one round here recognised him.'

'That unusual?'

'Round here?' He gestured around the tiny room. 'It's no exactly a metropolis.'

'Did you know Laura well?'

He nodded, eyes suddenly very soft and serious. 'Since she was wee. She got fostered by an English couple and stayed in the town from when she was eleven or so. They moved back down south when she was seventeen and she elected to stay put.'

'So that's her family, then.'

'No really,' he said, and Mal waited for him to elaborate. He didn't.

'Where did she stay?'

'With her pal. Freya McDonald.'

'They rent a flat or something?'

'Nothing like that round here. Besides, neither of them was earning properly. They both stayed with Freya's mum on Glen Way.'

'That night—'

He held up a hand. 'Don't ask me why I left her to lock up on her own, I've told the polis that until I'm blue in the face. She wasn't on her ain.'

'But the guy...' Mal pretended to consult his notes. 'Mr Pennycuick.'

'He was a drunk,' he said shortly. 'Aye. But a decent enough man and I didn't know he was drinking on duty.'

Mal tried to control his incredulity. If he had an alcohol problem, how could anyone expect him to resist while behind a bar for hours at a time?

'I'm surprised they didn't arrest him, though. I'd have thought he'd be a prime suspect.'

'He was, right enough,' he said. 'But thing is, he couldn't have done it.'

'Why's that?'

'When I came in that morning, the door to the cellar was locked.'

'And he was inside?'

'You're no getting it. It was locked from the outside.' He paused for maximum effect, to let this nugget sink in.

Mal obliged him by whistling through his teeth. 'That's weird.'

'I didn't even really twig until they started asking all the questions. I was a bit distracted, as you might imagine.'

'You found her, then?'

'Aye.'

'I'm sorry.'

'Not something I'm ever going to forget.' He gestured around the room. 'Had to get the room gutted. New flooring, new bar. Even got new curtains.'

That explained the cleanliness.

Mal looked down at his notebook, breaking eye contact in the hopes of setting his interviewee at ease. 'She was stabbed, is that right?'

'She was gutted,' he said, unconsciously repeating the word. 'There was blood everywhere. She was on the bar, laid out, like.'

'Were there any objects left around? Anything on her person?'

'I didn't look,' he said. 'I just yelled and then I heard Jimmy banging on the door downstairs.'

'Not easy to get over a thing like that.'

The man started polishing the bar, didn't meet his eyes. 'Worse for her.'

After a respectful pause, Mal returned to his questions. 'Can you think of anyone who might've wanted to harm Laura? Anyone strange hanging around, showing too much interest in her perhaps?'

'You mean a boyfriend like?'

'Or just a punter with an eye for the ladies. Was there anyone odd here that night? A stranger perhaps?'

Keith shook his head. 'I looked out for her. Everyone knew that. No one would've dared...' He trailed off as if realising the ridiculousness of the statement given the circumstances.

'She wasn't with anyone?' Mal said. 'Romantically?'

'No.' He shook his head. 'No way. She wasn't like that.'

Christ, Mal thought. No wonder this guy had been top of the suspect list. Not only did he find the body but he was channelling full-on creep mode.

'What was the nature of your relationship?'

His eyes narrowed. 'How d'ye mean?'

Keith's accent got more pronounced the more agitated he became. The plummy tones that he'd used to greet Mal as a customer had fallen away and he sounded more Glescae than borders.

'You were fond of her, that's obvious. Was that reciprocal?'

He flushed red. 'We were pals.'

'You didn't want more?'

'Christ, man. She was the age of my daughter.' He was flushed, looking like he wanted to take a swing.

Mal held his hands up. 'Fair enough.'

'I think you should leave,' he said. 'On your way.'

Mal slid from the stool and thanked him. He didn't hold his hand out as he figured the guy was more likely to punch him than shake it at this point.

CHAPTER EIGHT

Melody Wainright had been working in her parents Gas'N'Go station since she was eleven. Out in the middle of the Iowa fields, she thought she had seen every kind of driver that existed on the planet, but when the door opened on the cherry-red cab of the Western Star she did a double take. It wasn't just that the trucker was female, although that was still fairly unusual, but that she was very slight. As she jumped delicately down from the cab and landed in a crouch like a cat, Melody could hardly believe she could reach the pedals. Perhaps she used blocks under her feet like Short Round in Indiana Jones.

Melody pushed the magazine she'd been reading underneath the counter and pulled on the gloves she used for pumping gas.

The woman was young, too. She looked the same age as Melody but she guessed she must be a year or two older in order to have her haulage license. She had very long dark hair, which was braided in one thick plait, and was wearing skinny black jeans, a tight black t-shirt and thick-soled army boots. It was the kind of look Melody had seen on the gothically-inclined kids at school, but on the trucker it looked utilitarian rather than fashionable.

'Melody, right?' the trucker said, smiling.

'How do you know that?' Melody took a step back. The smile was not a good one. She could see that the trucker meant it to be a good one, something to put a person at their ease, but it hadn't worked.

'My daddy knows your daddy and he said I should look you up if I was in the area. And,' the trucker shrugged a little, as if to indicate uncertainty, 'here I am.'

Melody knew something wasn't right. There was a certainty deep inside, but she'd been brought up to be polite. Not just to customers, who were the lifeblood of their store, but to neighbours, teachers, church folk and family. Melody's father still believed in corporal punishment and she'd had her manners beaten in from an early age.

'May I use your restroom?' The trucker had moved closer and Melody took another step back. 'And I'd sure like to stock up on supplies while I'm here. I ran out of bottled water a while back and I'm thirsty as a dog. I got money, if that's what you're worried about. I'm not looking for handouts.'

As the trucker spoke, she reached into her pocket as if to show Melody her money, but she brought out a knife. 'I can see you're not buying this,' she said, and then sprang forward.

Melody was already running. She had a few steps

head start and was taller, longer-legged. She'd almost made it to the safety of the store, where she could've locked the door, pulled the security shutters and phoned the police, when she felt a hand on her shoulder and was jerked back.

She landed heavily on the ground, the breath knocked out of her lungs. She rolled over to face her attacker, bringing up her arms and legs in a defensive move just quickly enough to block the trucker, who was bearing down. There was a flash of silver in the trucker's hand and Melody twisted to the side just as she stabbed. The blade struck the concrete and a tiny chip flew into Melody's cheek.

Melody had been training in self-defence for years. Her father had paid for the lessons, thinking it would be a good idea for his daughter to be able to fight off would-be suitors or deal with dodgy patrons of the Gas'N'Go. Melody had happily learned the moves, knowing in her heart that she would be ready if her daddy ever decided to teach her any more manners.

She put her forearm up to block the next blow and bent her legs into her chest. If she could plant them on the trucker, she could use her strong thigh muscles to push her attacker away. Or, if the trucker came in too close, she would bring her closer with her legs, grab her hands and use her own momentum to flip her over-head. Melody had done the move several times in class but had never tried with a properly murderous opponent. She got her feet onto the truckers mid-section, but the girl pushed them apart and slipped between. In a single second, she was lying across Melody and the knife was at her throat. Melody went still. 'Please,' she said.

This close, Melody saw the delicate features and pale skin of her killer. Melody had thought she had hazel eyes, but now she could see that one was green. She looked so young, so pretty; it didn't seem possible that she was doing something this brutal. Perhaps she was frightened. Melody's terrified brain scrambled for reason. There had to be a reason for this to be happening. For this pretty girl to want to hurt her. 'I can help you,' she began.

'It's really nothing personal,' the trucker said, and slit Melody's throat.

Mary King's alehouse was squashed between a tattoo parlour and a Mexican restaurant on Cockburn Street. Its wooden front was painted black and faded gold and a couple of tables were placed somewhat hopefully on the pavement outside. It wasn't her only hostelry, of course, just her current favourite. She had always kept her money in tangible assets, property and pubs. Times changed and fashions came and went, but people always needed a roof over their head and liquor in their blood.

Mary King didn't put on airs and, as a point of pride, she put business first and foremost. Always had, and that was her secret. She was a man of the people. Well, a woman of the people. Creature of the people. Whatever.

Take the lowlife who was sidling into her bar at this very moment, Mary King thought. Many folk would think themselves above Robbie, a little man who drank meths for breakfast and had just enough wit to lace up his own shoes, but not her. Not auld Mary. She knew Robbie's value right enough.

Robbie was looking around the bar, his tongue anxiously wetting thin, chapped lips.

Mary King contemplated the scene with satisfaction, as her tongue played with one of the many piercings in her bottom lip. The fire was lit and gentle light flickered over the rows of wine bottles, the smell of garlic was thick in the air, and every single one of the creatures lounging at the tables would kill for her without thinking twice. Without thinking at all, in fact.

'You have something for me?'

Robbie shuffled forward. If he owned a cap, he would have been holding it in his hands. 'Missus.' He swallowed and tried again. 'Missus King, I got information.'

'Isn't that wonderful?' Mary King looked around, enjoying the rapt attention of her audience. The Sluagh were all very fine, of course, and she wouldn't think for a moment to disrespect Pringle's choice of army, but a human who could see her true self was delicious. The Sluagh were, she was forced to admit, loyal but dull. Humans like Robbie were physically repulsive and weak as kittens, but there was something about them, some sort of energy, that made their attention something worth having.

She drank in a little more, watching Robbie sag towards the floor. She ought to be careful. If she took too much of his spirit he would die before he had given her his present.

'Spit it out, Robbie,' she said.

'Mal Fergusson. He's looking for a girl.'

'And?'

'He's freelance, like, but he does work for Him. I thought you would appreciate it, ken?'

'Him?' Mary King was no longer feeling the glow of happiness. If Pringle was engaging the services of a mercenary like Fergusson, he was up to something. She had heard rumours, but had dismissed them. They had an agreement; Mary King had the unquiet spirits and property, Pringle had his beloved Sluagh and peace in which to play golf. They both had money and influence, more than enough for a thousand lifetimes, and as long as they stayed out of each other's business, all could remain in balance. If Pringle was looking to make a power grab it could be he was sick of harmony and wanted something a little more one-sided.

'What sort of girl?' she said. 'What does Pringle want with a mundane?' Want enough to jeopardise the pleasant arrangement she and Pringle kept with the mundane law enforcement; they didn't bother them as long as they kept civilians out of their business.

'He didn't say.' Robbie had gone beyond nervous and was, in fact, half dead. He was swaying on his feet and speaking automatically, the words coming from deep in his subconscious with no layers of thought or control to filter them.

'Right, then.' Mary King snapped her fingers. 'You can go.'

Robbie was holding his ground. He licked his lips. 'Something for my trouble, Missus?'

They could always surprise you, mundanes. She nodded to one of her audience and he fetched a bottle of wine from behind the bar.

Robbie narrowed his eyes as if he were considering arguing. Remarkable. But then his innate sense of self-preservation kicked in and he turned to leave.

'Wait.' Mary King had a thought. 'Do you know any girls?'

Robbie shook his head too quickly.

'One girl?'

Robbie looked at the floor as he spoke. 'There's a pretty one at Greyfriars. Speaks to the ghosts, like.'

'Really?' That was power. Could be the girl Pringle wanted. 'Tell me everything you know.'

'She's pretty,' Robbie said, smiling for the first time.

'What else?'

'I think she's a student.'

'A student?' Mary King's interest waned. A pretty student did not sound important.

'And she takes the tours. Out of Greyfriars.'

Mary King took a moment to understand his meaning, and when she did her disappointment was complete. He was talking about the idiotic but necessary tourist ghost shows. Robbie had a crush on a mundane. 'Get out,' she said.

Rose woke up with a start. She opened her eyes, which felt sticky with sleep, and tried to move. Immediately, there was a stabbing pain in her neck and she realised that she'd fallen asleep at the table again. She moved upright from her slumped position and looked around, trying to gauge how early – or late – it was. The beige curtains were glowing faintly orange from the streetlight outside and there was the swish of cars on the road. Evening, then, most likely. It felt like evening and her stomach was growling with hunger. Dinner time, perhaps.

She stretched her back and rolled her shoulders. The stabbing pain receded a little. She rubbed the sleep from her eyes but there was a great deal more of it than she expected. Her whole face felt unpleasantly sticky, in fact, and there was stuff on her hands, too. She looked at them in the half-light and her stomach lurched. It wasn't sleep-drool or eye gunk. Her hands looked black. And the smell that was coming from them was familiar in a horrible sort of way.

She stumbled to the hallway and into the downstairs loo. It was a tiny room with a mirror over a comically-small sink, and a plastic air freshener that lived on the cistern and smelled like the worst kind of fake lavender that had ever been invented. She pulled the light cord and blinked in the brightness. Her hands were covered in dark brown and the mirror confirmed that the same stuff was smeared on her face and neck and down the front of her t-shirt. It was mostly dry, flaking in places. A couple of patches were thicker and stickier. Her brain supplied the knowledge she had been trying to avoid. Blood. In the small room, the smell of iron was over-whelming. Bile rose in her throat and she leaned quickly over the sink to throw up. It splashed up the sides of the tiny basin.

Oh God, oh God. Was she hurt? There was so much blood. She was sore and scraped and tired, but nothing felt serious. After running the water to rinse the basin and washing her hands, she went upstairs to the big bathroom and stripped. She took a long, hot shower, keeping her eyes closed. She didn't want to see the blood swirling down the plughole. It had to be someone else's blood.

After shampooing her hair twice and scrubbing at her skin with a flannel until it was pink and slightly sore, she stood under the scalding water and tried to calm her mind.

There had been blood. It wasn't her blood. She wasn't hurt. At least, not like that. There were scrapes along her forearm and scratches like someone had caught her with sharp fingernails. A vivid purple bruise on one knee.

But where had the blood come from? More importantly, who had the blood come from? Perhaps she had a part-time job in a butcher shop and she'd blanked it out. Or, she'd done a bad thing. And she couldn't remember what it was.

Once she was swaddled in her towelling dressing gown, she made a mug of tea and got into her bed. She pulled the duvet up and concentrated on the hot drink until she felt strong enough to attempt rational thought. She could call Astrid, but she didn't know if she'd be able to say the words out loud.

She forced herself out of bed and picked up her skinny jeans. They were crispy with dried blood and she felt the panic rise up again. She knew she had to speak to

Astrid. She felt that she had just been with her, that something important had happened. Before waking up with the blood. Something else. Something which made her hands burn with remembered pain and her skin itch all over. She felt a lump in the jeans pocket and pulled out her phone. A slip of card came out with it, and she stared. It was a small rectangle with a few letters printed on it. She didn't recognise it, but she knew the word 'car- net'. It was French for a book of tickets.

Freya McDonald's family home was a two-bed semi on a nineteen sixties estate on the edge of town. Being such a tiny place, it was more a couple of cul-de-sacs than a full scheme, but Mal noted the usual suspects: rusted out car, forlorn-looking play equipment, and forest of Sky dishes.

He knocked on the door, hoping to get Freya rather than her mum. The young woman who opened the door could have been either, and he had learned not to make assumptions. 'I'm looking for Freya McDonald,' he said. 'David from the pub gave me this address.'

'Nice of him,' the woman said. 'What do you want with her?'

'I'm not from the papers, but I'd like to talk about Laura Moffat.'

The woman sighed. 'I bet you do. I'm not interested.'

'I'm writing a book on recovering from trauma. It's on the psychology of overcoming extreme experiences, trauma.'

'It was traumatic.'

'Absolutely. But Freya, by all accounts, has dealt with it extremely well and I'd like to profile her in the book. With her permission, of course. It's not really about Laura, it's not about the horror of that event, but about the psychological aftermath for those left behind. It's a self-help thing. Providing hope and guidance for others, you know?'

He couldn't tell if she was buying this particular brand of bullshit, but after a moment she opened the door a little wider. 'Do you want a coffee?'

The kitchen was overflowing with dirty dishes and a box of cereal with the top still open sat on the tiny beech-effect table. She didn't apologise for the mess and Mal found himself adjusting to the fact that this was a surprisingly mature Freya, rather than a youthful mother.

'You not in college today?'

'Gave up,' she said, flicking the switch on the kettle. 'You might not want to use me as a case study after all.'

'I wouldn't say that. You're still walking, talking and breathing. After what you've been through.'

She widened her eyes. 'You know, so many people don't understand that. It's not just the shock at the time, I feel it now. I feel, like, if something like that could happen to Laura, then what's the point? You know?'

Mal didn't know, but in his role as self-help guru he nodded understandingly. 'Did they offer you counselling?'

Freya turned away and poured hot water into two mugs. 'Sugar? There isn't any milk.'

'No thanks,' Mal said, as Freya dumped a generous

amount from a paper bag into her own mug and stirred vigorously.

'The polis sent a woman round and the college told me I could see the student counsellor, but I didn't bother in the end.' She handed Mal a mug which had a ring of dirt around the inside.

He set it on the table and got out his notebook. 'Is this okay?'

'I think so. I want full copy approval before it's published though.'

He nodded, trying to hide his surprise. 'No problem.'

'I did media studies,' she said, by way of explanation. 'I know what youse are like.'

'How are you doing these days?'

'All right.' She shrugged a little. 'Getting by like everybody else.'

'Keeping busy?'

'I'm working, if that's what you mean.'

'I meant, more, psychologically. Do you have any techniques you could pass on for getting over something like this?'

'You don't get over it,' she stated flatly, sounding much older than her years. 'Laura was my best friend. I loved her and she's gone. Not just gone, but taken. And no one knows why and no one knows who. It's fucking chaos.'

'The investigation?'

'No. The world is fucking chaos. No meaning to anything if that can happen.'

Mal suppressed the sudden urge to high-five the girl.

'That's a very understandable way to feel. I'm sure that a lot of people can relate to that sentiment.'

Freya put down her mug of coffee, untouched, and ripped a sheet of kitchen towel from a roll. She dabbed at her eyes, as if wary of smudging her makeup.

'Let's talk of happier times,' Mal said, covering his real motive underneath the guise of being kind, of caring about the victim. He didn't even feel a stab of guilt. He had long ago made peace with the necessary deceit that went with his chosen profession. He was a conniving bastard, but he owned it, at least. 'What was Laura like? I heard she was clever? Good at her schoolwork and that?'

Freya nodded. 'She was a right swot. Always did the assignments on time, never skipped class. Well, hardly ever.'

Her eyes had flickered, like she was remembering something. 'Had she started missing class sometimes? Maybe to meet someone?'

'You mean, did she have a "young man".' Freya's voice dripped with so much sarcasm she didn't need the air quotes.

'She didn't, I take it. What about admirers? Anyone hanging about her, anyone you were worried about?'

Freya lifted her chin. 'You sound like the polis.'

'That bar where she worked. Did she have any trouble there? Before.'

'Nah. Keith had a bit of a crush and half the regulars were eating out of her hand. She was lovely, you know. Just had a way with people so they liked her. She could get on with anybody. Any job, any age, didn't matter.'

'She was well liked.'

'She was well loved,' Freya corrected, emphasising the word. 'Golden aura.'

Something about those words made something click in Mal's mind. 'You two were an item?'

'Bingo,' she said sourly. 'I don't care if you put it in your book. I want the world to know that my love was taken away from me. I'm proper fucking grieving. My mum doesn't believe me, insists we were just friends. Round here isn't exactly enlightened. Even with equal marriage and Graham Norton.'

'How long had you been together?'

'Properly?' She slumped back in her chair, her voice dead. 'Eight months.'

'And was everything going well? No big fights?'

Her eyes narrowed. 'Why are you asking that?' She sat forward again. 'Are you suggesting I had something to do with her death?'

'No,' Mal said. 'Of course not. Just trying to build up a picture of her last few days.'

'Why? I thought this was a self-help book about overcoming grief?'

Fuck. In his haste to cut to the chase he'd forgotten his cover story. 'It is. I'm just trying to get as full a picture as possible. It's all relevant. What she went through is what you went through. Especially as you were so close.'

Freya seemed to relax again. 'It's funny you getting that. Being a bloke. Everything did happen to me, too. When she argued with her parents or whatever, it was like it happened to me, even if I wasn't there. I'd hear all about it and I cared, I wanted to make everything better.'

'Did she argue a lot with them? I heard they moved down south.'

'Oh, yeah. They up and left her.'

'I thought it was her decision.'

'Not really,' Freya said. 'They made it impossible for her to go. Made it pretty fucking clear she wasn't wanted.'

'But they fostered her. They chose her.'

Freya looked at him pityingly. 'You get money for fostering, you know.'

Mal wasn't in any great hurry to drive down to Wiltshire, but he had committed to digging around and felt a dogged determination to see it through. Besides, cases had sent him on far longer journeys in the past and eight hours on the motorway wasn't so bad with the right music playing.

It was significantly warmer when he stepped out of the car in the pretty town of Devizes. However, it had been getting busier and more congested on the roads, too, so living down south was definitely a trade-off. He would take freezing cold over crowds of people any day of the week.

Laura's parents lived in a semi-detached cottage towards the historic town centre. The building opened directly onto the street but the well-tended window boxes hadn't been nicked, which either meant an exceedingly low crime rate or that the Moffats put out new ones every week.

Mal generally didn't phone ahead, but he had checked that they wouldn't be away on holiday by pretending to be a cold-caller for PPI recovery. Now he was here, his back cracking from the long drive and diesel fumes from the motorway still lingering in his lungs, he wasn't at all sure it would be worth it. In his experience, the last people to know anything at all about an eighteen-year-old girl would be her parents. And these ones didn't even live with the girl in question.

Still, he rang the doorbell and gave his prepared spiel to Mrs Moffat, showing his fake warrant card and hoping there wasn't CCTV around recording this most illegal of deceptions.

'Do you want to come in?' She stepped away into the house without waiting for an answer. 'My husband's not here, I'm afraid. He's at work.'

'That's all right,' Mal said, following her inside and shutting the front door.

In a living room that was the polar-opposite of Freya's kitchen, so clean and tidy it looked as if was never used, Mrs Moffat perched on the edge of an armchair. 'Sit down, please.' She waved at the matching sofa.

Mal mimicked the way Mrs Moffat was sitting. Both to ressure her that he wouldn't stay long and to, hope-fully, engender trust. He opened his black notebook, the one that could belong to a police officer, a reporter or a traffic warden, and turned down the offer of a cup of tea.

'May I ask when you last spoke to Laura?'

Mrs Moffat took a deep breath as if readying herself for a horrible revelation. Then her shoulders slumped and she said, 'Four or five months. At least.'

'Had something happened between you?'

'We've been over all of this already,' she said. 'Why do we have to keep answering the same questions? It's so hard.'

'I'm very sorry,' Mal said, ignoring the needles of guilt. 'I wouldn't ask if it wasn't important.'

Mrs Moffat went very still. 'Has there been a development in the investigation?'

He nodded. He knew it was immoral to lie, to raise this poor bereaved woman's hopes, but that hope was the best way to ensure her full cooperation. And if she wasn't a poor woman, after all, but a suspect, then it would alarm her. A stone-cold professional would be warned, of course, but anyone less than that would just be wrong-footed, maybe into making a mistake. 'We have a new lead on your daughter's killer.'

Her eyes darted to the door, as if she was worried her husband would return. Mal filed this away and pushed, very gently, on his original question. 'I had the impression that there had been some kind of disagreement between you and your daughter.'

'Me?' Mrs Moffat shook her head. 'Laura and I got on very well. I mean, the early years when she first came to live with us were tough. Everyone warned us that they would be, but nothing quite prepares you...' She stared past Mal.

'If you could take me through the events which led

to you and your husband moving to England, and Laura staying in Scotland.'

'Of course.' She took another steadying breath. 'Truth is, there had been some friction between Laura and her father. Normal teenage stuff, though, nothing too major.'

'But you were still on good terms?'

She nodded tightly. 'As good as we'd ever been, yes.'

'You weren't close?'

'Do you have children?'

He shook his head.

'It's complicated. More so when they come to you as fully-formed people. There's only so much you can do... To mould, to teach...' She trailed off and looked down at her hands, clasped in her lap.

'How old was Laura when she arrived?'

'Eight. Very serious little thing. Very intense. I thought that if we gave her time and love she'd warm up, but she never really did.' She looked away. 'I know how bad that sounds. Believe me.'

'You did the best you could and you gave her a better life than she would've had otherwise, you've got nothing to be ashamed of.'

Mrs Moffat looked at him, surprised.

'Nobody is blaming you,' he said, not at all sure that was true. He hoped it was. There was true evil in the world, so many terrible things, he didn't see why someone who tried their best to make a family and give a kid a normal life should get grief.

'But I couldn't love her,' she said suddenly. 'Not really. Not deep down inside in the way you're supposed to. People talked about how they'd walk in front of a lorry to protect their kids and I never felt that.'

Mal didn't know what to say. It was an extreme way of measuring love, but very effective. Would he have walked in front of a lorry for Euan? Yes. He wished he had done.

'Forgive me, but I still don't understand why you were estranged. It all sounds very amicable.'

'There's more, but... I can't tell you. It sounds mad.' She was shaking her head.

It took Mal a moment to realise that she meant this literally. As in 'insane'. 'Is this something you didn't mention earlier? To the investigating officers?'

'I did,' she said defensively. 'At first. But I could see the look in his face – the first policeman I spoke to – so I didn't say it again. He didn't believe me. He thought I was in shock, I think.'

'I'm different,' Mal said. 'Try me.' He resisted the urge to lean forward.

She raised her chin, as if readying herself for a battle. Then she said, 'Laura could do things. When she was little she'd move stuff around her room. One time I opened the door to tell her to go to bed, it was past her bedtime, but she was in there. She was lying down with the duvet pulled up but she wasn't asleep. She was watching her toys moving about on the floor.'

'They were moving without anyone touching them?' She nodded.

'Okay. Anything else?'

'Just 'okay'?'

He nodded. 'Was that the only time?' He was

keeping outwardly calm while his mind was reeling. Telekinesis in humans was a myth. His father had never encountered a true case in all his years of hunting. Which meant that either things in his world were changing or he didn't know as much as he thought he did. Or, most likely, Laura Moffat hadn't been entirely human.

'No. I asked her not to do it in front of her friends, other adults. We were frightened it would get her singled out, picked on. Or something worse.'

'Good call,' Mal said. 'People aren't generally great with the inexplicable.'

She looked at him appraisingly. 'You don't seem very shocked.'

'I'm pretty much unshockable.'

'Right. Well, she did it to annoy me, she knew it worried me and she used it. Not at first, but as she got older. Then she got hormonal and moody.'

'That sounds like normal teenage stuff.'

'With flying objects,' she said. 'Not normal and not even a little bit funny. My husband couldn't cope. He shouted at her, kept setting all these rules. I told him that it was a mistake, that if he kept coming down hard on her she'd rebel, but he wouldn't stop. He was just frightened, I know, but the damage was done.'

'Did he hit her?'

'No!'

'Never?' Mal pressed. 'Not even a smack?'

She sighed. 'He tried to smack her once. He just lost his temper and lashed out. Just to smack, you know, but she lifted him to the ceiling and left him there for half an hour. After that, he avoided her as much as possible. As soon as she turned sixteen he said she had to move out. He didn't say it to her, he didn't speak to her if he could help it. But he said it to me. Said we had to. That we weren't safe, that she'd turned on him and she could turn on me, that we didn't know what she was capable of.' Mrs Moffat looked down at her hands. 'That's when we started making plans to move away.'

'How did Laura take the news? Was she upset?'

She looked uncomfortable. 'We didn't tell Laura.'

He sat back, half admiring their gumption, their sense of self-preservation. 'You did a flit?'

'She was round at her friend's house. Freya. We'd been planning it for a while, so we packed up the essentials and left.'

'Did you leave her a note?'

'Yes.' She was wringing her hands. 'I know how bad this sounds. I know you'll think we were terrible. I left money. I said I'd phone her in a little while but it was hard to find the words.'

'How long before you rang?'

'Three months.' Her voice was quiet and she didn't look at Mal. 'It got away from me and then it had been so long I was scared to speak to her.'

'By which time she'd moved in with Freya.'

'Yes,' she said. Her voice changed, became sour. 'If I'd known that we could've sold the house straight away.'

'Saved yourself some cash,' Mal said, his sympathy receding.

She pulled a face. 'We're not rich, it's not easy paying for two houses.'

'How did the phone call go, when you did speak?'

A long look. 'How do you think?'

'Fair enough. Was that the last time you spoke to your daughter?'

'Yes.' The voice was barely a whisper.

'Do you know if Freya knew? About her abilities.'

'I have no idea.' She shook her head for good measure.

'She never mentioned them to you, never came to you for advice?'

'We weren't close. Freya was a bad influence.'

'Freya was a bad influence on Laura?'

'She gave her ideas. Confused her.' Mrs Moffat's lips pursed and Mal lost a little more of his sympathy.

'You didn't approve of their relationship?'

'They weren't in a relationship,' Mrs Moffat said very quickly. 'They were friends. That's all.'

Mal nodded his understanding, wondering how much of this woman's distaste for her daughter's sexuality had coloured her opinion of her abilities. 'So Laura was different in more ways than one. That made you uncomfortable. Did you fight about it?'

'I don't know what you're talking about.' She got up. 'I think you should leave.'

'I think you should sit down,' Mal said, mildly enough. She sat. 'When you spoke to Laura, did she sound frightened?'

'No, of course not. If she had I would have done something.'

'She sounded normal?'

'She was angry. That we'd left.'

'Anything else? Did you talk about how she was getting on? Her life?'

Mrs Moffat closed her eyes. 'She talked about Freya. She knew it annoyed me and she was just trying to get back at me. Which was fair enough, really. I was in the wrong. I deserved it.'

Mal didn't say anything, didn't want to stop the flow of words.

'She was worried about something. I thought it was her college work. She was working in the bar in the evenings and didn't feel like she had enough time to get everything done. She drew, you know. Art. I didn't like a lot of it, but she was talented.'

When she stopped speaking, Mal asked if he could see some of Laura's work.

'I don't see what difference it would make. How can that help?'

'All the same,' he said. When Mrs Moffat didn't move, he added pointedly, 'If you don't mind.'

She got up and left the room and Mal settled in for a long wait. She must've known exactly where to look, though, as she was back in a couple of minutes. 'Her old portfolio. These folders cost a fortune.'

She unzipped the A2-sized leather folder and began spreading work out on the coffee table. There were charcoal sketches of horses and birds, studies of heads and beaks and movement. Mal knew exactly nothing about art, but they looked good. A blue sheet with strong black lines caught his eye, although it took him a moment to identify the subject of the picture: a face dissolving into the background. Underneath that was a watercolour study of seashells, and under that a piece of canvas with oil paint layered in thick swirls. They looked utterly different, as if each piece had been done by a separate artist. 'Are these all hers?'

'Yes,' Mrs Moffat said. 'We're not artistic.'

'Laura said this one was her brain when she had a migraine.' She pointed at the swirls.

'Did she get those often?'

'Monthly. Linked to her hormones, the doctor thought.'

'Did she take tablets for them?'

Mrs Moffat pursed her lips again. Shook her head tightly. 'She said they made her feel disconnected. Said she couldn't concentrate for days after. To be fair,' she added, 'when she did take them they knocked her right out. She'd sleep for twenty hours, no problem, then be all woozy.'

'Did she have them every month?'

'At least once a month, usually more.'

'Did she act strangely after them?'

'She seemed a bit downbeat, sometimes she would refuse to leave the house, even when she was feeling better. She cancelled plans with friends, didn't want to go into school, that kind of thing.' She sighed. 'She was like a different girl.'

'You've been a great help,' Mal said, putting away his notebook.

Mrs Moffat got up with him, her eyes bright with unshed tears. 'Can't you tell me anything?'

'Sorry?'

'About the developments. Do you have a suspect or a

lead or something? There's been nothing, no news for ages. Forgive me, but I thought you'd given up.'

You. The police. Mal shook his head. 'Never. We won't stop until your daughter's killer is caught and brought to justice.'

The light went out of Mrs Moffat's eyes. It sounded like a platitude to Mal's ears. Maybe it was something the police had already said to her. Maybe it was something she'd heard too many times on television crime dramas. Nothing was real, nothing was genuine.

At the front door, he thanked her again.

'Tell me the truth,' she said, her voice stronger, the tears still unshed. 'Is there truly something new in the investigation? I won't tell anyone, I swear,' she added quickly. 'I just need to know that it isn't over. That she hasn't been forgotten.'

Mal felt like hell. He reached for one of the woman's hands and held it lightly while looking her straight in the eyes. 'I'm the new lead in the investigation. It's not something the police can ever admit to in public, but I am a specialist in cases like Laura's. I have the knowledge to look in certain places and to study certain angles. And I will do everything I can to find the truth of what happened to your daughter.' He dropped her hand and turned to leave.

'You know about her abilities?' Mrs Moffat said, sounding slightly bewildered. 'You are a specialist in that?'

He didn't hesitate. 'Laura's abilities are just the tip of the iceberg. An iceberg I am intimately acquainted with.

I will find who did this, I swear. I won't forget Laura and I won't stop until somebody has paid for her death.'

Mrs Moffat's expression was a mixture of hope and mistrust. 'Do you really work for the police?'

'All the time,' he said, and got into his car, trying to look reassuring and dependable. Inside he felt something unfolding. Another life broken, shattered by loss. He started the engine and pulled away from the kerb, glancing in his rear-view mirror to see Mrs Moffat standing forlornly on the pavement outside her house, her hands clasped in front of her body as if she was praying.

CHAPTER NINE

Rose opened her eyes and the world rushed in. Sky. Pavement. Scottish Georgian architecture and a biting edge to the air. The dizziness and disorientation gave way to balance and comfort. She was outside the psychology building and just in time for Professor Lewis's lecture. Rose had the unshakeable sense that this exact sequence had happened many times before and that, somehow, it meant that all was well.

But then the fog in her mind rolled back. The world was spinning, faster and faster, and for a sickening moment she felt herself fall. There was the scent of baked bread and cigarette smoke, and the sound of someone speaking French. She tried to focus on the words, but they drifted away.

She shook her head lightly, as if to clear it. A group of students walked past her and into the building. It was reassuringly familiar and she felt the click as her thoughts realigned. She was Rose MacLeod. She was a student. She had been asleep in bed, or maybe some-where else, but then she had lost time. That didn't sound good, but it was all right. She was waiting for Astrid, her best friend, and everything was absolutely and completely fine.

Her arm itched, like a little reminder. She pushed up her sleeve and checked her inkless tattoo. It was barely there. A ghost of the image, picked out in silver lines, only really visible when she tilted her arm. From experience, she knew that was at least another week on from the last time she'd seen it. Probably more like a fortnight. What had she been doing in that time? She saw Astrid turn the corner and pulled her sleeve back over the tattoo. She noticed something at the same time – her fingernails looked dirty. Holding her hand up to her face for a closer look, she saw traces of something black around the edges of her nails and underneath, low down and untouchable by a nail brush. In that instant, she remembered: blood over her hands, trying to scrub it away, the water in the sink turning pink.

'Remind me never to drink again,' Astrid said, by way of greeting.

The words seemed to be coming from far away. Rose lifted her hand and inhaled. The smell of iron was there and, at once, it was everywhere. She was seeing a girl outside a petrol station. Bright sunshine. A knife.

'Something's wrong with me,' Rose said. She felt as if she wanted to sit down, right there on the pavement.

'Oh, dear,' Astrid said, frowning at Rose. 'Is it still happening? I was worried about this.'

'Still happening?'

'Are you remembering weird things? Things you're not supposed to remember?' Astrid grabbed one of Rose's hands and squeezed, not very gently. 'You're Rose MacLeod. You are a student at Edinburgh University.'

'We were in Paris,' Rose said. 'We just – sort of – zapped there. Like magic.'

'Fuck,' Astrid said quietly and dropped Rose's hand. 'I need a drink.'

Fear flooded Rose and, for a moment, she thought she might fall down. A student with a bright red backpack glanced at her and frowned as he passed. He looked like a child. No, even younger than that; a baby. Unformed and barely alive. There was something very wrong and even Astrid looked like an alien – her features just a jumble of odd, fleshy parts with no coherence.

'It's going to be okay,' Astrid said. The words sounded stilted, false. But then she patted Rose's arm and things shifted again. At once, Astrid seemed like the girl Rose knew and loved. 'I promise,' Astrid said. 'You're safe.'

Rose didn't know how long they had been outside, but the stream of students entering the building had slowed and then stopped. The lecture must have started. They ought to be in the theatre, Rose thought, sitting in their usual places. Rose would have an open pad of lined paper and Astrid would be complaining about her hangover. Rose felt an itch, as if she was about to remember something important, but she was distracted by Astrid's hand in hers, towing her along the pavement and away from the psychology building. 'How did we get to Paris?' This seemed important.

Astrid kept on walking, dodging people on the pavement and half-dragging Rose until she moved faster. Astrid was taking an odd and twisty route through the city, seeming to just walk for the sake of walking. 'Power,' she said finally, not looking at Rose. 'You can do things that other people cannot.'

'But I'm a person?' Rose hadn't known she was going to say those words until they were out. Now that they were, she felt afraid.

'Of course,' Astrid said quickly. 'You just have some extra powers. It's not that odd.'

Rose opened her mouth to say 'it really is', but Astrid had ducked down a narrow close and she was already too far away to hear.

'We need help,' Astrid said once Rose had caught up with her. She was bouncing down the steep steps of the close as if she was dancing, while Rose felt as if she would fall at any moment. The muscles in her legs quivered and she felt off-kilter. When a couple stopped abruptly in front of them and turned to go back up the steps, Astrid swerved around them without breaking pace, but Rose almost collapsed with the effort of halting and moving to the side. Her head began to pound.

Astrid cut up through the Grassmarket and Rose concentrated on keeping up and not passing out. Astrid had said that she had 'powers' but she had never felt so weak.

'Who was the man we ran away from?' Rose said, once she had enough breath to do so.

Astrid glanced at her, slowing as she thought. 'I don't know.' She tapped her lip. 'I wonder if he did something—'

'To me?'

'Mmm,' Astrid said. 'Your memories are protected. You're not supposed to be able to access them. It's to keep you safe.'

That made no sense.

'There aren't many with the juice to mess with the mojo I laid down.' Astrid sounded petulant.

'You laid down?'

Astrid stopped. They had reached Candlemaker Row and Greyfriars Kirk and Astrid pulled Rose close, lowering her voice. 'You have power that a lot of very bad people would want if they knew about it. I am your guardian, I keep you safe. I figured out a long time ago that the best way to protect you from other people was to hide your true nature from everyone. Even you.'

'So you want to hide it again? You want to wipe my memory?' Rose still felt oddly calm, as if all of this insanity was perfectly reasonable. She felt tired and spacey and very, very weak. A small part of her mind was insisting that this was huge, important, frightening, but her overriding feeling was of exhaustion. She wanted to have a lie down.

'The tour folk might know,' Astrid was saying. 'They see a lot, and if that guy knows the life he might have been poking around. Somebody put him onto you.' Astrid looked suddenly terrifying. 'And I want a word with them.'

'Tour people? Drama students know about this

stuff?' Astrid was usually pretty scathing about her ghost tour colleagues. They corpsed rather too often for her professional tastes.

'Got to get my head torch,' Astrid said, which didn't make things any clearer. The booth was shut up for business, but Astrid produced a key. Rose kept watch at the door and Astrid passed out a slim torch that was a lot heavier than it looked, and a pewter flask with a cross on the side.

Feeling ridiculous, Rose asked, 'Is that holy water?'

'Close enough. It's Ardbeg. Matured for fifteen years in a sherry cask.'

Rose turned the flask over and found a skull etched in the metal. 'If you say so.'

'Trust me,' Astrid said. 'We'll need it for bribery. These folks don't give out intel for free.'

'Intel?'

'Intelligence. My God, Rose, do you never watch CSI?' Astrid sounded so much like herself, then, that Rose felt some of the weirdness shrink away. It was like they were messing around, playing a game to alleviate boredom in a dull tutorial.

It was significantly colder by the time they reached Blair Street. The weak sun had been swallowed by dark clouds and there were spots of stinging rain. Rose wrapped her arms around herself and wished she'd had the foresight to buy a hot drink.

The entrance to the vaults looked innocuous. Just another doorway in the city. 'This is the way we bring the punters out, but it's the quickest way to get to the deepest tunnels.'

'Oh, goody.' Rose injected as much bleak sarcasm into her voice as possible, but Astrid just flashed her a grin. A couple walked past, arm in arm, their heads close together. Astrid waited until they were a few feet away, then unlocked the door.

The passageway inside was dimly lit with electric bulbs, but was much darker than the overcast day outside. Rose blinked, trying not to freak out.

'Make sure the door is shut properly. We don't want anybody following us.'

'Like who?' Rose said, but Astrid was already way ahead and disappearing through a wooden door at the end of the passage.

Uneven steps led downwards and into another, narrower passage. It was clearly old. The stonework was weathered by the trickles of water that appeared to have been running over them for decades. The air was mouldy.

'People lived down here?' Rose felt like ducking even though there was easily a foot of soupy air between the top of her head and the curved stone ceiling.

'Lived, traded, whored, died.'

The passage opened out into one of the vaults, an area the size of a box room with the remains of some neon green paint on the walls. It was colder in here. Rose shivered, wishing she had a thicker coat.

'What's with the paint?'

'After the vaults were reopened some of them were used as practice rooms by musicians. Mostly punk bands – they were the only ones who didn't mind the incumbents.'

'Incumbents?'

'The residents. Like our friend Mr Boots.'

Rose felt a hard pinch just above her right elbow, and cried out.

'Manners, Mr Boots,' Astrid said severely. She was looking at the empty space to Rose's side, and it was creepy.

Dust on the floor swirled, forming a spiral that rose upwards in slow motion. 'What the fu—' Rose began, but the dust coalesced into a small dense cloud and rushed at her face. She choked down a mouthful of ancient dirt and started coughing.

'If you don't behave, you won't get any of this.' Astrid held up the flask.

Rose straightened up, her eyes streaming. Astrid was tucking the flask back into her bag. 'After,' she said, as if in response to something. 'I want a chat first.'

Rose wiped her eyes and blinked. They felt coated in grit. That was when she saw the man. He was the same colour as the brownish-grey stonework and not much taller than she was. He wore a dirty coat and a shapeless, squashed-looking hat.

'No.' Astrid was shaking her head. 'I might stretch to some ciggies if you stop hiding and start acting like a gent.'

'I'm no gent.' The voice was raspy and deep. The voice of a man who most certainly did not require any more cigarettes.

'That's a good trick,' Rose said, trying to work out how

his costume was semi transparent, and how his feet were floating a couple of centimetres above the floor. 'I bet that wows them on the tours.'

Astrid shot her an exasperated look.

'Those bloody tours,' the man's expression twisted. 'You're always bringing them through here. Disturbin' me. Cain't a man sleep in peace?'

'Oh, hush,' Astrid said. 'You love the sport.'

The man called Mr Boots turned and gave Rose a slow, filthy smile. 'I haven't seen you before, darling.' His voice wasn't just raspy. It was hollowed-out.

Rose's mind stopped fighting the evidence of her senses. It was the voice of a dead man.

Her hands curled into fists and her fight or flight response kicked into overdrive.

He stepped forward, his rheumy gaze suddenly intent. 'What are you, gurlie?'

Astrid stepped in between them, blocking Mr Boots from coming any closer. 'What do you see when you look at her?'

'Hard to say.' He glanced pointedly at Astrid's bag. 'I'm awful thirsty, ken?'

'You're just awful,' Astrid said. 'Forget about my friend, I want the news. Anything out of the ordinary you want to tell me about?'

He turned his head and the motion made Rose feel a bit ill. 'There was a ground-shaking. And blood ran down the walls.'

Astrid didn't seem to be thrown by this alarming statement. She sucked air through her teeth. 'When was this? Last couple of days?'

He stuck out his bottom lip, sulking. 'I can't keep track of time. It jumps. Gives me a powerful sore head.' He turned big eyes to Rose. 'Telt her to give ma drink, missus.'

Perhaps one day, a long time ago, Mr Boots might have been a good-looking man. It was difficult to say, but Rose would've laid money that his bad personality had always darkened his features so that even in life they'd never appeared wholesome. Now, his pock-marked and craggy visage was nothing short of horrific.

'Okay,' Astrid said. 'How about this. Remember the last tour group I brought through here? The one where you tripped that old man, broke his ankle. Remember that?'

He shrugged.

'Was it before or after that tour?'

'After, mebbe.'

Astrid took the flask out and unscrewed the lid. Mr Boots licked his lips, his eyes wide and excited. She took a healthy swig and he made a grab for the flask, but she caught his hand and took another drink. He howled. Astrid seemed to have grown several inches. She towered over Mr Boots, who appeared to be in genuine pain. Her wrist flicked and his arm twisted. He sank to his knees in front of her.

'Forgive me, missus.' He was blubbering now, ghostly snot bubbles popping from his nose.

'I need someone higher up the food chain,' Astrid said. 'Where can I find something older than you?'

'Dinnae ken.' He shook his head violently then let out a howl.

'Don't lie to me, Peter.'

'I dinnae. I swear.'

'Come, now, Peter,' Astrid said. She smiled and Rose felt afraid. 'I just want a name.'

'Mary King.' Mr Boots snapped his lips shut, but the words were out.

'And where, pray, will we find fair Mary?' Astrid said, and took another slug from the flask, smacking her lips after in a pantomime of pleasure.

Despite the tears that were flowing down his face and the twist of agony on his lips, he looked suddenly obstinate. Astrid seemed to sense it, too. She gave a wide smile and upended the flask so that the last few drops of whisky fell onto the floor.

Mr Boots howled again, an inhuman sound that made the hair on the back of Rose's neck stand up.

She didn't pay any attention to her surroundings as she stumbled back through the vaults. She didn't check to see if Astrid was following her, either. Outside, the cold rain and dark sky was welcome. It wasn't underground with a howling spirit. When Astrid appeared, shutting the door carefully behind her, Rose looked at her friend with new eyes. 'For Christ's sake, Astrid.'

'Cake,' Astrid said. 'And a hot chocolate. I need sustenance.' She plucked a packet of Benson and Hedges out of her jacket, crumpled it up and put it in the bin. She set off, then paused and turned around. 'The thing you have to remember about Mr Boots is that he's a complete bastard.'

'I see that, but I just...'

'You don't see anything, Rose. You're just skipping

along in your perfect little bubble while I do all the hard work. You have no idea—' She broke off, looking away for a moment. When she spoke again her voice was controlled. 'You have no idea of the dangers I'm protecting you from. A little shit-weasel like Boots is just a disgusting pustule that I had to squeeze for the common good.'

Rose lost her grip on her own temper. 'Well, I wish you'd tell me. Stop with the cryptic need-to-know nonsense and Just. Tell. Me.'

Astrid let out a sigh then began furiously re-doing her hair. 'I wish I could.' She stabbed a kirby grip so hard that Rose winced. 'But if I do, your tiny mortal mind will most likely break into a thousand little pieces and I'll be stuck doing the fucking Rose jigsaw for the next six hundred years.'

Rose stared hard at the ground for a few moments. Her stomach felt as clenched and cold as ever, but her mind had gone strangely clear. She was used to living with uncertainty. She'd been hiding her weirdness and time lapses from her parents and her best friend for as long as she could remember, which wasn't very long, but what was life except what we knew and remembered? So. She could do this a bit longer. At least she felt she was getting closer to revelation. At least it appeared that she wasn't the strangest thing she knew – there were ghosts in the world, and goodness only knew what else.

'So, ghosts, huh?' She tried to make her voice upbeat, to cut the sudden tension between them.'

'It's all about attention for these apes,' Astrid said, still twisting curls of hair with a fierce concentration.

'Ever wondered why celebrities get a kind of sheen? Even minor ones, ones who have no talent for anything except being known, being on telly in some reality show?'

'That's the makeup,' Rose said. 'And the botox. They get all buffed and camera-ready. Makes them more attractive than the rest of us. And we prize beauty.'

'No.' Astrid shook her head. 'It's more than that. They've been watched. They've had the attention of hundreds of thousands of minds. That polishes them right up. And it's a spiral. They get a bit of energy from the attention and that makes them shine a little bit. That little bit of shine makes people watch them more carefully and their shine grows.'

'Shine?'

'Energy, magic, holiness, shine. Same thing, different lexicon.'

They began walking, heading back up to South Bridge. 'It can't just be attention,' Rose said after a moment.

Astrid shrugged. 'You know that plants grow better when we talk to them?'

'Is that true?'

'There was a study,' Astrid said. 'And think about the rise of mass media. It's a way of getting a load of attention from millions of people all at once. It's got a power of its own, something above and beyond the content it provides.'

'Are you saying television is sentient or something?'

'Television? Are you living in the dark ages? The internet is the most powerful force on this rock at the moment.' Astrid shuddered. 'I hate the fucking internet.'

'Is that where Mr Boots gets his energy from?'

'The ghosts? Yeah, I suppose. They had a bit of juice left over when they kicked the bucket, a bit left in the battery, and then a couple of people saw them and had a strong emotional reaction...'

'They were scared,' Rose said. 'They saw a ghost.'

Astrid formed finger guns, which she proceeded to fire at Rose. 'Exactly. That energy was enough to make them burn a little brighter so they were seen by a few more, and a few more, and so on until they were practically alive again.'

'So the ghost tours—'

'Feed the ghosts at the same time. Bingo. Symbiotic kind of thing.'

Rose had often wondered why there seemed to be a handful of 'well-known' ghosts like the Grey Lady of Glamis Castle or the little girl down in the old streets beneath Edinburgh. Now she knew: they were maintained by their fans. There was a strange kind of comfort to that, a symmetry. She had seen a plaque once in a gift shop which read 'you travel in the direction you are facing'. Whoever wrote it probably had no idea just how right they were. Question was, which way was she, Rose MacLeod, facing? She didn't know. She didn't know anything. And with that, the panic was back.

She stopped walking as the panic stopped her breath. Black spots danced in front of her eyes and she doubled over. Then Astrid's hand was on her shoulder and she felt the tide of fear and confusion recede. She straightened up and took a full breath, and then another.

She had the feeling that she had been about to ask Astrid a question, something important, but the words had drained away. She felt calm again, as if everything was going to be all right. Ghosts were real and that was fine. At least she had Astrid.

She looked into her friend's beautiful face. 'You mentioned hot chocolate?' Her voice came out weak, though, and she felt a spurt of loathing. Why was she so pathetic?

Astrid took Rose's arm. 'Sounds good.'

'Whipped cream?' Rose said, picturing those tiny marshmallows spilling from a tower of sweet white foam, the smell of sugar and cocoa and the comforting warmth as it slipped down her throat.

'With extra sprinkles,' Astrid said, still gripping her arm. Truth be told, she was squeezing a little too tightly and it hurt, but Rose wasn't going to say anything. Astrid was her world.

CHAPTER TEN

When Mal arrived back in Edinburgh he was too wired to sleep. His body was tired, he knew, and his eyes felt gritty and sore, but his mind was racing. Laura had some kind of power, that was clear, and he thought it was a fair bet that was the reason she had lost her life. While lots of people had enough sight that it could be trained into becoming useful, like himself, very few had a natural gift. And those that did tended to struggle with their mental health. The image of Aislinn came to him, gazing up at him from her seat on his sofa, eyes wary but resigned, as if all the bad things had already happened. And another image – Aislinn's face as the life drained away with the blood that ran down her arms and onto the pub floor.

He swallowed a handful of painkillers and downed a pint of coffee while he contemplated his next move. He needed to find the target for Pringle and draw a line under that particular job, but – and he found that he could finally admit this to himself – he wasn't sure he could do it. Yes, Rose MacLeod was certainly not entirely human, but the fact remained that she looked the part. And Aislinn had called her 'pretty', which was not an adjective Mal associated with the true face of a demon.

The thought reminded him of something Freya had said. 'Golden aura.' He had snagged on it as a sign of her deeper feelings for Laura, but what if she had meant it literally? What if Laura and Rose were connected somehow? What were the chances that Pringle was after some girl that wasn't quite a girl and who definitely had juice, and another girl with a power he had never encountered before in a human had been killed only fifty miles from the city, and they weren't connected? Was Pringle working his way through a bunch of psychic kids? It wouldn't be the first time. Maybe killing them released their energy or whatever to Pringle, made him stronger. Mal felt his face twist. Now that wasn't a good thought. What kind of legacy was he, Mal Fergusson, going to leave the world if he carried along this path? Killed a girl and made the biggest non-human bastard he had ever known even more of a threat. Good fucking job, man.

Of course, Pringle had told him that Rose wasn't human. That she was an object in disguise. It didn't generally do to question the boss. And if Pringle was telling the truth (something which was far from likely) and had all of the available information (again, not a given by any stretch of the imagination), Mal would probably be kicking a hornet's nest for no good reason.

On the other hand, he'd always liked to do his own research and couldn't shake the habit no matter how much of a pain in the bollocks it inevitably turned out to be.

'Can't help yourself, you poor stupid bastard,' he told his yellow-skinned reflection, then went to pay his respects to one of the best business minds in Edinburgh.

Mary King looked amazing for her age. Lush, ripe, devastatingly sexy. She held out a hand for Mal to kiss, but he grasped it in his gloved hand and shook it bracingly. He wasn't a fool.

Mary King shrugged and laughed, the sound spreading down through his body and straight to his cock, which rose in response. She did this every fucking time. One of her games. It was embarrassing, but the knowledge that she was playing a power game made no difference. Even the sickening knowledge of what she was made no difference. His body responded in the same, predictable way, sending him straight back to the horrific days of puberty when he could get an erection looking at a suggestively-shaped piece of fruit.

'How can I help you?' Mary sat down on the low sofa and patted the upholstery in invitation. Her gaze lingered on his crotch, a small smile playing around her lips as she enjoyed the effect she had on him.

He took the desk chair and turned it to face her. He was higher than her now, so she couldn't do any *Basic Instinct* leg-crossing routine. Not unless she was acrobatic. Part of him wanted to see if she'd try, anyway. Part of him that he wished didn't exist and was probably responsible for nine-tenths of his worst decisions.

'Missing person,' he said. 'A girl.' He had already decided to concentrate on Rose, and not mention Laura unless Mary King did first. Despite his hunch, he had no real reason to connect the two and didn't want to put ideas in Mary King's head. Didn't want to send any visitors to Freya's doorstep.

'A girl?' She raised an eyebrow. 'Bit pedestrian for you, isn't it?'

Mal tilted his head and waited. He knew it would piss her off but he was too tired and sore to play the usual verbal games. Most of all, he wanted to get out of this office and back into the relatively fresh air of the street. Mary's flunky knocked quietly and opened the door. 'Coffee? Tea? Water?'

Mary King waved him away. 'Mal isn't staying.'

Perhaps it had been a mistake not to kiss her hand.

She leaned back in her chair, regarding him for a moment before speaking. 'Can you tell me anything about this lost girl?'

'Long dark hair, wears it like a rope.'

Her mouth quirked. 'A plait?'

He waved his hand. 'Yeah. She looks about nineteen or twenty. She was using the name Rose MacLeod. Pale but not artificially so.'

'No makeup?'

'Don't think so. Can't always tell.'

'Glamour?'

'Didn't feel one.'

'You might not,' she said, not altogether kindly. 'Why do you want her? Search and destroy?'

'No. Strictly recovery only.'

'I'm sorry,' Mary King said, clearly not sorry in the slightest. 'I meant, why does your employer want her? What's the end game?'

'Strictly recovery only,' he repeated.

Mary King leaned back. 'I hate talking to the monkey but, in this case, the organ grinder is worse. How is dear old Pringle these days? Bet he's feeling those aches and pains. Bet he's hungry.'

Mal told his face not to react, but Mary just laughed. 'I'm teasing you, darling boy. I know Pringle would turn you inside out if you so much as used his name.'

'Can you help or not?'

'Well, now. I haven't seen your mystery girl but I'll keep a lookout, let you know straight away if I get the eyeball. Unless you want me to recover her for you – for a fee, of course.'

'No,' Mal said. 'Information only. Highly prized information,' he added. 'Excellently priced.'

She nodded. 'Fair enough.' Mary King stood in one fluid motion. 'Always a pleasure.' But she didn't hold her hand out this time. He was dismissed.

Outside, he wondered about that. Mary King never usually missed an opportunity to make him uncomfortable. Getting away from her was always a performance. She would hold out her hand, and he'd have to pretend to kiss it or brazenly shake it like he had first thing. Or she'd lean in for a cheek kiss, her smell almost knocking him out, and then she'd laugh as he swayed on his feet like a punch-drunk boxer.

Walking towards town, he mulled it over. Perhaps he'd really pissed her off this time. No, if it was that bad, he wouldn't have made it out of the building so easily. He'd checked for a tail, too. Nothing. In fact, he decided as he came in sight of Calton Hill, it was almost as if she'd suddenly wanted him gone. As if she was hiding something.

The bad feeling wouldn't leave, the skin on the back of his neck prickling. He always trusted that patch of skin, so he doubled back to Mary King's office, took a seat by the window in a nearby cafe, and watched. After a couple of hours he was rewarded by the sight of a car pulling up to the kerb outside and one of Pringle's lackeys getting out of the back. The creature was buzzed into the office building, and stayed for half an hour before getting back into the waiting car and being whisked away.

Mal was preparing to leave the cafe when the main door opened and Mary King herself stepped out. She looked relaxed, but he knew that her surface appearance meant less than nothing. She projected whatever she wanted to project – her skin and bone was just a borrowed suit, animated with dark magic and a well of power she had sucked from the world over decades.

She was alone, which was unusual, and she moved away down the street rather than hailing a taxi or getting into a private car. Mal left the cafe and began following her, still not sure what he was hoping to achieve but working on instinct, when he saw something far more interesting. His mystery girl.

She was walking with her blonde friend in the opposite direction and on the other side of the street. They were moving fast and within seconds they were swallowed by the crowds of people on the pavement. He made his decision instantly. He had a job to do for Pringle. His last job, he had now definitely decided. He would apprehend Rose MacLeod and, assuming she was as non-human as he expected, pass her straight onto Pringle and wash his hands of the whole situation. If she was human but with some sort of power, like the unfortunate Laura Moffat, he would rethink. He liked that word. He knew, deep in his heart, that it would end the same way. If he didn't complete the job, Pringle would have him killed, and, besides, he couldn't protect her from Pringle for more than a week or two. There was no option which ended well, no puppies and rainbows to aim for, but the word 'rethink' gave him the smallest, briefest illusion of choice.

Mary King didn't often walk the streets – she preferred a nice ride in a flash car. Something red and shiny like fresh blood. Although, she had to admit that strolling the pavements was a far more pleasant experience now than in days past. No more wading through filth, no more odour of unwashed human and sewage. Well, she amended, as a vagrant-scented individual with questionable personal hygiene sloped past, less odour, at least.

She needed to think. Mal Fergusson, the broken-down son of a hunter, had dared to visit her office and, although she could scarcely believe it, he had appeared to be asking for her help. What could be so important about a missing girl? Then, to make matters worse, she had called for Pringle but he had insulted her by sending one of his whelps. She felt the flush of fury and embarrassment and something darker beneath – fear. Pringle may as well have removed his trousers and waved his member in her face. Disrespect. The lackey had come bearing lies, saying that Pringle hadn't engaged Mal Fergusson for a job in months. Mary King had hoped the feel of the city stones beneath her feet and the arching grey sky above would help, but as she took a cobbled lane deeper into the New Town, her mind remained unquiet. Was Pringle challenging their truce? Or had he simply grown old and sloppy and uncaring? Was it an act of war or the ravings of a old monster?

She arrived at her destination and felt the knots of tension in her neck loosen as she gazed upon it. It was half past midday, and a bell sounded somewhere within the school. Children flowed from the doors and into the playground. They wore dark green sweatshirts with the school crest embroidered on the front – a unicorn and a stag up on hind legs facing one another.

Mary King barely registered the symbolism, though. Her entire being was focused on the faint glow which came from the very young. When she had first settled in the city, there had been enough shining light to go around. It had been a haven of superstition and ignorance and blind faith. People left bowls of milk out for the pixies, wore white heather for luck, and washed their faces in the dew on the first day of May. Mary King had grown fat and strong, enough to last her through the lean years which had followed.

Children under the age of ten, as most of these primary kiddies were, had a little shine. They were open and ready to believe with attention that was sparky and new. They had an intensity which would wane soon enough. Ordinary children didn't have much, it was true. The glow which Mary King could see was barely even detectable in most of the small people who were currently engaged in a spirited game of wall tig, but amongst the grey, small lights shone. They were murky, like candles at the bottom of a muddy lake, but they flickered nonetheless, and she felt her hunger sharpen in anticipation of a meal.

The gate to the playground was locked but it was more a visual comfort to the law-abiding and something to stop the smallest and stupidest of the small people from running into traffic. Mary King gave thanks that she hadn't washed up in America, where an armed guard would doubtless have barred her way, and reached over the top of the gate to slide the bolt open.

The tots nearest were three girls. Seven or eight, perhaps, although children had been getting steadily larger and they may have been younger. Either way, she had only to lay her hand briefly on top of their heads to siphon their meagre gleam. The girls were staring at her, now, suprise just beginning to show on their round faces, but she moved on.

There was one adult supervising the playground, a tired-looking woman clutching an insulated mug with fingerless-gloved hands. She glanced at Mary King and then, as Mary King wished to remain undisturbed, her gaze slid over her and away.

A boy was stood over by the wall of the grey school building. He was slight and pale with gingery hair and a half-eaten banana clutched in one fist. 'Hello,' Mary King said, and the boy looked up. His face wasn't open and trusting like a well-fed milksop, but sharp and wary like the kiddies who used to swarm her streets. She felt a pang of nostalgia for the old city, the streets which had been built over in the name of progress. The cramped accommodations which had been deemed insanitary and unmodern had held a certain crammed-together convenience, and the atmosphere had been thick with power. Folk fervently believing in anything and everything to ward off death's icy fingers and shiny attention had been easy to come by when the biggest form of entertainment and wonder had been a vagrant in a bright coat pulling a half-dead rat out of his stinking hat. She smiled one of her nicest smiles and the boy visibly relaxed.

'May I?' She gestured to the boy's hand, the one not mangling a piece of tropical fruit.

He reached out his hand, as if in a dream, and she took it. The moment their skin touched, the current began. Oh, this little one had a lovely spark. She closed her eyes in pure pleasure. With training he could even have had the sight. There weren't many of those left; she and Pringle had swallowed them all. Choked them down quick as they could to keep their edge. Now it had been years without a decent meal. They had formed their truce, consolidated their own little corners and developed their interests to keep busy, but they were both bleeding hungry and that was the truth.

The spark snuffed out far too quickly. The little one's eyes glazed over and he sat down on the black asphalt. Mary King was already turning away. The hunger at her centre had quietened, but she knew it wouldn't last and that it would soon be baring its teeth. She was back out on the main road, her phone to her ear, ready to summon a car, when a thought dropped into place – what if the missing girl had a spark? If Pringle was lying to her about the girl then maybe she had more than a spark. Maybe she was a flame, or even a bonfire. A bloody feast. Mary King licked her lips.

Back across town, Mal caught up with his target and her diminutive blonde friend. He stayed a cautious distance behind, and followed them along the busy pavement of Princes Street. They cut up to Charlotte Square and, as the streets grew quieter, Mal allowed the distance between himself and the girls to increase. It was harder to follow unobtrusively with fewer bodies to act as shields, but he was well practised in the art.

Luck was on his side, too, as the girls appeared deep in conversation and oblivious to their surroundings. He got close enough to catch Rose's expression as she looked at her friend. She looked frightened and Mal was surprised to find himself responding to her fear. Sympathy. It had always been Euan's weakness, not his, but it seemed his brother had passed on the gift when he'd sunk into his permanent sleep.

There was no time for that now though. They had turned down a side street, a cobbled cut-through with a closed French restaurant, a couple of boxy metal bins and no people. Mal slid his hunting knife from inside his jacket and sped the last few steps. He would grab Rose, hold the knife to her throat, and tell the other girl to run. In the unlikely event that she tried anything heroic, he would disable her with a blow to the head. Knock her out as carefully as he could.

Time expanded, as it always did in the moments of action. Mal had no trouble in closing the gap, taking Rose and pulling her against the front of his body, his arm up in one smooth movement to hold the knife at the optimum angle a hair's breadth from the vulnerable skin on her exposed throat. He had time to note how light she was, lighter even than he expected from her small size. He had time to feel her human warmth, the biological scent of her sweat and hair that was like a wrong note in a symphony. Demons didn't smell like humans. When he grappled with a demon, no matter how they looked at first glance, he was under no illusion that he might be hurting a human being. This was different. Every signal Rose gave was of a human woman – a young, frightened human woman – and it took every ounce of will in his considerable reserve not to let her go and apologise.

He was going to tell the other girl, Astrid, to get away, but in the next second he felt a warmth spreading through his body. It was like sunshine and he had the ridiculous urge to glance up, check the sky.

'Rose,' the other girl said, her voice gentle. 'You can stop him any time you want.'

And then the warmth was abruptly heat, far too hot, running under and over his skin like fire. He dropped his knife and let go of Rose, stumbling back. The last thing he saw, as the pain increased with the heat, licking every nerve ending and setting it screaming, was Rose's pale face as she turned to look at him, her eyes wet with tears and her mouth forming words he couldn't understand. He felt himself fall and he welcomed it, opening his arms and diving into the cool darkness, desperate to get away from the burning pain.

CHAPTER ELEVEN

Rose stared down at the man on the ground, trying to ignore the buzzing in her ears so that she could think. She recognised him from that day in the bar, when he had chased them. Adrenaline was pumping through her body and she felt as if she were on her tiptoes, almost floating. She hoped she wasn't about to zap somewhere like she had on that day. She wondered if it was under her control and, just in case, thought, 'stay here'.

One of the man's jeans-clad legs twitched and she hoped that meant he was still alive. Not conscious, not about to leap up and attack her, but alive. His knife was on the ground where it had had fallen, and she kicked it further away from the prone body, aiming for the handle but missing the first time she tried, her foot scuffing along the pavement next to the weapon.

'Okay.' Astrid had her hands on her hips and was studying Rose intently. She didn't look surprised, more interested. 'How are you feeling?'

'Sick,' Rose said. She couldn't tear her eyes away from the man. She had been so frightened but now that he was unconscious, he looked so young. There was blood coming from his temple, where he must have hit the pavement. Quite a lot of blood. It kept flowing steadily from just beneath his hairline, and something snapped inside her. She pulled a wad of tissues from her bag and folded them into a pad. She knelt next to the man and pressed the pad onto the wound. He didn't groan or wince or grab her by the throat, and she felt something else mixed in with the relief that she wasn't being attacked. Concern.

'Leave him. We need to move.'

'No.' Rose spoke without looking around. The man's face was grey. His skin looked waxy and there was a layer of sweat. She could see pain etched into his face. 'We need to phone for an ambulance.'

'For the man who just tried to kill you? I don't think so.'

The tissues were soaked through but the blood seemed to have slowed down. Rose took a cautious peek.

'Head wounds bleed a lot,' Astrid said, sounding impatient. 'He'll be fine.'

'Are you a doctor now?'

Astrid sighed loudly but Rose felt her kneel down beside her. She put her head on the man's chest, her blonde curls splaying out and covering part of his face. 'His heart is beating at only slightly above normal speed and he's breathing.' Astrid began searching the man's pockets, bringing out a flat wallet and flipping it open.

'Mal Fergusson,' she muttered. 'Why are you buzzing around?'

'We need to do something,' Rose said.

'Nonsense,' Astrid dropped the wallet onto the man's chest. 'Look at him. He'll be awake and ready to kill us in no time.'

On cue, the man's eyes flickered and his head twisted to one side. He let out a groan that sounded like a name.

Astrid stood, pulling Rose with her. 'We have to go.'

'I'm going to throw up,' Rose said. She had done this. She had let something out and it had hurt this man. Badly. He could have internal injuries or brain damage or broken bones—

'All the more reason,' Astrid said. 'Come on.'

Rose allowed Astrid to tow her a few feet down the alley, back towards the main street, but then she planted her feet. 'Dial 999,' she said.

'He's awake,' Astrid said, but her phone was already in her hand and she was hitting buttons with her thumb. She spoke rapidly, giving the street name and saying 'some guy collapsed' before hanging up.

A bus came into view on the road and Rose imagined faces pressed up against the windows, looking at the man lying on the ground and the girls who were walking away from him.

'Perfect.' Astrid held out her arm.

'It's not a taxi,' Rose said, but the bus was already slowing down. It stopped with a grinding noise and a hiss from the brakes. The doors unfolded and Astrid half-dragged Rose up the steps and inside.

Sitting on the fuzzy seat of the bus and hearing the hum of the engine, the familiar sight of the castle looming over the road, Rose felt the urgency of the moment drift away. Her habitual calm was flowing back, slipping over her mind like warm water. She shook her head, trying to stay clear. 'What just happened? Who was that?'

Astrid patted her hand. 'It's all right. It's over now.'

'It's not all right,' Rose said, and Astrid's eyes widened in surprise. 'What did you do to him?' Rose fought harder against the numbness. She pushed her sleeve up and looked at her tattoo, rubbing her fingertips across the raised skin and not even caring that Astrid could see her.

'I didn't do anything,' Astrid said. 'It was you.'

'No. I didn't do anything.' Rose frowned, trying to remember. They had been in an alley. Cobbles and bins. A slice of grey sky high above and a faint smell of onions and cooking oil. There was a light. A flash, maybe, and a man falling to the ground. 'Was he hit by lightning?' She knew the words were stupid as soon as they left her mouth.

'No.' Astrid started speaking quickly and quietly. 'There's an energy inside of you. Some of it must've leaked out. You're not in control at the moment because you can't remember what you are. It's not good. It's like in those moments when you're just waking up from a really deep sleep and you maybe talk nonsense for a bit or your limbs spasm and you kick the wall.'

'I didn't do it. I didn't do anything.' Rose knew she

was lying. Deep down, she knew. 'I've got to get out of here.'

She stood up and made her way to the front of the bus. 'Stop,' she said, not even looking at the driver. The bus lurched as the driver braked. Car horns sounded and there was a ripple of discontent in the bus, passengers shifting and muttering. Rose ignored it all, her eyes on the doors which seemed to be taking forever to open.

Finally they unfolded with a flapping noise and Rose was back on the street, a fine drizzle instantly soaking her hair and sticking her fringe to her face.

She began to walk but then Astrid was there, clattering down the steps of the bus and grabbing her arm. Rose shook her off.

'Rose,' Astrid said, her voice weird and breathy. 'Let me help you.'

'How?' Rose said, fear and confusion giving way to anger, pure and hot and overwhelming.

Astrid swallowed. 'I can protect you. Explain what is happening. We just need to go somewhere quiet.'

'I have to go,' Rose said.

'That's what I'm saying.' Astrid looked relieved. 'I think we should—'

'Not you,' Rose said. 'Me. I've got to go.' She pointed at Astrid. 'Don't follow me. Keep away from me.'

She turned away and began walking. She half-expected Astrid to follow, to tug on her sleeve and argue, or, more likely, to simply walk alongside her for a wee while and then start chatting as if nothing had happened. Truth be known, she was thrown when that didn't happen.

She reached the corner and, unable to resist, glanced back. Astrid looked tiny. She was stood next to a black litter bin and was too far away for Rose to make out her expression. She had the impression that it was anguished and felt a stab of guilt. It was closely followed by anger though. Why was she just standing there? Deserting her? Rose ignored the fact that she was the one doing the deserting and stomped around the corner, out of sight and view of her best friend.

Ex best friend.

Mal opened his eyes just as the paramedic was preparing to insert an IV. He jerked his arm away, sending the needle clattering to the floor of the ambulance. There was something restrictive on his face and it took his brain a second to realise what it was. He ripped the oxygen mask away and looked around, trying to work out how much time had passed. There was no sign of Rose, or her friend with the curly blonde hair.

'Hey!' The paramedic was a man in his forties with a shaved head and a five o'clock shadow. He looked like he could wrestle Mal back onto the gurney with one arm tied behind his back. 'Take it easy. I'm here to help.'

'I'm fine,' Mal said, trying to placate him. His mind had clicked into life and was racing through an inventory of his physical state. His head hurt like a bastard and a stabbing pain in his chest suggested he had re-broken his healing ribs. Not fun, but he would live. 'Thank you.' He sat up carefully. 'I need to go.'

'Nae chance, pal. You're needing to get checked oot.'

Mal reached into the pocket of his jeans, wincing as moved. He pulled out a crumpled twenty and offered it to the paramedic. 'Couple of painkillers and I'll be on my way.'

The paramedic glanced towards the front of the ambulance where his partner was in the driving seat, then plucked the money from Mal. 'Aye, suit yerself.' He rooted around in his bag. 'Paracetamol do you?'

Mal tried a winning smile. 'Be serious.'

'Co-codamol then. Just two, ye ken? I'm no having an OD on my hands.'

'I'm not going to top myself over a kicking,' Mal said. 'You got something stronger?'

The paramedic had made the twenty disappear and now he shook his head. 'You feel that bad, you can take a wee trip to A&E.'

Mal held up his hands in surrender. 'No, thanks.' He swallowed the pills dry and climbed out of the back of the ambulance, ignoring the instant increase in pain. A meaty hand on his arm stopped him for a moment. The paramedic's face was suddenly uncomfortably close. Mal got a view of the large pores on his red nose. 'You'd better no be a journalist, pal.'

Mal started to shake his head but the pain made him stop. 'Nope,' he said instead. 'I just want to go home. To my own bed.'

The paramedic retreated, looking mollified. The doors slammed shut and Mal was alone on the street. He waited until the ambulance had pulled away before searching for his knife. He had assumed he had dropped it during... Whatever the fuck had just happened. But it must have been flung some distance. The hilt was sticking out from underneath one of the big metal bins and he dried it on his jeans before stowing it inside his jacket. He tried to feel victorious about that, at least. It was a good knife, one of his favourites.

He ignored the pain in his head and ribs and began walking, hoping for a taxi but without any real optimism. He probably looked like hell, and the Edinburgh drivers could afford to be picky during the tourist season. In the depths of winter, then they'd pick up a guy bleeding freely from a head wound. *Mebbe.*

The thing that he wasn't thinking about – very carefully and deliberately not thinking about – was the fact that the girl had beaten him so easily. He'd had his arms around her, the knife in position, and she had – what? He couldn't remember exactly. That was what was truly frightening him. He couldn't afford to lose his marbles, couldn't get cloudy. If you got cloudy you got dead.

So, how had a girl who looked like she'd disappear if she turned sideways, knocked him out? The simple answer was that she wasn't a girl, just as Pringle had said. But she had smelled human, felt human. A technicolour, full-sensation memory came back to him: Rose's body against his, the scent of her skin, the intense shine of that long black braid and the curve of her pale neck.

He had to find her.

As if on a psychic link (a horrifying thought), his mobile rang and he saw Pringle's number on the display.

He thought about not answering it for a split second but knew that would be suicide. 'Yes?'

It wasn't Pringle, of course, but one of his 'men'. 'Have you found it?'

'It's in progress,' Mal said. 'Patience is a virtue.' He forced himself to keep his voice level. He knew that Pringle would probably be listening to the exchange and he didn't want to give him any hint of his feelings. He pushed the image of poor Laura Moffat laid out on a bar, her body opened up with a knife, just to release a little burst of energy. That poor kid with her telekinesis would have been like a snack for Pringle, a fucking Big Mac meal to go. An unexpected surge of anger shot through him as he thought of the demonic bastard.

There was a silence and Mal felt the anger flip into fear. Pure cold terror ran through his system to a liquid place down low in his stomach.

'Just a reminder,' the voice said. It was flat, emotionless, which somehow made it worse. 'We don't want you getting distracted.'

He forced himself to breathe deeply, control the fear. So Pringle knew he had been to Wiltshire to talk to Laura's parents. 'I'm not distracted,' Mal said. 'I will finish the job.' He wanted to add 'and then we will be finished' but he couldn't quite get the words out. His hands were shaking, and he clenched them into fists.

Another pause, and then, 'We know your brother is alive.'

Mal felt nothing for a second, just numbness. 'What?'

'Pringle said to let you know, just in case you were

thinking of going off-job. He knows you've been to see Mary King.'

'Information gathering,' Mal said, pleased with how even his voice was. 'But I don't know where you got the intel on Euan. He's deid.'

The demon hung up.

Mal put his phone back into his pocket and carried on walking. He was not going to fall apart. There was every chance that Pringle didn't know that Euan was lying in the infirmary, that he was simply taking a punt. 'He's just trying to freak you out,' he told himself. 'He doesn't know.'

As he walked, he went over and over the conversation, angry at himself for using Euan's name. It wasn't a new detail – Pringle had known Mal and Euan and their father for as long as Mal could remember but it still felt like a betrayal. Pringle shouldn't think about Euan, shouldn't hear his name spoken aloud. Euan didn't belong to Pringle, he belonged to Mal.

Back when his dad was alive, Mal had thought the very worst thing that could happen would be losing him or Euan. When he died, Mal thought the axe had fallen, that nothing would ever hurt him as much again. He and Euan had gone all out for a few months, taking down demons in a way they never had before. It wasn't their job, anymore, or even their mission. It was revenge and redemption, guilt and anger. Euan had always been the sensible one, had always been the one to suggest caution. His most overused phrase was 'let's check it out first'. But it was like a switch had been flipped. He was like one of those Viking berserkers, all flailing fists and snapping teeth.

The worst thing was that Mal had loved it. All the strictures he had chafed against were gone. The wildness he had always sensed inside himself was set free and his big brother's restraining hand was gone from his shoulder. Side by side they hunted until their injuries forced them to rest for a while, holed up in an anonymous hotel on the motorway, almost at the English border and away from Edinburgh and the monster's nest they had kicked.

They had been careless. Unheeding of the long-term consequences. Having been brought up to bring down these creatures, one at a time, they had no concept of how wide the organisation ran, of how the threads bound up every aspect of the city and its people. When they had healed enough to head home, Mal could only think of getting stronger. He had heard of a man who peddled 'upgrades' in a little room above one of the shops in the Grassmarket, and he sought him out. Euan had been against it and had refused to come along. He said it was stupidly dangerous, that Mal didn't know what the upgrade would do to him or what it would cost. When that didn't work, Euan had told him that using supernatural elements, rather than destroying them, was completely against everything they stood for. He delivered the final blow just as Mal was heading out of the door: 'What would Dad say?'

Mal hadn't bothered to reply. Their dad wasn't saying anything ever again. What did it matter? With hindsight, he could identify that moment as the point at which he changed. The singular moment in which the good and the bad blurred a little. He passed over a tight wad of banknotes to a man who was not entirely human, in exchange for a tattoo which would improve his natural healing capability by over fifty percent, and in so doing became a little less human himself.

Rose checked her tattoo as she walked fast away from Astrid. It looked pretty much the same as the last time she had looked, meaning she hadn't missed a chunk of time. She ran her thumb lightly over the bumps where it was healing and waited for the usual rush of comfort. Instead, she could feel her anger drain away and fear step into its place. She was utterly alone. She doubled back, looking for Astrid, dodging the people who all seemed to want to get in her way. The pavements were empty. Not empty of people but empty of Astrid. She was too frightened to double back too far. What if she bumped into the man again? He had looked in a bad way, but perhaps he could have recovered and be ready to attack her again. He could be waiting in one of the doorways or side streets right at that moment.

Walking so fast it was almost a run, she made it to the end of Princes Street, where she got into a black cab. She would go home. She would take a nap, and perhaps when she woke up all of this would have changed. After fighting against the blanket of calm which had dulled her thoughts and lulled her senses, she craved it. Maybe, if she went to sleep, she would lose some time. Skip this horrible now. Perhaps she would wake up outside the university, ready for a lecture, or in a cafe with Astrid, both of them with mugs of hot chocolate and the world reset to a safe and known thing.

Outside her house, she paid the driver and climbed out of the cab. She hesitated on the pavement for just a moment and then unlocked her front door with the Yale key and stepped inside.

The hallway looked just the same as always. Light came through the stained glass panel at the top of the front door and dappled the floor with splotches of colour. The familiarity of it was like a balm and she took a deep breath, inhaling the scent of home.

She sagged against the wall, suddenly weak. At once, she was ravenously hungry and desperate with thirst, but she went straight up the stairs to her mother's study. There was a wild hope that she could prove that this was all insane. That she was having a hallucination. She no longer cared that she would be rushed to a psychiatric hospital, pumped full of drugs, that she would have to drop out of her course, ruin her life. This was serious. She had believed that she had travelled to Paris and back. That a man had wanted to kill her. She could still feel his hands on her skin, the kiss of the knife blade on her throat.

Now that she was back in the house, her instincts for normality had woken up. Something was telling her to stop climbing the stairs. She stopped, one foot raised to take the next step, a hand on the banister.

She knew that she always called 'I'm home,' and then went into the kitchen. That was the routine. That was what every part of her body wanted to do right at this moment. She was hungry. She was thirsty. She should turn around and go back down the stairs to the kitchen. She could make a cup of tea, wrap her hands around the mug, feel the comforting steam on her face as she tipped it to her lips to drink.

No. She was going to break the routine. Everything had fractured. She knew, deep in her bones, that something was very wrong and that this was her chance. Astrid had left her and she had to do something different. Was it Nietzsche who said that stupidity was doing the same thing and expecting different results? Or had that been Oprah? Was Oprah on the television anymore? She tried to remember the last thing she had watched on television, but there was nothing there. Just a blank. She tried to picture the television in the living room – everybody had a television, after all – but she couldn't. She felt like she was flying apart. She was anxious. She was panicking. She needed help.

She took another couple of steps. The urge to call out 'I'm home' was almost overwhelming. She actually clamped a hand over her mouth to stop herself from doing it. She had the irrational feeling that if she called out in her usual way, she would simply go back down the stairs and into the kitchen and everything would regain its smooth running. That was tempting, of course, but the thought that Astrid knew an actual ghost – knew more, in fact, than she would tell Rose, and had just abandoned her – jolted her back to her mission. Change the routine. Shake things up. Get help.

The door to her mother's study was closed. It was an ordinary interior wooden door in a light oak finish with a brass lever-style handle. There was no reason for Rose to be afraid of it, but sweat had broken out across her forehead and she felt cold all over.

She reached out, pushing down the fear and the desire to shut down, to walk away. She pictured Astrid. Astrid smiling at her with her crooked mouth. Astrid spooning the whipped cream from her hot chocolate and talking a mile a minute, making Rose feel normal and loved. She had to change the routine, had to ask for help in order to find Astrid. She pushed down on the handle before the fear could overtake her sense of purpose. The door swung open.

The room was empty.

Not in the sense that her mother wasn't inside, sitting at her desk and frowning at her laptop screen, but completely empty.

There was no desk. No chair. No laptop. Rose blinked. She had an image of her mother's room. There should've been piles of paper and books. There should've been a big pinboard on the wall with coloured notes and photographs.

She stepped into the room. There was a faint scent of chemical air freshener. The curtains were shut, but they were flimsy and there was a fair amount of light coming through. She could see dust motes in the air. Every detail was crisp and real and there was no reason to believe for one second that it was not. She dug her nails into her palms, squeezed her eyes tightly shut, and then opened them.

The room remained empty.

She went downstairs and into the kitchen. She no

longer felt hungry but she forced herself to open the cupboards and look for food. There was an ancient jar of mustard on one shelf, individual salt and pepper packets which had been taken from a chain restaurant, and a single tin of sweetcorn. The smell from the cupboards was of old air.

She opened the bread bin and wasn't surprised to find it empty. She felt as if she had broken into two pieces. One half of her could almost see the loaf of sliced wholemeal and the open packet of crumpets which usually sat in the bread bin, but the other half could see the empty space. The ancient crumbs gathered at the edges. The hint of mould. When had she last eaten something? She could picture herself taking two crumpets from the packet and then toasting them, spreading them with butter and honey. Her fingers remembered the action, the smell of the honey and the way it melted into the hot crumpet, the sensation of the plastic packet as she put it away. She hesitated, trying to focus on what was in front of her eyes, not her memory. Something wasn't right with it, something that was so close she felt she could almost touch it.

The crumpet packet was always open. There were always five out of the six remaining. She always toasted two and folded the edge of the packet under as she put it back into the bin.

Every time.

But if she always ate two, how could there always be five left in the packet? She couldn't recall a single time when there had been one or two or three left. Or when there had been no crumpets at all. All at once, the half of

Rose which saw the full bread bin and her mother in her study and the jar of honey in the kitchen cupboard fell away. None of that had been real. She had never made food in this room. Never spoken to her parents. Never had parents. Every time she had called out 'I'm home' it had been to this empty house.

CHAPTER TWELVE

Fuck. Shit. Bollocks. Astrid walked in the opposite direction to Rose. She had no choice in the matter and knew better than to try to resist. She had been given a direct order and her body would obey.

A group of men were walking behind her on the pavement and she slowed to let them pass. They were young, with tight muscles and loud voices, swaggering along the road as if they owned the world. She breathed in the pheromones and considered a brief distraction from her problems. An hour of pure physicality would clear her mind. For a moment she let her imagination go to that happy place of tangled limbs, sweat and screaming sensation.

No. She resolutely turned down another street, away from temptation. She had been enjoying the holiday spirit for too long and she had become sloppy. Somebody had blabbed about Rose and sent that boy. And she, Astrid, had to accept some blame for the situation too.

She had let Rose become too aware, and now she was alone and disorientated. Maybe even in danger. Astrid felt a stab of real pain and used that to sharpen her focus. She would sort out this mess in no time and then things could get back to normal. Then she would flag down the nearest good-looking body and take it for a spin. With that cheerful thought, she turned on her heel and headed for Greyfriars. The tour folk always had the gossip.

Mal had decided to risk a trip to his flat. He kept a bag packed in his car, but he wanted to check to see if anyone was hanging about, scoping the place. His brain was spinning, trying to work out how much trouble he was in, and his ribs and head were chiming in. Not helpfully.

He checked his wards and found no sign of entry. His birds were as healthy and happy as a bunch of reanimated dead creatures could reasonably expect to be. Monty ruffled his feathers in a way which suggested he was saying 'where the bloody hell have you been?' and Mal stroked his soft head, drawing more comfort from the action than he liked to admit.

At least he kept good pain killers in stock. He congratulated himself on his forethought while he swallowed a handful. The headache from hell had wrapped itself tight and was squeezing his temples in time with his pulse. He also flipped through the scraps of paper, business cards and old index cards which constituted his filing system. He wasn't sure what he was expecting to find. Some forgotten ally who would be able to keep an eye on Euan until Mal could finish the job for Pringle. Someone who could keep Euan safe and then help Mal to move him somewhere new. It wasn't much of a hope, and he wasn't surprised to confirm that his best names were dead or on the other side of the world.

He threw a few clothes into a holdall and emptied some bird seed onto the coffee table. 'Be good, pal,' he said to Monty, then reapplied the wards and protections, as well as re-bolting the deadlocked and reinforced front door.

He drove around the city for a while, letting his thoughts settle. He was good for nothing while he was still thinking about Euan, so he parked near the parliament building and hiked up Arthur's Seat, passing joggers and tourists.

Euan had been their father's golden boy. He was the one who could hit a bullseye, strip a gun in military-grade time, run for the longest without getting out of breath. Mal had never been envious, though. Being the golden boy meant even more of Dad's attention, and Mal had quite as much of that as he could handle. Their dad was intense. That was the polite way of putting it. Batshit crazy was another. Total fucking heidbanger was the most accurate.

When he was very young, of course, Mal didn't realise this. That was just his father. His life was just his life. It wasn't until high school that he grasped that not everyone got a knife for their birthday and a weekend-long lesson in using it to kill things. When Mal was twelve and Euan fifteen, he'd taken them on a camping trip in the highlands. Mal had never seen scenery so beautiful outside of a calendar picture, and the sky when they'd sat out around the fire that first evening had been so big and star-filled that it felt like magic.

Euan had brought marshmallows from a corner shop and they threaded them onto sticks, toasting them in the fire until they were blackened and crusty on the outside and gooey sweetness in the middle. Mal had never been happier and, if pressed, he would find it hard to say he'd ever been happier since. As he went to sleep in the tent that night, Euan on one side and his dad on the other, he allowed himself to get excited about the rest of the holiday. It seemed it was a real trip. The kind of thing he'd read about. Perhaps his dad would teach them to fish in the loch or maybe they'd just climb one of the giant hills, stand on top of the world and shout at that massive sky until their voices went hoarse.

The next day, of course, it turned out that they weren't on a special holiday after all. It was a job. Their father put up some protective charms and told Mal to stay in the tent while he took Euan to kill something horrible in the woods. Mal didn't know what was worse; that their father had brought them on a job or that he'd left Mal behind like a spare part. When Euan had come back he'd been pumped up and full of swagger and tales, but he'd also been pale and there was a gash along his arm that Dad had stitched using his first aid kit. Euan hadn't cried but Mal could see it had been a struggle.

Six years after that, Euan was as good as dead. The thing that had got him was just an ordinary demon. Nothing special. Nothing unusually strong or fast or clever, just one of the Sluagh. Just a routine job in a backstreet in Leith. Euan moved to the right and it went to the left and managed to get a blow past his defences. It was a lucky shot (or unlucky, from Euan's point of view). Mal had seen Euan double over and moved closer as quickly as he could. He dispatched the demon he had been fighting and hit the one in front of Euan. It was too late, though, just a fraction. It had already landed a blow onto Euan's temple, and the light went out of his eyes as he swayed on his feet. Mal had been experimenting with charms and they were both wearing ones which kept them upright. One of the worst things in a fight was to go down. You were vulnerable on the floor. Plus, the sight of a never-falling opponent helped psychologically. Gave you the element of surprise and an edge – something that said 'I'm human but I'm indestructible'. But something Mal hadn't factored in was the curiosity factor. The part that marvelled at the still-standing human and wanted to know why they had their eyes closed. Euan was in a dead faint but the charm was keeping him upright. Maybe if he'd been on the floor, the demon would've left him alone, turned its attention to Mal. Instead, it wanted to know why the human was sleeping standing up and what, exactly, would make him fall down. The demon punched Euan a couple of times in the head. Euan still didn't fall. He was unconscious but upright, held there by the charm Mal had traded from a guy in a bar, and as a result the demon hit him a couple more times, probably causing the damage that put him into a coma.

Of course, it might have made no difference. If he

hadn't been wearing the charm and had fallen to the floor when he fainted, the demon could've kicked him in the head and the result would've been the same. Or perhaps the demon would have kicked him in his vulnerable soft belly, ruptured something vital and watched him bleed out from the inside.

There was no way to tell and no point in playing the blame game. Or another round of 'what if'.

Didn't stop him doing it, though. Didn't stop him from blaming himself. The facts remained: Euan, the smarter, stronger brother, was laid out in Edinburgh Royal Infirmary. Mal was way past borrowed time and he knew it.

Mal walked a little way back down the hill until he got phone reception and called Robbie. 'You ken those girls?'

'Aye.' Robbie managed to sound both wary and glaikit, but at least he seemed halfway sober.

'I think there's a target at the infirmary. I need you to scope out the place, let me know if you see anything unusual.'

'Any demons, like?'

Mal closed his eyes. 'Yes, Robbie,' he said with exaggerated patience. 'You're not to engage or alert them. Just call me. I'll pay the usual rate.'

'I want more,' Robbie said, sullen. 'If it's the thing that knifed that girl it could be dangerous.'

'If it's the thing that's killing young women, then I think you'll be safe,' Mal said. 'Being neither of those things.' He was about to hang up, but something Robbie had said tickled the back of his mind. 'Why did you say 'knifed'?'

'What?'

Robbie's voice sounded suddenly quiet, as if he'd looked away from his phone when something caught his eye. Or someone. Mal was getting paranoid, he knew it. Didn't help. 'You said she had been strangled.'

'Aye, the French bird was.'

'But you knew how Laura Moffat died too?'

'I telt you it before,' Robbie said, his voice stronger. 'Are you feeling all right, man?'

'Fine,' Mal said. He stuffed his paranoia down deep. He knew he couldn't trust Robbie but he was sure he wasn't working for Pringle. Even demonic entities had standards. He hoped. 'Get away to the infirmary now. Let me know if you see anything.'

Robbie didn't say goodbye, and Mal slid his phone back into his pocket with the horrible feeling that he might have just made a mistake. Every molecule of his being wanted to go straight to Euan's bedside and stand guard, but he knew that if Pringle had been bluffing he certainly had suspicions and nothing would confirm them faster than Mal heading to the hospital at this very moment.

The best way to keep Euan safe was to finish the job for Pringle. Find the girl. Get the girl. Deliver the girl. He swallowed hard, trying not to think about poor Laura, about Aislinn and his part in her death.

There was a stiff breeze but the sky was bright blue and he knew that there was only one place he would really be able to talk to his brother. Not in the overly hot room of the infirmary, but up on Arthur's Seat, looking down over the city and remembering all of the times they had climbed the hill together.

There were a few folk with the same idea, but once he was on the summit he moved away from the main path and found a quiet space. A lunatic with a yen for extreme fitness ran past him, head to toe in performance gear, and Mal resisted the urge to shout after him, 'You're still going to die, ken? Why not go and have a beer?'

At the edge of the hill, where the land fell steeply away, Mal kicked away an empty bottle and sat down on the scrubby grass. Edinburgh was laid out beneath and the blue sky arched above, but the view wasn't as soothing as he had hoped. His arms were resting on his knees and his hands dangled in between. The sunlight picked out the tracery of scars on his knuckles and the disc-shaped pale patch below his right thumb where he had been burned on a hunt when he was sixteen.

He glanced around, checking that he was still alone, and then pulled the piece of leather string around his neck out from underneath his t-shirt. The charm attached looked like something you would buy from a stall during festival time. Some cheap piece of silverish metal, shaped into a vaguely Celtic symbol. He ran his thumb over the surface, feeling the indents and the smooth patches.

Euan buried his kindness under an unwavering devotion to the principles set out by their father. Magic, charms, undead birds; all of these things were supernatural and therefore bad. He wouldn't have liked Mal using a charm to conjure his image, but then, there was precious little about Mal's life he would approve of. He squeezed the charm and closed his eyes and, after a moment, he felt his brother sit next to him. He was dimmer and less tangible than the last time – the charm was obviously almost out of juice – but it was better than nothing.

'Hey.'

'Hey,' Euan said. 'Am I still asleep, then?'

'Aye,' Mal said. 'Lazy bastard.'

Euan smiled and, for a moment, it was like old times.

'I'm in trouble.' Mal didn't want to see the judgement in Euan's eyes, but he didn't want to waste a single second of seeing him upright and animated. Alive.

'There are rumblings. Even where I am, I'm hearing them.'

'What is Pringle after?'

'The usual, but it seems there's a new source in the world. Twenty years ago everything shifted.'

Mal felt his stomach swoop. Twenty years ago, their mother had died.

Euan smiled sadly. 'Not that. I mean on, like, a bigger scale. Massive.'

'Pringle is challenging Mary King. If those two start, it will be a war. I don't want to give Pringle what he's after, but I can't protect you.'

Euan nodded. 'Or yourself.'

'I don't much care about that,' Mal said.

Euan was fading. Already Mal could see the city buildings through his body. It was too quick. He wasn't ready.

'Stay with me,' Mal said, willing himself not to cry.

Euan shook his head. 'You have to wake me up.'

Mal couldn't speak. The lump in his throat was choking him and Euan was almost gone. Only the faintest outline of his face remained, his features just a light sketch against the grass of the hill and the view of the city beyond.

'Things are gearing up, all right.' Euan's voice was very quiet, almost lost on the wind. 'It's not a good time to be in the life.'

'Has it ever been?'

He waited to see if Euan could tell him how he could get out, describe an alternative path, but there was just wind and faint traffic noise from below. He sliced the leather string and stuffed the spent charm into his jacket pocket.

He hadn't chosen the life, his father had chosen it for him, and now he was stuck in it, all alone. Once upon a time, it had been different. Mal and his big brother, slicing and dicing in a demon nest over in Corstorphine. Getting beers on the way home and playing FIFA on the Xbox to celebrate a job well done. It had been good for a wee while there. Just for a precious few moments.

Rose couldn't stay in the house. She had gone through the rooms in the vast terrace and found them all as empty as the study. The only room which looked the way she remembered was her bedroom. She had curled up under her duvet and tried to sleep, to block out all the strangeness and, maybe, zap things back to the way they were, but it hadn't worked. All she could see were the lies. The framed photograph of Rose with her mum and dad which sat on her bookshelf. Two strangers posing for a picture. The line of battered Penguin children's paperbacks which she'd thought she had read as a child but now meant nothing to her. The faded stickers on her wardrobe door. It was all set dressing. She pressed one of the books to her nose, inhaling the old-paper scent and willing it to transport her back to childhood. To the childhood she had carried with her as series of snapshot memories. Memories which were as flimsy and fake as the Photoshopped family picture.

She packed a rucksack with a change of clothes, some toiletries and her toothbrush. She checked that she had her purse and, without thinking about it too much, she shoved the framed photograph into the bag and went down the stairs and into the street. As she closed her front door for what felt like it would be the last time, she missed Astrid with a physical pain. It radiated from her stomach and travelled along every muscle, pulling her down to the ground with grief. Why hadn't Astrid followed her? She must have known Rose was just hurt and upset, hadn't really meant for her to leave.

If she had a phone, she could call Astrid, but there wasn't one in her jacket pockets or her bag. She pulled out her purse, instead, and looked through it. Some cash, a debit card for her bank account, and her student identity. She looked at her face on the card and tried to remember the time of her next lecture. She could meet Astrid at the university. Slide into the seat next to her and say 'hey' and they could sort all of this out. Astrid would have an explanation for the house, would make everything all right.

She couldn't remember her timetable. She had always just appeared at lectures. Woken up waiting for Astrid outside the psychology building or in the middle of a lecture, some professor droning on at the front and Astrid snapping her cherry menthol chewing gum.

Okay, then. She would go to the psychology building and wait. Sooner or later Astrid had to show up there. She pushed down all the bad feelings and told herself that this plan was a good one and that it would work. She was always waiting for Astrid, always standing in the same places, waiting to see Astrid's shining blonde curls appear in the distance. She would follow the pattern and Astrid would be delivered back to her, a miracle in tiny spike heels.

CHAPTER THIRTEEN

Astrid arrived at the booth just as one of the other tour guides was closing the shutters. She stepped back from the entrance and waited behind the kirk wall until the young man had gone on his merry way.

The smell of the booth – pine resin, paper, and the rubber that made up the cheap souvenirs – was comforting. She re-opened the shutters and sat on her stool, thinking how much she had come to like this part of the charade. What had begun as a convenient way to acquire fresh meat, a constant stream of day trippers and foreign tourists, had become part of her life. That she thought in phrases like 'my life' was another warning sign. She had become complacent.

Robbie, one of her many admirers, hung around this part of town in the hours before the pubs opened. He was grey-haired and greasy and as aesthetically pleasing as a pustule, but he was useful. He roamed all over town and heard all kinds of interesting titbits on his travels.

He had an obsession with Astrid and would turn up to the booth several times a week to get his fix. Just to be certain he wandered by for a glimpse today, she put out a bit of extra shine, something to draw him in. Sure enough, after only forty minutes, which she spent enjoying her third favourite pastime, napping, Robbie's unkempt figure shuffled up to the booth's open window.

'Hello, you handsome devil,' she said, stretching her arms above her head and tilting her head to each side. Robbie looked around as if expecting to see somebody else. She drew a quarter bottle of cheap whisky from the inside pocket of her leather jacket and handed it to him. 'Let's have a blether.'

He straightened himself up, obviously pleased. The bottle disappeared into his ratty grey army surplus bag.

'Mal Fergusson,' she said. 'You know him?'

'Mebbe,' Robbie said, his eyes flicking up and to the left.

'Come now, sweetie,' she said. 'I thought you knew everyone.'

He looked momentarily pleased and then the guarded look was back.

'He looked like a military type.' She leaned forward, ignoring Robbie's perfume of sweat and booze. 'He official like that?'

Robbie shook his head. 'Nuh-uh. He's trained, though, ye ken?'

'Dangerous?' She widened her eyes, then wondered if she was laying it on too thick.

'Not to me,' he said, puffing out his emaciated chest.

'He was kicking around with a girl,' she said.

'Looked like she'd been kept in a hole for the last five years. I want to speak to her.'

'You cannae,' Robbie said, wincing a little as he spoke as if expecting retribution. 'She's deid.'

Astrid paused to digest this piece of inconvenient news. 'He killed her?'

'Nah, she did hersel.' He shrugged. 'She was crazy, like.'

'Don't be so quick to label,' Astrid said, wagging a finger at him. Privately, she thought the girl had the right idea. If she had woken up human, she would probably top herself too. Didn't know how the monkeys managed.

'She was staying in the hospital. Mal took her out.' He shrugged again. 'I dinnae ken why.'

Mal had used the girl to take a peek at Rose. Astrid had thought it was a coincidence that she had the sight, but it seemed he had been using her. Smart boy. Unfortunately for the girl, she wasn't just touched with the sight. She was one of them, and pointing her at Rose had been like making her look at the sun through a magnifying glass.

'What else do you know about him?'

'He's got a brother in the hospital.' Robbie smiled an unpleasant little smile. 'Vegetable. And he's on, like, a mission. Used to be a hunter like his da, and he likes to play the big man still. I told him about that Moffat gurlie in Peebles and he was aff on one. You ken the type.'

'Moffat girl?'

'Aye. Another deid one.'

Astrid had spent a fair amount of time in the underground places talking to the dead, and she knew her history. Back in the day, this world had been populated with plenty of shine. Plenty of people had the sight and could fix a little cursework if the need arose. It was rich pickings, and the soulless creatures which had grown up right alongside humankind had thrived, feeding on the shine and enjoying the sport. Around the eighteenth century, though, the humans had grown a little cannier and had found ways to fight back. A few trained hard and focused their cursework and invented weaponry to even up the odds. These hunters passed on their knowledge and trained others, keeping the fight alive. Now, in the twenty-first century, most humans knew the soulless only as folk tale and legend, superstition and whimsy. And the hunters that were left were out of step, clinging onto old ways and a world that no longer existed.

'Why would a hunter be interested in a dead girl—' Astrid stopped. There was precious little shine left on this rock. And scarcity brought value. Astrid had assumed that Rose's true power had simply dissipated back into the ether and was zooming around somewhere in the galaxy, exploding stars and whatnot, but perhaps she had been too complacent. Perhaps it had hung around on Earth instead, giving a few humans a bit of shine, and this hunter was killing them, releasing the power back in little packets. He probably hoped to take it for himself, but what if it was going back to Rose? Waking her up. Astrid let out a sigh. That was irritating. 'I meant, who does he work for? I'm assuming he's not his own man.' She would find the hunter and stop his murderous rampage. That ought to fix things nicely.

'I cannae say,' Robbie said, looking alarmed. 'It's no

worth it.'

'You can't or you won't?' she asked.

'Cannae,' he said, and his lips compressed into a tight line.

'That's okay, sweetie,' she said. 'You don't have to say it, just think really loudly.'

She touched his pitted cheek, making a mental note to wash her hands after. The name came instantly, Robbie being not what you might call especially strong of mind. Pringle. Ridiculous-sounding name.

Robbie was swaying slightly and his pale skin had taken on a yellowish tinge. 'You can go,' Astrid said, wiping her fingers on a tissue. In that moment she missed Rose more than she thought possible. She didn't belong here, wiping human grease from her hands. She had only intended to have a little holiday, after all, and now here she was trapped in this body with Rose AWOL, trading for information with a scabby little man. In every possible sense, it was beneath her.

Rose had been at home, she was almost sure of that. She had been in a very empty house and she had been upset. She squeezed her eyes shut and tried to remember what had happened next, but there was nothing. Another blank in her memory, another lost piece of time. And now she was stood on the steep curve of Cockburn Street, blinking and confused. She looked around, instinctively expecting Astrid to appear.

When she didn't, Rose began walking. As she emerged onto the Royal Mile, the clouds parted and the sun shone upon the cobbles. And the crowds. The street was always busy, but the clear sky gave a view across the Forth and a sense of space. Her panic, barely held in check, swelled with the proximity of so many people, and she focused on the distant water to try to keep it at bay. The sounds of feet on stone, voices rising and falling, the smells of humanity; it all compressed against her until she felt sick. She looked at the water and imagined floating up and away, into that vast blue expanse.

'Fucking watch out,' a woman with a toddler in tow said, brushing Rose's arm as she pushed past. Rose felt her nausea rise with the contact. She stumbled away from the crowd, hugging close to the wall in an attempt not to get in anybody else's way. There was a shop window filled with bottles of expensive whisky, and she felt a sudden urge to go inside, buy one, and get drunk. Astrid had said getting drunk was fun and that she ought to try it at least once. 'Let it all hang out. Go wild.' Of course, Rose wasn't sure who Astrid was anymore so perhaps it wasn't the best time to start following in her footsteps.

Three men in polo shirts with red faces and sweat patches underneath their arms lurched towards her. 'All right, hen? You look offy lonely.'

Rose turned away. After everything she'd seen, the way her world had broken into pieces, she shouldn't have been frightened by three pissed-up locals, but her heart hammered anyway. There was an entrance to a close in between the overpriced whisky shop and a juice bar, and she started down the stairs. The men behind her called out but didn't follow.

It was cool in the close, the tall buildings blotting out the bright sun. She got halfway down the flight of steps before she felt she could slow down. She took several deep breaths, feeling annoyed with herself for panicking. There was a fresh spurt of annoyance with Astrid, too, for leaving her. Dumping crazy words and explanations that explained nothing and then leaving her to walk alone. Why hadn't she followed? Why had she let Rose walk away when everything was so serious and scary? It made no sense.

Looking at the narrow steps below her, she felt her anger transfer to herself. She was a fool for making such a stupid escape choice. If those men had followed her, she'd be isolated on this dark stairway. No one near to hear her or come to her rescue. When she and Astrid watched horror films and one of the characters did something idiotic like go into the woods on their own, Astrid declared them 'too stupid to live.' That's me, Rose thought miserably. She had to start being smarter, had to start looking after herself.

She passed a doorway, propped open and releasing scents of stale beer and cigarette smoke. She moved down a few more steps, her hand lightly on the wall, steadying her while she tried to catch her breath and slow her racing heart.

Then she heard a footstep, much closer than she'd have thought possible, and her mind scrabbled as she turned. She hadn't seen anyone in the doorway she'd just passed, nobody had been coming down the steps behind her. It wasn't possible for there to be a figure there but, impossibly, there was.

She was slammed from behind against the wall, her arms pulled roughly behind her back. There was a solid body behind her, pushing her against the damp brick. 'Try anything and I'll cut you, I swear to God.' The voice was deep, male and familiar.

Her mouth went completely dry.

'Turn around. Slowly.'

Her hands released, she rotated, as if in a dream. Nothing about this felt real anymore. The fear had pushed reality right out of the park.

It was the man from before. The one she had hurt. He was so close it was like they were embracing, but his expression was stone cold. He wasn't lying about the knife, either; it glinted in his hand. Smaller than she expected but serrated and very sharp-looking.

'Please don't hurt me,' she said. She was amazed her voice still worked, although it came out more as a dry whisper.

He smiled quickly and without humour. 'Funny. Last time we met you almost killed me.'

She shook her head, swallowing hard. She wanted to explain that she hadn't meant to hurt him and that she didn't know how to do it again or even if she could.

'We're going for a walk,' the man said. 'No sudden moves, no trying to run, no screaming for help.'

It was exactly as she had thought. The attack she had imagined as she'd run away from the drunk men. 'Please,' she tried again.

He frowned, just for a second, before the cold mask slipped down again. He leaned closer. 'Do you think you can play me?'

She froze. She pressed against the brick, using the wall and the effort of her will to stay upright and conscious.

'I've been hunting things like you my whole life. There is nothing you can say, nothing you can do to fool me, so don't try.'

One of his arms was braced against the wall, blocking her escape, the other held the knife. He had pale skin inked with curling black shapes, and arm muscles which bulged under his close-fitting t-shirt. With his cropped dark hair and strong jaw he looked like a squaddie from an American film. Good-looking, wide-shouldered and deadly.

'I didn't mean to hurt you. Before. I don't know how —' She wanted to say 'and you attacked me with a knife' but she didn't think that would help. It wasn't as if he wasn't aware of the fact, wasn't as if he wasn't doing exactly the same thing right at that moment.

'Quiet.' One word. She could see the black stubble on his jaw, the fine lines around his eyes. He smelled of clean, male sweat and she felt her stomach flip in a completely different way. Pheromones. Astrid was always going on about those and how the right sort made her weak at the knees. Suddenly, Rose knew what she meant. She was terrified of this man, but some obscene part of her wanted him to touch her. That wasn't a normal reaction. She was holding onto enough of her wits to recognise that fact. And she shouldn't be thinking this much, either, she realised. She ought to be more terrified, not observing the sensations. The wildly inappropriate sensations. Somehow, that was the most frightening thing she had experienced in an already terrifying day.

This whole time, Astrid had been coaching her to notice men (or women – Astrid had been equal opportunities when it came to dragging Rose out of her virginal exile) and she hadn't been interested. She'd felt all the raw sexual interest of a soft toy, but now, now her lust appeared to have woken up and roared. Mortal danger, that's the ticket. I'm delirious from the fear, she thought. I'm babbling.

'I'm babbling,' she said out loud.

'What?' A noise at the top of the stairs made him look away. A muscle jumped in his cheek as his jaw clenched. Without warning, he moved away, gripping her arm to take her with him. A thought appeared, as if transmuted by the grip of his fingers on her arm: his name was Mal.

She thought about the last time he had attacked her, tried to make her mind focus. She had done something, shot some kind of energy that had made him let her go. If she had any idea of how she had done that perhaps she could do it again. Zap him.

She stumbled on the steps as she tried to keep up with his pace and tried to feel cheered that he didn't let her fall. Surely that meant he didn't mean to kill her? She ignored the voice that told her he was simply covering ground in the quickest possible way, getting somewhere private where he could slit her throat. 'Mal, please,' she said, using his name without conscious thought.

He stopped and looked at her. 'You know me?'

She shook her head, trying to catch her breath, get some oxygen into her lungs. 'Just your name. I don't know how.'

'Fuck,' he said, running a hand over his head. 'What are you?'

'A girl,' she said automatically. 'My name is Rose MacLeod, I'm twenty years old and I live in Bruntsfield with my—' She stopped before the lie 'my mum and dad' came out. She didn't have any parents. What kind of person didn't have parents?

'Well, Rose MacLeod,' Mal said, his voice surprisingly soft. 'I'm not going to hurt you. We're just going somewhere for a little chat. Don't mess me around and everything will be fine.' But his eyes flickered slightly and she knew he was lying.

The bottom of the steps were in sight now, and she wondered if she dared to try to break away from him once they were on a busy street. He wouldn't hurt her with witnesses, surely?

As they reached the last step, a young couple turned off the street and began to climb. Rose's heart leapt. Perhaps they could help her, call the police. They were holding hands and the woman was carrying several shopping bags. There were only seconds, Rose knew, before they would pass and her moment would have slipped away. Should she try to attract their attention subtly or just scream?

The moment was passing. Rose reached out to pull the woman's sleeve as they hurried by, but then something unexpected happened. The woman dropped her shopping bags and lunged for Rose. And Mal threw himself between them, blocking the woman and throwing a punch into the side of the man's head which dropped him to the ground.

'Run,' Mal said to Rose. He had let her go the moment he began fighting, but she hadn't registered it immediately. He was facing the couple, who now appeared less like people and more like something else. Rose's brain refused to fill in the 'something else'. It wasn't possible. It just wasn't possible.

She stumbled down the last step. The main street with its bright sunshine and shoppers was a small step away. She heard a dull thump followed by an grunted exhalation and turned to see Mal grappling with the things that she'd thought were a human couple.

She knew this was her chance to get away, and she told her legs to stop acting like jelly and take it. Mal had hit the male thing and it dropped to the ground. He was just turning when the female thing swung an arm that no longer looked like an arm and he sprang away, his back thudding into the wall of the close.

Rose forced herself to move. She turned onto the street and began running, dodging between and around people on the pavement, stumbling and almost falling more than once. She was halfway down the road, wondering whether she dared ask a stranger for help or whether there were more of those things behind her, around her, walking past right at this moment, when a hand on her arm made her cry out.

'This way.' It was Mal, a bruise blooming on one cheek. He spun her around and pulled her to walk in the other direction, away from the shopping centre.

Rose was glad he wasn't dead. It wasn't rational, but it was true. And in her terror over the creatures and her strange relief that he was all right, she forgot to be as scared of him. 'What were those things?'

He glanced at her. 'You don't know?'

She shook her head. 'Were they going to hurt me?'

'They were going to gut you,' he said.

She swallowed. She didn't want to ask the question but she couldn't prevent it from spilling out. 'Why did you stop them?'

His pace didn't slow, and she was struggling to keep up. His grip on her arm was strong, almost painful. She watched his profile, his serious expression and the way he was looking around, clearly a hundred different things on his mind. He wasn't going to answer her.

'Have you got a death wish?'

Rose had so given up on a reply that it took a moment to pick up her place in the conversation. 'No,' she said, wondering if it ought to be this easy to talk to one's kidnapper. 'But wouldn't it have saved you the job? I don't understand why you'd save me just so that you can kill me yourself...' She trailed off, horrified that she might've just answered her own question. He was a psychopath. He enjoyed it. The fear came back, stronger than ever, as if it had just been gathering energy in that brief hiatus. Although it hadn't been like the fear had gone away, she'd forgotten for a moment that she ought to be scared. If she didn't remember to concentrate, she didn't think like a person should think.

He shook his head but didn't answer her question. 'Here.' He paused at the entrance to a building. The door plaque was cheap looking and had several logos. She read 'chiropractor' and 'yoga studio' before he dragged her inside.

'Please, let me go,' she said as he marched her along a corridor. Just because she had accepted that she was mentally unstable and that, most likely, all of what was happening was an elaborate hallucination of some kind, that she was probably back at home with her long-suffering parents or lying in bed in an institution, didn't mean she wasn't going to try to stay alive. He held onto her tightly as he unlocked a door which said 'S. Lewis. Chiropractor' and then pushed her inside, ahead of him, locking the door behind him.

It was a plain room, filled with furniture but still managing to seem barren. There was a beech-coloured office desk with a swivel chair, and a single bed crowded against one wall with a black duffel bag sitting on the bare mattress.

'Sit,' Mal said, pushing her towards the swivel chair.

She did, glad to sit down before she fell. She knew that her adrenaline should still have been pumping but it had drained away. She was in terrible, life-threatening danger and she just wanted to close her eyes. To let it be over. The instinct of self preservation was there, though, however weak, and she made another appeal. 'If you let me go, I swear I won't go to the police. I won't tell anybody. Please.'

'Stop it,' he said. 'Just stop pretending.' He opened the duffel bag and took out a thin rope which he then used to tie her to the chair.

Rose began to cry. She couldn't help it, the tears just

sheeted down her face in a steady stream. Terror, exhaustion, misery. The appropriate reaction had finally arrived and it felt awful. She closed her eyes so that she wouldn't have to watch the man anymore. The beautiful man who was going to kill her. Torture her? Her heart stuttered and every part of her tensed, waiting for the attack, the touch of a knife against her skin, perhaps a blow to the head.

She felt instead, something against her lips. She opened her eyes and found him close, holding a glass of water to her mouth. She drank. Her throat hurt with crying and as soon as she tasted the cool liquid she realised she was desperately thirsty.

After she'd finished the glass he put it carefully on the desk, then, moving a laptop with a dented case, sat on the edge of the desk and looked at her. His expression wasn't hostile and his voice was gentle. 'What are you?'

'My name is Rose MacLeod.'

He glanced away, irritation flickering across his face.

'I'm twenty years old,' she said. 'I live at 223 Bruntsfield Close. I go to Edinburgh University.'

'What year are you in?'

'First,' she answered immediately. Then she hesitated. Or was it second? It couldn't be third because that would mean she'd nearly be finished and she hadn't been thinking about life after uni. If she'd been nearly finished her degree she'd be worrying about final exams and the dissertation and job fairs.

He was looking at her intently again. 'You're not sure?'

She shook her head. 'No. Yes. First year. Definitely.'

'What are your parents' names?'

'Mum and Dad.' She didn't want to think about her parents. Her not-real parents. Who had doctored that photograph and put it in her bedroom?

'Their names.'

Again, there was a tiny blank before the names came to her. Then she said, 'Rosemary and Philip. I was named after my mum.'

'Christ,' Mal said. 'You really don't know, do you?'

'Know what?'

He shook his head. 'You're not human.'

She tried to laugh but no sound came out. Her throat closed up completely and the air seemed to disappear from the room. Her ears were ringing.

'You're a monster. A demon, probably, although I'm not sure. You don't exactly follow the pattern.'

'You're insane,' she tried to say, but her throat had closed up. It made a kind of sense, after all. She had been struggling to find an explanation and now Mal was providing one.

'Okay.' He shrugged. 'We'll have to agree to disagree.'

She closed her eyes again. 'If you're going to kill me could you please just do it.'

There was another pause and she could feel him looking at her. She kept her eyes closed and concentrated on breathing.

'I'm not going to kill you,' he said. His voice sounded tired. A little sad, perhaps.

She opened her eyes. He was looking at her with a

strange expression. There was resolution there, and something else. Regret? 'Thank you?'

'Unless you try to kill me again.' He smiled a little. 'I think that's fair.'

The smile made him look less of a thug and she felt her fear recede. She shook her head. 'I didn't mean to hurt you, I swear. I just wanted to get away.'

'You might not have meant to do it,' he said.

'I didn't,' she said, eager to make that crystal clear.

'But you are really strong. And the fact that you don't know it, or don't know how to control it, won't make me any less dead if you use it.'

'What do I do?' she said, her voice a whisper. 'I don't want to hurt anybody.'

Again, that look of surprise. Who did he usually spend time with?

'How did you get away from those people?' In her last glimpse of the fight, Mal had been raining down blows, but there were two of them and they had been twisting and stretched, no longer human shaped, moving all around him in deadly tendrils.

'They weren't people. They were the Sluagh. And I killed them.'

'In broad daylight?' Like that was the strangest thing.

'In a close.' He smiled again, as if he was thinking the same thing. 'And the Sluagh don't have bodies, so no evidence left at the scene.'

'They had bodies. I felt that woman's arm.' The word he had used again, 'Sluagh', sounded strangely familiar. She felt the tickle of a memory at the back of her mind.

He leaned down, looking deeply into her eyes. 'Not a woman. And once they've been killed they burn up. They leave traces, but nothing that the human world is equipped to identify or even notice. Unlike demons, which remain corporeal after death. Annoyingly so.'

'You keep talking about the human world. Like it's something separate.'

'It's not,' he said. 'Not exactly. There's just another layer that most people don't know about. Most people never touch it, or, if they do, they aren't aware.'

'And where do you fit in?'

'I'm human but I was brought up to hunt the things that aren't.' He slid off the desk. 'Okay. We need to keep moving. This is a safe house but it won't fool the Sluagh for long. They have our scent now.'

She felt the fear rush back. 'I thought you killed them?'

He held up a hand and made a seesaw motion. 'It's complicated. If I untie you are you going to try and kill me again?'

'I told you, I didn't do that. I didn't do anything.'

'You know something? I'm starting to believe you didn't mean to do it, but that doesn't make you any less dangerous.'

That was it. Something released inside Rose and she laughed. 'You're the one with the scary knife. You're the one who attacked me, tied me up.'

An almost-smile appeared on Mal's face and he reached behind her to loosen the rope. She caught a blast of his scent and felt her head swim, even as she rubbed her wrists where the rope had chaffed them.

'We could do with a disguise.' Mal reached for her plait and Rose jerked away.

He frowned. 'Your hair is pretty noticeable. We should cut this off.'

'No.' She didn't know why, of all things, her hair felt important, but it did. Something familiar to hold onto. She realised that she was gripping the end of her plait and forced herself to stop.

'It'll grow back,' he said. 'And there isn't time to dye it.'

She shook her head. She didn't know why she didn't want her hair cut, especially when it was such a lucky escape compared with having her throat slashed. She backed away. 'I'll wear a hat.'

'This is serious,' he said, but he was moving around the room now, pulling objects from drawers and studding them into his jacket pockets. He pulled a black moulded case from underneath the desk and opened it to reveal weaponry, nestled in specially-shaped foam. She identified guns and knives and a few other scary-looking things she didn't recognise.

'You need to look different, throw them off. It will buy us time. I mean, they get close enough and they'll smell you, but from a distance...'

Rose felt the weight of her hair in her hand. She coiled the plait up behind her head and reached into her pocket for a hair pin.

'No.' He glanced at her. 'Not up, gone.'

'Fine,' she snapped, the panic morphing into anger. 'Fine. Gone, then.'

And the coil of hair disappeared beneath her palm.

Her fingers grasped thin air and her brain stuttered over the sudden lack of sensation. She felt the back of her head frantically, denying the reality of what had just happened.

'Mirror.' Her voice was as panicky as her scattered thoughts.

'What?' Mal looked up. His expression changed as the colour drained from his face. He seemed to be clenching his jaw.

'Mirror. I need—'

'Yeah.' He smiled without a trace of humour. 'You're totally human.' He stabbed a finger at the door in the corner. 'Bathroom's through there.'

She stood in the tiny room with a cracked basin, a toilet, and a window that was too small for her to fit through and looked at herself in the mirror. Her hair had gone. She twisted her head to try and see the back but could only see the sides. It was sticking out in rough tufts. It looked kind of good though, like a hairdresser had been chopping away and had blow-dried it so it stood out. It made her look older, more fierce. Or perhaps that was just how she felt. The anger was still there. Why was this happening? Who was this man and what the hell did he think he was doing? She splashed water on her face, used the facilities and considered locking the door and refusing to come out again. It was a flimsy little bolt, though, and she knew he'd probably kick the door down without a second thought.

In the main room, he was leaning against the desk, bare-chested. His clothes were bundled on the chair and there was a box of first aid stuff open on the desk. He was cleaning out a wound on his side. It was a three-inch gash and he didn't even wince as he sluiced it out with a squeezy bottle of water, starting fresh bleeding as he disturbed the clotting. He obviously wasn't a stranger to injury. There were large bruises on his left side, spreading over his ribs and in various stages of healing. His body was so sculpted that, if it wasn't for the evidence of harm, it would look unreal, and that, Rose told herself, was why she couldn't stop looking at it. Scientific interest.

'From them?' she asked.

He pinched the edges of the wound and applied butterfly strips to keep it together. 'Just a nick.'

'I think I'm going to throw up.'

'Bathroom,' he said, without looking up.

She took a step towards him instead. He wasn't wincing or crying, but his muscles were tense. Everything about his posture and the set of his jaw radiated pain. She didn't know how it was possible, but she actually felt sorry for him. 'Does this happen a lot? In your life?'

He smiled briefly. 'Occupational hazard.'

'Did you do something to me?' Her hand strayed back to the bare nape of her neck.

'What do you mean?'

'To change me,' she said. 'I never cut my hair without using scissors before. And I never hurt anybody or—'

'No.' He turned his attention back to his work. 'You were a special little snowflake long before I came along.'

She digested this. 'Why are those things trying to hurt me?'

He didn't look at her. He was sticking the last of the butterfly stitches to his wound and his face was tense. 'My boss probably sent them. He sent me first but I guess he got impatient.'

'Your boss?'

'Client, really. I'm freelance,' he said. 'Pringle.'

'What?'

'That's his name.'

'It doesn't sound very demonic.'

He glanced up, a grim expression on his face. 'He's powerful now, but everything starts somewhere, and I think he needed a name which disguised his nature. If you want to lure kids into your van, you don't call yourself the childsnatcher.'

'Is that what he did? Hurt children?'

Mal looked back at his wound. 'I don't know, that was just an example, but probably. There's probably not a single awful thing you can think of that he hasn't had a shot at.'

'And you work for him?'

'It's complicated.'

'Not really,' she said.

'Fair enough,' he replied after a moment. 'You're right. I work for anyone who pays, which makes me worse than them. Happy?'

Rose didn't think there was a good answer for that, so she kept her mouth shut. Instead she took another step towards the desk. He was strapping a pad of white cotton to his side, struggling slightly. She picked up the adhesive tape and cut a length.

His eyes widened. 'Thanks.'

She was close enough to catch the scent coming from his skin, and when he twisted to pick up his t-shirt she felt herself leaning towards him. Which was insane. She did have the weirdest feeling that she knew him, though. Or had met him at some other time, a time she couldn't recall exactly. She had the feeling that he had rescued her before. Not today with the Sluagh, but from a prison. At night.

She took a step back, putting her hands behind her back in case they betrayed her good sense and reached for him. No matter how odd life had been before, she had never truly felt unhinged. She had never thought she needed psychiatric help. Now, for the first time, she wondered if there was something truly wrong with her mind.

He pulled his t-shirt on and stood up, suddenly very close to her. She reached out a hand and smoothed the front of the shirt, then snatched it back. Yes, she was unhinged.

He put his hands on her shoulders and looked into her eyes. For a moment she thought that he was feeling the same weirdly intense attraction, but then she realised that he was peering at her with a scientific interest. The lines between his eyebrows deepened as he concentrated, his gaze flicking from her eyes over her face, and then back to her eyes again, searching.

She tilted her face up and put her hands on his chest. It

was solid and she could feel the heat of his body through the thin material. If he wanted to examine her like she was some strange breed of cat, she would take the opportunity to give in to her base human instinct. Or base demon instinct, if that was what she turned out to be. She didn't feel demonic or evil, but then maybe that's just how being evil was.

His face was so close that when he spoke, she felt his breath warm on her skin. 'What are you doing to me?'

She swallowed, unable to look away from his eyes. Which were narrowing in suspicion, rather than widening with attraction or closing with lust. Not ideal. He let go of her shoulders and stepped back, like she'd become radioactive. 'Is this one of your things? Powers?'

'You think I'm using my special supernatural powers to get you to kiss me? You seriously think that's what is on my mind at this moment?'

'I don't know.' He shook his head. 'Get me off guard, mebbe?'

'You're an idiot,' she said. She had a horrible feeling she was blushing.

He looked at her for a beat longer and then turned away. She wasn't sure if she was relieved or disappointed. She crossed the room and sat in the chair. The rope he had used to bind her was still sitting on the table and she picked it up, passing it through her fingers, feeling the rough surface and using the sensation to bind her to this place, this moment. She had to break out of this fog, try to start thinking rationally. Astrid wasn't here to look after her anymore, she had to look after herself.

CHAPTER FOURTEEN

Mal's side hurt like a bastard where the Sluagh had caught him. They didn't need weapons, could simply mould their bodies into sharp shapes, and the thing had moved so quickly. He had been distracted, too, by the girl. Rose. He had cautioned himself to stop thinking of her as a young woman, a girl, a human female. She wasn't Sluagh, he knew that, but she wasn't just human, either. He had to see her as the object of power or whatever Pringle had her categorised as, the thing he was going to deliver so that he could tie up his obligations and move on with his life. First job would be to move Euan to a different hospital in a new city, get away from any bad thing which might know about him. Pringle wasn't likely to forget about some leverage.

Of course, this wasn't a simple delivery job. If Laura Moffat hadn't already proved that, then Pringle sending the Sluagh was the candle on the fucking cake. Mal couldn't pretend to himself that this was object recovery.

Not when the object in question was a girl and that girl was gazing up into his eyes like he was the answer to a question she had been asking all her life. Like he was the light in a dark room.

It was messing with him. The girl-object was using tricks, maybe a glamour or a charm. Something strong enough to get through his training. Didn't change the fact that she felt human, though. And if she was human with a touch of power, how did that make her any different from him?

He finished packing his bag and paced the room for a couple of turns, waiting for the answer to come. His father would have slit her throat. He wouldn't have delivered her to Pringle because he would never have made any kind of deal with a demon, never have worked for one in a hundred million years. Euan? Mal didn't know what Euan would do. When Rose had emerged from the bathroom, her pale skin had lost some of its luminosity and there were dark shadows under her eyes. She looked frightened.

Euan would save the girl. But then, he'd always been the heroic one.

Now Rose was sitting in the chair by the desk. She kept touching the back of her head, self-consciously. She looked so much like a person it physically hurt to look at her – the disconnect between the energy which radiated from her, the kind Mal had always associated with evil, and the prosaic normality of her body. He had been so close he had seen the pores on her skin. The tiny scar above her left eyebrow that looked like a chickenpox mark. Flakes of dry skin on her lips.

'We have to move out of here,' he said, trying to ignore the urge to wrap his arms around Rose, to touch her newly-shortened hair. His instinct for self-preservation was at war with his desire to protect. He thought that part of him had died the day Euan was hurt, and he ached with the unfamiliar emotion. As a result his voice came out harsher than he intended. 'Unless you want to stay and fight.'

She flinched, and he felt like hell. 'I don't know how,' she said. 'I told you, I don't know—'

'Okay.' He held up a hand. 'We'll go.' He crossed to the window and looked down to the street, taking a sharp breath inward when he saw how many Sluagh had gathered. They were milling about on the pavement, looking like the cattle they were. A couple were working on the door, though, and it wouldn't be long before they had broken through the protective seal.

'Can't someone help us?' Rose said. 'Astrid took me to see a ghost, but that's probably not helpful. He mentioned someone called Mary King. Could she hide us or something?'

Mal paused. 'Astrid knows Mary King?'

'I don't know.' She shook her head, as if trying to clear it. 'She knew the ghost. Mr Boots.'

'Small blonde Astrid? Your student friend?'

'Yes,' she said, looking surprised. 'She knows lots but she wouldn't tell me. She wouldn't explain and I got angry. You recognise the name?'

'Oh, aye' he said. 'And she is not the place to go for help.' He stopped. An unwelcome thought arrived: If Mary King knew about Rose, then the Sluagh circling

the building might be the least of their problems. *Fuck.*
'We need to get moving. Now.'

There was a crashing sound from the ground floor. Rose's face was a picture of terror and he felt another stab of concern, responsibility. He had dragged her here.

'They're in,' he said. 'This door is warded, too, but it won't take them long.' He hefted his bag onto his shoulder and looked out of the window. When he looked back, he was pale. 'The roof was my backup plan, but one of them is climbing the wall. It will see us if we go out of the window.'

The thundering sound of shoes on the stairs seemed to fill the room. It rang in Rose's head and made it impossible to think clearly. She opened her mouth to ask what they were going to do. This man, who had seemed so terrifying and strong, suddenly looked small and young. But the flash of fear in his face was gone as fast as it had appeared and he reached out his hands to her, pulling her gently from the chair to a standing position. He squeezed her hands, dipping his head to look into her eyes. 'You can escape. You did it before.' Fists were pounding on the door to the office now, the door shaking in its frame.

'I don't know what I did. I don't know—'

'You can. You were running away from me and you just disappeared. You can do it now. You'll be all right.'

'What about you?' Rose knew that she had held Astrid's hands and they had ended up in Paris together but she didn't know how or why. She didn't know if she could make a repeat trip.

'I'll be fine,' Mal said. 'They're only after you.' But she knew he was lying.

She hesitated, wondering if there was something she could do, like click her heels together or say the magic word.

'Come on,' he said, smiling a little. 'I'll chase you around the room. It worked last time.'

He was trying to help her, and she felt something tugging in her chest. A feeling. She gripped Mal's hands more tightly, wrapping her fingers around his and resisting when he tried to pull away. She heard the door crack and knew that there were seconds before those things were in the room. She closed her eyes.

Nothing.

The sound of splintering wood. She opened her eyes, terrified now. 'I can't. I can't do it.'

'It's okay.' He pulled his hands free and she let him go. He pushed up the sash window and gestured to her. 'You first.'

Her legs carried her to the window, while her mind shut down. A blank white space where thought ought to be. She looked at Mal's face, drawing strength from his concentration, the way he was acting and moving and trying.

'Face me and get hold of the top of the frame. You're going to stand on the bottom part and then reach up to the ledge that runs along the building. From there you'll be able to get hold of the roof edge and pull yourself up.'

'Why aren't you going first? So that I can see how it's done?'

Mal glanced behind her as another blow made the door shudder and splinter. 'No time.'

She sat on the window frame and grabbed hold of the top of it. She brought her feet up to a crouch and prepared to stand on the frame, her body outside and sixty feet in the air. Her last view before she flexed her muscles and pulled herself upwards was of Mal, looking tense and unsmiling, but giving her an incongruous thumbs up.

Flattened against the side of the building, Rose felt the wind buffeting her back, and when she looked for the ledge, her eyes began watering. She couldn't stay here though, and knew that she would have to move. Every second that she remained still was another moment to think about what she was doing, and to freeze in place. She reached up, half blind, and her hand scraped rough stone. There was a definite protuberance, though, and she decided to assume this was the ledge and gripped it with her fingertips. She brought her other hand up and held on. Now she was pressed tightly against the wall and window. She had to move her feet to the decorative stonework to her right. She shuffled along the window frame to the corner, moving her hands carefully along the ledge.

Then, the thing she'd been afraid of happened. She froze. Every part of her body locked in terror. Her right leg, the one she wanted to move to her foothold, began to shake.

Mal's voice, from below and to the left, said something which was snatched away by the wind.

Then, she had a comforting thought. She could just

let go. She didn't need to be frightened, clinging to the side of a building in the freezing cold. She could just let go and it would all be over.

'Rose.' Mal's voice, clearer this time. Just her name.

The pleasant thought of oblivion receded and she moved her right foot, catching the foothold on her first try. She had to move both feet before she'd be able to get enough height to catch the edge of the roof, so she had to trust the stonework would hold her. She moved her left foot across and then reached upwards straight away, as if she could trick gravity with speed. Miraculously, her hands made solid contact with the edge. It was a lovely proper place to hold on. She pulled with her arms and scrabbled her feet up the wall until she could swing her body over and onto the roof ledge. It was narrow, just a foot or so, but the gently sloping tiles and little horizontal space seemed like heaven after the sheer cliff face.

She moved along so that there would be room for Mal when he made the same manoeuvre. She didn't allow the possibility that the Sluagh were already in the room below, that he might not make it. His head appeared first, the short dark hair a welcome sight, and then the rest of his body.

He pulled himself almost silently onto the roof, indicating with a gesture that Rose should move forwards, along the roof towards the next building. She obeyed, crawling, leaning towards the sloping roof and away from the edge. Sounds from the street drifted from below and the wind picked up, whipping strands of her new hairstyle into her face. After what seemed like an hour but was probably no more than a few minutes, she reached a roof valley between the buildings. It wasn't deep or especially wide, but it looked very smooth. It looked, in fact, like a chute which had been especially designed to funnel climbers off the roof and to their deaths.

She twisted her neck to look at Mal and found him closer than she expected. He leaned in so that he could speak directly into her ear, mindful Rose assumed of his voice carrying to the Sluagh below. 'We could go up,' he said, pointing. 'Climb to the ridge tiles.'

She put her mouth to his cheek and said, 'No more up.'

She turned back to the channel of smooth leading and tried not picture herself slipping on it.

'We have to keep going,' he said. 'Unless you've got a better idea?'

Staying put, she thought. That's a good idea. Just wait here in the peace and hope they go away and forget about us.

'When they don't find us inside, they'll start checking outside. We have to keep moving.'

'I know,' she said, feeling a burst of irrational anger that the world was this way and not some other, more convenient arrangement.

She turned back to the valley and then, without thinking about it anymore, she moved across it. It wasn't as slippy as she'd expected and the roof on the other side was wider.

'Bloody hell,' Mal said from behind her, and then he had crossed the channel and was crouched next to her.

There was definitely more room on this side, and

Rose felt less in danger of slipping and tumbling over the edge. And it was in that precise moment, when some of her clenched muscles relaxed the tiniest amount and she shifted her weight to relieve the pressure on one leg, that her foot slipped on a tile. It skidded out with such force that her balance toppled and the other leg followed. In less than a single second, she was flat on her stomach on the roof, both legs over the edge and without purchase. The breath had been forced from her lungs with the impact of falling but there was no time to contemplate the pain in her body, only to realise that she was still moving, slipping down the sloped tiles, her fingers desperately scrabbling on the smooth surface, trying to find purchase.

Mal grabbed hold of her wrists and she felt the tug in her arms as he stopped her from moving. One leg was off the roof and dangling into space but she was able to pull the other up, getting her knee onto the edge and trying to push up from it.

Mal was still holding her, but then she felt them both begin to move. He was slipping too. His greater weight gathered momentum quickly and within moments her body was shooting down, over the lip of the roof and freefalling into space. Mal was still gripping her wrists and it hurt where he was holding so tightly, but she knew that he couldn't save them. They were both falling.

CHAPTER FIFTEEN

Mary King had been running businesses in Edinburgh for a very long time. She remembered when thieves were hanged in the Grassmarket and Waverley Station was nothing but a swampy loch. The same stinking loch which was used to drown witches and to drain the filth from the piss-reeking tanneries and back-room stills. She remembered when the air was black with soot and the tenements ran with cholera and she would have thought that a soul departing from that world would be glad to leave. The city hadn't quite loosened its grip, though, and the spirit that became Mary King endured.

She hadn't always been called Mary, of course. She had taken that name from a woman in 1616, and it pleased her to see it on the street sign in the city and in the tourist guide books. It made her feel like an institution, all respectable and proper. Of course, those nobs in the New Town still wouldn't have anything to do with her directly. Pringle always used intermediaries, like he was above all that gutter stuff, like he was above her. She licked her lips. He was going down a peg or two and that would be bleeding delicious. That would be a feast, all right.

Mary King ran her hand over the can again. It was definitely the real deal. It was humming with the stuff. The can was black and orange, with '48-hour protection' printed on the side. It was a spray to stop you from sweating, a twenty-first century, mass-produced object, with a thousand identical copies available in supermarkets and chemists around the country, but this one was special. It had been taken to a remote tribe in South America, a place the people had never seen microwave popcorn, tarmac roads or television. They had played with the can, stared at it, wondered at its smooth surface and glossy black. She could feel all that interest and attention, all that wonder. It had seeped into the can and she could feel the tingle of power it had left behind. That was the thing with objects, they picked stuff up. Even mundane humans instinctively liked old things or, depending on their sensitivity and the object's history, feared them. People felt it when they held something random like an arse-ugly little troll doll or a shiny foreign coin, and had the sudden urge to close their fingers tight and keep the thing forever, even though there was no logical reason. Attention and desire, clinging to the object, making it shine.

She tucked the can into her pocket and adjusted her butter-yellow cashmere wrap more securely across her shoulders. A hundred people would walk past the deodorant can and never think to touch it. If someone picked it up, even a pedestrian little human would feel a tingle, a slight thrill of otherness and longing. For Mary King and her kind, it was like putting her hand in a flame. Of course, there was a world of difference between sensing something other and knowing what to do with it. Luckily, she had the wisdom to go along with the sight. It was what had made her an unstoppable success and now, finally, she had enough juice to wash away the last pretender to her crown. She smiled, imagining Pringle's expression when he realised his mistake. If he had joined Mary when she invited him, he would get to survive and thrive. Now, she was going to destroy him utterly and then she was going to Valvona & Crolla for an early dinner.

Back at her office, Mary King dealt with the client who had been waiting for an hour and who had the clout to move forward the property development deal she was cutting in Leith. After the hand-shaking was finished and she had a fresh coffee, she opened her hidden wall safe and put the deodorant can away. The small opening expanded to the size of a door which led to a small storage room, lined with shelves. The can sat next to a plastic doll with a hole in its rosebud mouth and a Bucks Fizz seven-inch record in a plain black paper cover. She touched a finger to a couple of items, as if greeting them, then picked up a ball of gardener's twine on an old wooden spool. Books were often powerful. People assumed this was because of the words inside, but that wasn't quite correct. People held books for long periods of time, they concentrated on them, they communed. They worshipped. That was what gave books – some books – power. The hush in a library was reverential for good reason.

A knock on the door disturbed her pleasant ritual and she closed up the safe room, stepping back into her office as the door swung open to reveal her assistant, Edward, looking flustered. She hesitated – she hadn't known Edward could look anything except composed – but there wasn't time to ask him what was wrong.

A tiny blonde girl, no more than five feet in her high-heeled boots, squeezed past Edward, who shrank against the wall.

'Astrid, my dear, what a lovely surprise.'

The girl's name had appeared to Mary King and she had used it, expecting the small human to look frightened and confused. Instead, the girl tilted her head to one side and said a single word. 'Interesting.'

Mary King hesitated. This was not the reaction she had expected. She looked carefully, but the girl still looked like a girl. Undersized by modern standards, with pale yellow curls and a kissable Cupid's bow mouth. 'How can I help you?' Mary King said, playing for time.

'My friend has gone AWOL,' Astrid said, looking around the office with open interest.

'Oh dearie me,' Mary King said automatically. She was peering at Astrid with all of her sight and then, just at the edges of her perception, she caught it. A glimmer of light. 'That's careless,' she said. 'Lots of bad folk in the world. I assume your friend is... delicate?'

'Not really.' Astrid's mouth twisted. 'She's attracted attention, though, got herself a fanclub.'

'Who might belong to that club?' Mary King

cautioned herself to stay calm. This girl had a glimmer, would make a tasty meal, but there was something off about her too. Something that was making Mary King want to step backward, not rush in.

'An old-school hunter. Mal Fergusson,' Astrid said. 'But first I'd like to hear more about this Pringle fellow.'

Mary King sucked in her breath. A human throwing Pringle's name around as it were nothing. 'How do you—'

The girl smiled widely looking, suddenly, nothing like a girl at all. 'Oh, you'd be amazed at the things I know.'

Blinding white. Like a hundred LED bulbs shining into her eyes. Rose blinked to try to clear her vision. She wasn't falling anymore, but perhaps that was because she was dead.

As the bright white light faded, she realised that she was no longer in Edinburgh and that her body ached in a way she didn't think it would if she was dead. Surely spirits didn't feel pain. She must have travelled, but she didn't feel sick the way she had in the catacombs in Paris. She didn't know if that was because she was getting used to doing it or whether it was because there was a cooling breeze on her skin and she wasn't under-ground and surrounded by bones.

Everything was still white, though, until she lifted her chin and saw bright, azure blue. Mal was sitting on the ground a few feet away, his hands on his knees. He was taking deep breaths like he was trying not to throw up.

'It's the sea,' Rose said, finding the word for the vast bright blue, sandwiched between the white sand and the pale blue sky. The sun was shining and the turquoise water belonged in some exotic location in the tropics. 'Where are we?'

'Scotland.' Mal was looking around with a strange expression.

'No chance,' she said. The breeze sprang up, and it contained a chill. 'Really?'

'We're on Iona. I came here with my family once.'

'Holiday?'

'Work,' Mal said. 'But we did stay on for a couple of days after. Survival training.' He turned, shading his eyes from the sun, and looked back towards the land. 'This looks really familiar. It might have been near here.'

Rose sank to the ground and raked her fingers through the fine white sand. It was real. The salt on her lips was real.

Mal came and crouched next to her. 'How did we get here?'

'It seems to be a thing I can do. When I did it before, we landed in Paris.'

'But you can do it, not me. Why am I here? And how did you move Astrid?'

'Astrid said I stay still and change the world around me.'

'That doesn't help.'

'I know,' Rose said. 'Sorry.'

'I've never known this kind of power before. Not without symbols and objects. Spellwork.'

He was looking at her with admiration and fear. It stirred memories. People had looked at her that way before, long ago. Rose swallowed. 'But I don't know how to control it. I don't know what I'm doing.' A thought occurred to her. 'Would symbols help me with that? What can they do?'

'I've got this one.' He pulled up his sleeve and showed her a black-ink tattoo. 'It means that I heal faster.' He put his head on one side. 'Have you really not heard of them?'

Rose shook her head.

'And you don't have any tattoos?'

'Just this.' She pushed her sleeve up and showed him her rose. 'It's made without ink so it just fades over time.'

'That's not a symbol I know.'

'It's a rose,' she said, feeling stupid for stating the obvious.

'I know that.' He gave a small smile. 'I mean I don't know it as a power symbol.'

'Oh, I don't think it is,' she said. 'I just started getting them to help me mark time. When I blank out, I lose time, sometimes lots. I don't always have a watch and it all felt a bit unreliable, so I thought this would be a good way to be sure. Sometimes it's completely gone, the skin totally healed, and then I know it's been months.'

'You've forgotten months of your life?'

'I think I've probably forgotten years,' she said, forcing the words out. It felt good to say them. Frightening but honest. And they had the ring of certainty.

Her mind felt as if it was clearing, here in this wide space, with the wind blowing and the smell of salt in the air. 'Astrid knows something about it,' she said, feeling her mind getting clearer with every breath. 'We never argue. Never. But I was angry and I told her to leave me alone and she walked off and I haven't seen her since.'

'I'm sure she's fine,' Mal said.

Rose took another deep breath. 'You don't understand. She's never left me before. I don't remember the last time I went more than a few hours without seeing her.' Except when she was asleep. Or having a blackout. And those times didn't count in her mind, because the time slipped past in the blink of an eye.

Mal hunched his shoulders inside his jacket, like he was trying to make himself smaller. 'Okay. Putting that aside, what do we do now?'

She loved that he'd said 'we'. Loved it but felt the guilt like a two-by-four hitting her around the head. 'You don't have to do anything. Walk away. Get as far away from me as possible.'

He looked towards the dunes as if searching for a path, a way out. She smiled encouragingly. 'I'll be fine,' she said. 'Thanks for not killing me.'

'We need to get moving. We don't know if the Sluagh can follow us here.' He stood up and held his hand out to help Rose to her feet. His grip was warm and she found herself wishing he hadn't let go once she was upright.

'I don't think they can,' she said, trying to hide her relief that he wasn't walking away. She felt the loss of

238

Astrid like a hollow and, selfishly, she didn't want to lose the only other person she knew.

'Still,' he said. 'I'd feel happier on the move.'

Rose's legs buckled and she sank back onto the sand. It was all too much.

'Rose?' Mal was frowning. 'I really think we should move on.'

'In a minute,' she said. She still felt shaky and weak. She sat on the beach and looked out to sea. The sky met the sea and the sea met the land and it was all of one piece. Images were clicking together. Thoughts and memories rising, rebuilding structures which had fallen into disrepair. She was in an empty room. A second later she identified it as a pub. There was sunshine coming through the windows, throwing squares of light onto the floor. A young woman stood behind the bar, stacking glasses from a trolley onto the shelves. She turned, her mouth forming a perfect 'o', a comedic expression of surprise.

Then Rose was back on the beach. She felt as if she had been tugged back, like a rope was connecting her to this place and it had been yanked hard.

Mal sat next to her, his hands around his knees. He looked so young. Beneath the stubble and the scars, his bones were so fragile. She had to tell him but she knew it would be the end of their partnership, friendship, whatever had begun to build. 'You were right,' she said.

'About what?'

'Me. There's something wrong with me.'

'Well, that makes two of us,' he said. He leaned over and she felt his arm around her shoulders, his warm hand on her arm. 'I was raised to hunt demons and now I'm working for one. I've betrayed everything, done bad things...' He trailed off for a moment and Rose waited. After a few moments, with the sound of the waves lapping the shore, he said: 'I just sometimes wish I was normal, you know? That I didn't know the things I know. That I had never been taught to see.'

Rose reached over and took his hand, squeezed it for a moment in lieu of speaking. Her throat felt thick and she knew that any words would be clumsy.

'Anyway,' Mal said, giving a little laugh as if he was embarrassed. 'Everyone hates their lives. It's the human condition.'

'What about demons? Or things like me. Are we happy?'

'I've never met anything like you before,' he said.

She took a deep breath. 'And your boss wants me because of the things I can do?'

Mal looked out at the sea for a moment. 'I'm supposed to take you to him. It's my job. But I think he killed other girls. Girls with powers like you. There was a girl down in Peebles who had telekinesis, might have been psychic, too. I don't know.'

'He killed her?'

'I think so,' Mal said. 'And now he has sent the Sluagh.'

'I don't want to die,' Rose said. His arm tightened and she wished she could lean into him, put a head on his shoulder and pretend she was a normal girl. A human who could kiss and love and feel and live.

'It's all right,' he said. 'I won't let anything hurt you.

I'm not going to take you to Pringle. I'm sorry I frightened you but I'm going to help you. I just need to get back to Edinburgh so that I can move my brother. You can go wherever you want. I'd recommend far away.' He gestured around. 'This isn't a bad start, but I think you should keep moving. For a while at least.'

'You were right about me,' she said. 'I don't know if I can control it. What if I hurt somebody?' She didn't say the words she was most frightened of – what if she already had?

'There are people who can help. I see this guy for my spellwork. There's probably a symbol that will give you the control, and if not, there are other places we can go, people we can ask.'

'I'm remembering things, places I think I've been.' Rose kept her gaze on the sea. She felt his arm tighten around her for a moment. 'But it's all fractured. I don't know who I was or what I've done. It could be anything. If your boss wants to own me or kill me, that doesn't sound good, does it? That suggests that I'm something bad.'

'He's a bad thing. Doesn't mean that you are.'

'I feel sick,' she said. 'I'm so frightened but there's a part of me that is acting frightened. I feel like I'm going through the motions, but I haven't even got a script to follow. I can't remember if I'm the kind of person who would panic or be calm, be cruel or kind. I don't know what films I like to watch or books I read. The more I think about my life the more insubstantial it seems.' She took a breath. She didn't say the last bit, but she thought it. 'What if I'm not even a person?'

She felt Mal's hand leave her shoulder. He leaned forward and she thought he was preparing to stand up. Instead, he took her hand in both of his and pushed something into her palm.

'Here,' he said, closing her fingers over the object. 'Can you feel this?'

She closed her eyes for a second, then nodded.

'This stone is real. It's from this place and this moment. Whoever Rose MacLeod was in the past, this stone is for the Rose MacLeod who is sitting here on this island with me.' He frowned with concentration as if willing her to understand. 'Keep it with you. It means you have a choice. You can choose to be this Rose MacLeod.'

'But how?'

He leaned closer and placed his forehead very gently onto hers. She felt his warm breath on her skin. She closed her eyes and moved her head so that their lips brushed together. When she opened her eyes, Mal's were staring into them. 'I don't know,' he whispered.

CHAPTER SIXTEEN

Astrid had appreciated the wide entrance hall, plush reception area and thickly carpeted stairs, but Mary King's office was something of a disappointment. She had expected a bit more decadence, a bit more va-va-voom, but the room was sleek and anonymous in shades of grey and pale blue. The receptionist was excellent, though; a young man with good teeth and an expensive-looking suit. He was ridiculously handsome, like a Hollywood actor, and Astrid wondered what little extra services he performed for his boss. She had enjoyed brushing past him as she walked into the office and made a mental note to pay a return visit when all this was sorted out.

Right now, however, Mary King was avoiding her question. Annoying.

'Edward,' Mary King said. 'Bring us some coffee, darling.'

Edward opened his mouth as if to argue, giving

Astrid another view of his outstanding dental work, then clearly thought better of it and nodded instead.

Obedient. Astrid could do with someone like that around. She sat on the only comfortable-looking item of furniture, a dark grey velvet sofa which was pushed against one wall like an afterthought.

Mary took the more businesslike chair behind her desk and steepled her fingers. The piercings in her face ought to have looked out of place with her business suit and the fancy office, but somehow they didn't. 'Is your lost friend like you?'

Astrid thought about her and Rose, spinning through the stars, surrounded by cosmic dust and swirling gas. She didn't know how she would answer that question even if she was inclined to do so. 'I need to find her urgently,' she said instead.

'You seem like a clever girl,' Mary King said. 'Why do you need my help?'

Astrid thought about Rose's direct order: 'Stay away from me.' She had no choice but to obey, until Rose countermanded it, but she wasn't about to tell Mary King that. 'A man attacked us,' Astrid said. 'I'm assuming he was sent by one of the big players in this town. As far as I can tell that means you or Mr Pringle.'

Mary King didn't answer. Her gaze was intense and Astrid felt a tickling as she tried to delve behind the surface.

'You need help.' Mary King leaned back in her chair, light glinting on her nose ring, and smiled. 'Well, isn't that a treat.'

The door swung open to reveal Edward with a tray.

He put it on a side table and delivered a creamy-looking drink to Mary King.

Astrid was just about to say that she didn't want coffee (she hated the stuff and didn't know why any human would drink it in a world which contained hot chocolate), when Edward placed a delicate china cup onto the arm of the sofa. It was filled with creamy chocolate. The rich smell rising from it was intoxicating, and her hand reached out automatically to take it.

She lifted the cup to her lips but, just in time, her gaze flicked to Mary and saw that she was being watched with something that felt, suddenly, like hunger. She replaced the cup carefully on its saucer.

Mary King sat back, clearly disappointed. Then she arranged her face into an expression of concern. 'When you say attacked...'

'I just need to speak to Pringle. Assuming that you haven't been stalking my girl yourself?'

'No such luck,' Mary King said. She closed her mouth straight after as if trying to stop herself from saying anything else.

'Fabulous,' Astrid said. There were all kinds of undercurrents in the room. Plans. Rivalries. A hunger for power that, had it not been directed at Astrid, she would have found admirable.

'Does your friend have something valuable? Or is she in trouble of some kind?' Mary King attempted an expression of concern. 'I would be happy to help a nice girl like you. I don't like to think of your friend out there alone, unprotected.' She hesitated. 'Is she very like you? You didn't say.'

Astrid saw the naked avarice in Mary King's face and another possibility fell into place. This Mary King creature had a little power. Maybe she could combine it with whatever Pringle had and that would be enough to help Astrid lock Rose back into her box. Keep her safely contained so that Astrid could get back to enjoying life. 'Pringle,' she said, allowing a little impatience to enter her voice. 'Where might he reside?'

The struggle was clear on Mary King's face.

'Time's a wasting,' Astrid said, pushing a little extra oomph into her words.

'I can bring him here,' Mary King said, flashing the first genuine smile of their encounter. 'It would be my pleasure.'

On a tiny island with a beach of pure white sand, Rose was waking up from a long, deep sleep. No, not just waking up; more than that. It was like being resurrected. Everything was clearer and brighter than before. She found her mind kicking into gear, turning over the information available. Her thoughts clear for the first time, as if the seaweed-tinged air had woken her up. 'How many other girls have died?'

'Two that I know of for sure,' Mal said. 'Pringle said he wanted you alive, though.'

'That could be a lie,' she said.

'True, but the others were killed in situ, not brought to him.'

'Tell me.'

'Laura Moffat, killed in the pub where she worked.

Françoise Hellier, doctor.' Mal shrugged. 'And I heard there were more.'

'So, either I'm different for some reason, or they aren't connected to your boss.'

Mal dug his hands into the white sand and lifted a handful, letting the grains fall back to the beach 'Scotland's a small place, and when you take out the mundane side it gets very small indeed.'

'You don't think it's likely a coincidence, then?'

'Nae chance,' he said. 'And Laura Moffat definitely had power. Pringle would have been drawn to that.'

'Can we go to the police?' Rose mimicked Mal's action, digging her own hands into the soft sand. As if it might anchor her in a reality that made sense.

He pulled a face. 'The link between the cases is supernatural, so no.'

'Might there be more? Could we work out who is in danger and warn them?'

'You are in danger,' he said. 'We need to worry about that right now.'

'I am,' she said, brushing the sand from her fingers. 'But there's plenty of room up here.' She tapped her head. Then an awful thought hit her. Astrid. For a moment she couldn't speak. Astrid was in Edinburgh. Alone. Unprotected. 'What about Astrid?'

Mal's face changed as comprehension dawned. 'You said she took you to see a ghost.'

'She spoke to it. That's psychic, right? And she's my best friend. If your boss knows about me, he knows about her. Oh God. Oh God.'

Mal was rooting through his pockets. He brought out

a bundle of notes. 'You take this. I think this is as good a place as any to hide out for a wee while. I'll get the boat off the island and go to Edinburgh. I will find your friend, if I can. I promise.'

'No.' Rose was absolutely certain. 'I'm coming with you.'

'You can't,' he said. 'Pringle controls the Sluagh and they don't sleep or eat or stop. I can't protect you. Hell.' He ran a hand over his head. 'You know that. If you hadn't zapped us here, we would both be broken on the pavement.'

'We will zap back,' she said, standing up. 'There isn't time to travel any other way. He could have her already. She's never left me this long. What if that's why?' She felt suddenly as if she would throw up.

'You'll be safer here,' Mal said. 'I'll go.'

'I'm not leaving her,' she said.

He blew out a breath. 'Fine.' He began walking inland, toward the dunes.

Rose followed. 'There isn't time,' she said. Astrid was alone right now. Maybe the Sluagh had already found her. Maybe Pringle had her captive. Rose refused to contemplate the possibility that she was dead, that they were already too late.

Mal didn't break stride. 'That's why I'm moving quickly.'

A vision from her dreams flashed into Rose's mind. A figure looming over her, knife in hand, the knowledge that she was about to die coursing through her veins. She reached out and grabbed Mal's wrist. 'Let me try to move us.'

He stopped then. 'I don't think so. I'm sorry, but I don't understand how you do it and that worries me. You don't even know how you do it.'

'I know,' she said. 'But—'

'What if we get split up?'

'We'll find each other.'

'No. What if we get split into pieces?'

'That's pessimistic,' she said, trying to make him smile. 'Anyway, the real trouble is getting it to work. I couldn't do it until we were falling.'

'I'm not flinging myself off a cliff,' he said.

The wind had sprung up, and it made Rose shiver. 'Fair enough.' She could feel the adrenaline surge waning. He was right. She didn't know how to do anything. Each time she had used her so-called power it had been an accident.

'Although,' he said, hands on his hips and brow furrowed. 'Perhaps there are other things we could try. If you're certain you want to.'

'I am,' she said.

He moved so quickly that she almost didn't have time to be surprised. One moment he was stood in front of her, scowling as he tried to work out the angles of their situation, and the next he had his hands on her waist and was pulling her hard against his body.

'Oh.' It was a small sound, instantly eclipsed by the feel of his lips on hers. Rose closed her eyes and wrapped her arms around his shoulders, letting her fingers find the back of his neck and the soft hair there. Salt air and male sweat mingled with a base note of something else, something she wasn't sure she had ever encountered before. Pure Mal.

She felt him gasp a little as she kissed him back, giving it all she had, reaching up on tiptoe the better to press herself against him, to fit her body to his and her mouth to his. Her mind was singing and she felt the gaping sense of need and fear deep in her body get filled with something else.

He ran his hands over her back and hips, and lower, and she thought she might pass out from the pleasure of it. He broke the kiss, pulling back to look into her eyes. 'Is this okay?'

His breathing was erratic and Rose knew that hers was exactly the same. 'Don't stop.'

CHAPTER SEVENTEEN

In her townhouse in Edinburgh, Mary King had just finished making the call. When she looked up, Astrid had gone. Mary King felt instantly a little better, although she hadn't heard her office door opening and shutting. She pushed that worrying realisation to one side and concentrated on preparing the office for her visitor. Her plan had not changed and Astrid's arrival was simply an added bonus; if she was as strong as she seemed, Mary King wouldn't even have to break a sweat. She could take the shine from Astrid and use it to pin down Pringle long enough to hoover up whatever he had left in the tank. And then she could go looking for Astrid's little friend.

Pringle arrived on time. He was wearing a pink pastel jumper and beige chinos underneath a wax jacket. When he was sat in the office, a double-shot espresso on the desk in front of him, and the pleasantries had been dispensed with, Mary cut to the chase. 'I know where your girl is,' she said, enjoying the flicker of desire which crossed his face. Not his real face, of course, but the human one he was wearing.

He didn't move. 'Is that so?'

'And you won't get her. You need to drop out of the race.'

'I have that in hand,' he said.

'You have Mal Fergusson following her around town like a puppy,' Mary King said. 'Not the same thing.'

'He is bringing her to me,' Pringle said. 'But why this is any of your business, I don't quite understand. We've had a long and profitable relationship in this city by not getting in each other's way. You don't want to jeopardize that now, trust me.'

Mary King allowed herself to smile. This was what living was all about, small moments of true pleasure. 'She's not what you think,' she said by way of an opening, but before she could continue, another voice spoke, cutting across Mary King and sending a vibration of energy through the room.

'She's off limits.'

Pringle turned at the sound of this new voice and Mary King drank in the sight of his discomfort. She was the one holding all the cards, she was the one with the friends in high places. Or, more accurately, powerful friends in low places. The tiny blonde girl had not been visible a moment before and now she stood in front of Pringle, regarding him coolly. That kind of glamour took serious shine, more than the glimmer Mary King had been able to see. Her mouth was dry with anticipation.

'Do you know who I am, little girl?' Pringle said. His voice was strong and even, but his face betrayed his concern. He was scrambling, Mary King was certain, trying to work out who Astrid was. He couldn't be missing the power that shone from Astrid and was probably trying to work out how he could use her too. How he could acquire her. Mary King felt her smile widen. That, she would like to see. Mary King was going to wait until Astrid was off guard and gobble her up in the blink of an eye. That was the only safe way to tackle a predator that was bigger than yourself. Better yet, Pringle might have a go and weaken Astrid. Then Mary King could feast at her leisure.

'Rose is my charge,' Astrid said. 'She isn't an object for you to acquire.'

'We can do a deal.' Pringle licked his lips. 'There's always a deal.'

Astrid put her head on one side. 'You sent the boy, didn't you?'

'No harm meant.' Pringle spread his hands wide. 'I can call him off just as quickly.'

'Leave her be,' Astrid said.

'Done,' Pringle said. 'As soon as we agree the terms.' He smiled as if he still thought he was in control of the conversation.

'And the other girls too,' Astrid said.

'What other girls?' Pringle sat forward and Mary King realised that she had mirrored the movement. Others like Rose? Like this Astrid? The thought was deliciously exciting.

'The others,' Astrid said, a note of impatience in her

voice. 'Mal Fergusson has been snuffing them out. It's inconvenient and I want it to stop.'

'There are others like Rose?' Pringle said. 'That's interesting, but I assure you it is entirely new information.'

Astrid was staring at him. After a moment she said, 'You are telling the truth.'

'Of course,' he said smoothly.

'You didn't kill them?'

He smiled a little, and Mary King, who had seen a thousand evil things and crushed them all beneath her red stiletto heels, suppressed a shudder. 'You will have to be more specific, babydoll.'

'The things like Rose,' Astrid said slowly.

He shook his head. 'I swear upon the city.'

'Bugger,' Astrid said.

'I'm sure I can be of help to you,' Pringle said. 'If it is information you need, or protection—'

Astrid stepped up and touched his cheek. 'Shush, pet,' she said, and the thing which called itself Pringle, and had walked the streets of Edinburgh in one guise or another for over three hundred years, crumpled to the floor. It was over so quickly that Mary King didn't have time to enjoy it, which was a shame, and the pile of ash and bone which spilled from the pale pink cashmere sweater was going to leave a horrible mark on her antique rug.

'Now,' Astrid said, turning a bright smile onto Mary King. 'Let's talk about those other girls, shall we? Have you been messing with my stuff?'

Mary King wanted to stand up but her legs suddenly

felt weak. Truth was, the small blonde girl no longer seemed to be any of those things, and Mary King felt something she hadn't felt in a very long time: pure fear.

Hannah woke up to the sound of a dust cart being dragged along the street outside her building. There was shouting, some kind of argument, but she couldn't hear clearly enough to know what it was about. It might not even have been an argument. Sometimes, especially when she was still half asleep, she mistook enthusiasm for aggression or sadness for excitement. Even after four years in Alexandria, she could still feel like a tourist on a day trip to the pyramids.

It was Saturday but she dragged herself to the tiny bathroom to wash and get ready. Saturday was one of the busiest days at the international school and she had back-to-back classes until Asr, the mid-afternoon prayers. There was a small mirror propped on a shelf in the bedroom and she used it to apply her eyeliner, staring at her reflection without really seeing, only concentrating on the thick black line. With her black hair and tanned skin, she could pass for a local, and it made everything that bit easier if she did. The kids still tried to sell her stuff, of course, but she could swat them away for minutes at a time. When she had first arrived, and hadn't yet shaken the tourist vibe, walking down the streets had been like wading through a primary school playground. She'd had five kids hanging off each finger, each with a story to tell or a knotted leather bracelet to sell, and another three trying to pick her pocket.

Her building was on a narrow backstreet, the heat of the sun kept mainly away by the tall walls that enclosed it. The slice of sky was bright white, and she braced herself before joining the main thoroughfare, ready for the onslaught of summer sun. Even at seven in the morning, it was scorching through her white long-sleeved top and the scarf she wore over her head. She stopped at the hole-in-the-wall bakery. The guy lifting trays of sweet-smelling baklava gave her a thumbs up and an extra pastry. 'Too thin.' He shook his head. 'You work too hard, I think.'

'Says the man who's been baking since three,' Hannah said, smiling back.

'Ah, but that is good work. Body work. Not up here.' He tapped his head. 'That's what is making you sickly.'

Hannah had become used to this concern from near-strangers and didn't even bat an eyelid at being described as sickly. She loved it all. The foreignness of it was exhilarating and that it was so familiar made her feel fearless.

The international school occupied an entire building on El-Tawheed. The sign outside was written in several languages and little flags were printed along the bottom to further underline the multicultural experience it offered. Students, nurses, and teachers all flowed through the blue-painted main entrance, most of them eager to improve on their English. Hannah had started working for the school when she'd run out of money in Thailand. She'd done the post-uni gap year, travelling with a bunch of friends through Europe, to America and Australia, and had ended up in Asia, enjoying how far the last of her funds would stretch. Friends went home, got jobs, started their adult lives, and Hannah kept telling herself that she'd do the same. And then another fresh load of travellers would come through Phuket and she'd show some of them around, introduce them to the best midnight beach parties and get bought drinks and food for her trouble. Then, as she passed her mid-twenties and then her late-twenties, she stopped telling herself she was going to go home and began planning a new trip. When a vacancy at the international school came up in Egypt she thought 'why not?' and took it.

She'd lost touch with most of her friends back home, keeping tabs via the pretend-friendship of Facebook. Her family had stopped asking when she was going to get a career, and her mother just asked, forlornly, at the end of every Skype session whether there was someone 'special' in her life and whether she was missing the British weather yet (ha ha).

Truth was, Hannah didn't know why she was still in Egypt, why she was still teaching English or why the thought of returning to England made her skin crawl. She avoided thinking about any of it. Today the sun was shining on the traffic-clogged streets. Despite the smog, the city was beautiful and exotic and, after work, she could visit the Museum of Fine Arts, or take a siesta with her current bed-buddy, Omar. She could have kushari for dinner and eat it outside with a cold bottle of lager. That was enough for now.

Taking the steps to the classroom, she concentrated on going slowly and on breathing. During her first summer, she had made the mistake of continuing at her usual pace and had almost passed out halfway up. You just had to make adjustments, that was the key.

'Hannah!' Jeremy, ex-Etonian and business manager of the school, appeared on the top landing. His linen shirt was crisp and Hannah had a perfect view of his Italian leather shoes as she climbed the last few steps.

'I've been waiting for you.'

That was typical Jeremy. He always liked to put people on the back foot. Hannah didn't have a meeting booked with Jeremy, nor was she late for her first class, but somehow he managed to convey that she had done something wrong. She was irritated to discover that she wanted to apologise. Instead, she straightened her spine and pulled her shoulders back a touch.

'Marking scheme is due on the twenty-first,' he said.

This was not news.

'I trust you've got it in hand.'

'Yep,' Hannah said. She pressed her lips together to prevent herself from adding anything else. Ever since Omar had pointed out that Jeremy walked all over Hannah in team meetings and staff appraisals, she'd been practicing assertiveness. Strength. Poise. Knowledge. She repeated the mantra a couple of times while Jeremy ran on, saying the same things about the importance of the standardised marking scheme that he'd said a hundred times before.

'Oh.' Jeremy paused. This was another of his tricks – just when he seemed finally ready to move on, like he'd run down his list of things he wanted to say, he'd find something else lurking at the bottom. It was usually something unpleasant. He patted Hannah on the arm.

'There's a girl in your room. Says she wants to sign up for intro to business English.'

What Hannah wanted to say was 'why didn't you direct her to reception?' That was where the student sign-ups happened. Speaking to a prospective student wasn't, strictly speaking, her job. However, the last thing she wanted to do was to delay Jeremy from leaving, so she just nodded and said, 'Okay.'

The classroom windows were open but the air was completely still. It felt baked, tasted slightly scorched on the inside of Hannah's mouth. The sun glanced off every reflective surface, creating little flash flares that could blind the unwary. She would have to pull the shutters before the students arrived or no one would be able to concentrate. She dumped her camel leather messenger bag onto her desk and smiled at the girl sitting on one of the tables near the window. 'You're interested in signing up?' She spoke in Arabic first, although the girl didn't look local. She had the palest skin that Hannah had ever seen in the city. Even the tourists had more colour. 'You need to head back down the stairs and take a left to the reception desk. They will help you.'

The girl smiled, standing up in a graceful movement. 'I wanted to meet my teacher first,' she said.

'Well, you sign up for the course and then you'll be assigned a teacher, depending on class sizes and timetabling. You might not get me.' Hannah spread her hands to indicate regret. Manners cost nothing, after all.

'Ah, but you seem nice,' the girl said, smiling a little wider. She seemed sweet. Shy. Hannah felt instinctively protective.

She tilted her head to one side, a gesture that made her look even younger. 'May I have your name so that I can request you?'

'Hannah Weston.'

'Great.' The girl stepped closer, one hand held out as if for a handshake.

Hannah reached to take the hand, hesitating as some part of her brain fired off a warning signal. She looked towards the windows, expecting a bird – they flew in sometimes and caused havoc – or for whatever noise had bothered her to reveal itself. Instead, the girl was suddenly very close. The hand that Hannah had thought was heading for a business-like gesture of greeting or gratitude or the conclusion of a contract (Business English, module three), instead grabbed Hannah's arm and wrenched her around so that she was pulled up against the girl. She was taller than Hannah had realised and the hand that held her was strong, the fingers digging in painfully to her flesh.

Hannah had been so surprised that just a small sound had escaped, not much more than an exhalation. Now she drew a breath, ready to shout for help or to yell at the strange girl for hurting her. She'd been in some dodgy situations before; once a guy who was either reacting badly to the ecstasy he'd popped or had mixed it with some bad LSD had tried to strangle her. She'd stamped on his instep and kneed him in the balls, left him in a whimpering pile while she ran.

She couldn't twist around and, of course, the girl didn't have a scrotum to aim for. Some part of Hannah was holding back as she tried to twist and kick at the girl

– the teacher part that knew she mustn't use violence against a student, even one who hadn't enrolled yet.

'I'm sorry,' the girl said into her ear and, at the same time, Hannah felt a pressure drawing a line across her neck. A second later it began burning. She hadn't shouted, she didn't think. She'd meant to but it had all happened so fast. The darkness was rushing up, she was falling or flying. There was something beyond the darkness. A bright light. She understood, then, that she was dying. People talked about a light, didn't they? Lights and tunnels and their loved ones waving to them. Life flashing. Hannah just saw the light. It was beautiful and powerful and it filled her completely until there was no place where Hannah ended and the light began.

CHAPTER EIGHTEEN

Rose opened her eyes to find Mal above her, looking worried. She was lying on the sand next to a line of long spiky grass, his jacket bunched underneath her head. It was warm down here, sheltered from the wind.

'Bloody hell, I thought you were gone for a moment there.' Mal was white with worry.

'I'm fine.' Rose's voice seemed to come from far away and she had the feeling that she had been dreaming. She felt torn, as if she wanted to dive back into it.

'You just collapsed,' Mal said. 'Like you fainted.' He tried to smile. 'I knew I was a good kisser, but still...'

'What were the names you mentioned before?'

'There was a moment when you weren't there at all. I know that sounds crazy,' Mal was talking at full speed and it made him sound several years younger. 'I swear you disappeared for a second, like your body just flickered.' He rubbed a hand over his face. 'Did you mean to do that? Did you feel it?'

Rose felt utterly calm and she waited for a break in Mal's flow to repeat herself. 'The names you mentioned before. What were they?'

'What? When?'

'The dead girls.'

His frown deepened but he answered her. 'Laura Moffat. Françoise Hellier.'

'Laura.' There was a little tweak in her mind. Squares of light on a floor. A girl behind a bar, stacking glasses. She reached across the bar and closed her fingers around the girl's throat. The sound which had been half out of her mouth was cut off as Rose compressed her windpipe. She pulled hard, lifting the girl's body from the ground with no effort. The glass she had been holding smashed on the ground. She was across the bar now, her legs flailing in the air. With one movement, Rose spun the body so that it was laid out on the bar. It had brown eyes and they were wide with fear and pain. Rose felt nothing. She went onto tiptoe to gain a little height and then brought her knife down.

'Rose!'

She refocused on Mal. His hands were on her shoulders, and he was lifting her.

'Do you feel sick? You keep zoning out.'

Rose could still feel the cold emptiness of the Rose in her memory. She hadn't felt anything at all. The blood didn't horrify her, even now. She prodded herself, trying to make it matter, trying to feel the disgust and guilt she ought to feel. Slowly, it began to seep in. Slowly.

'I should take you home,' she said, sitting up. Mal moved back, giving her space. He looked so young.

Beneath the stubble and the scars, his bones were so fragile.

'Rose, what is it?'

She had to tell him but she knew it would be the end of their partnership, friendship, whatever had begun to build. It had just been a brief moment and it wasn't hers to keep. 'You were right,' she said.

'About what?'

'Me,' she swallowed hard. 'I'm dangerous.'

She didn't look at his face, didn't want to see his expression. Rose wished she could close her eyes and lean into his shoulder, block it all out, and play at being a real human girl for a while longer. Instead she felt sick. She could still remember the blood, feel the grip of the knife in the palm of her hand. She blinked back tears. She didn't deserve to cry.

Instead, she pushed herself upright. 'It's time to go.'

Mal stood up too. 'But how?'

'Hit me,' she said. As soon as she spoke the words she knew how right they were. She was a killer, after all. A monster.

'I'm not going to do that,' he said.

She put a hand to his shoulder and shoved. 'Come on. Frighten me. Attack me.'

'No,' he said, horror on his face.

He stepped back and Rose followed. 'It's the only way. We know it works.'

'I'm not going to—'

She pushed him again, harder this time so that he stumbled back. 'Come on. It's not the first time. And I'm not human. I'm a thing. You hunt things.'

'I'm not going to hurt you,' he said.

She got closer, grabbed his shoulders and brought her knee up. He twisted so that the blow hit him in the thigh and not on target. He spun her around. 'Stop it.'

She kicked back, her foot connecting. It was like kicking a tree.

'Will you just stop. Jesus...'

She twisted in his grip and pushed her hands inside his jacket. He would have a weapon. He was that kind of man.

He grabbed her wrist just as her fingers made contact with a shape in his pocket. 'No.' He squeezed and a bolt of pain shot up her arm. She didn't stop. She forced herself to keep struggling, forcing the pain higher, the desperation. She was a thing, a dangerous thing, and she had to make him understand.

He pushed her away in one violent movement, and her head snapped back. In that moment, everything went white.

Back in Edinburgh, Astrid watched as Mary King licked her lip ring. Her eyes were wide with fear and Astrid felt happy. She had played the subordinate, had considered using Mary King's appetite as a way to siphon off Rose's energy when she showed signs of waking from her half-slumber. Now, Mary King was beginning to see more clearly.

'I don't know any other girls. Not like you and Rose. I can help you find them, though. Let me help.'

'I can feel her,' Astrid said. 'Rose is my other half. We are one and the same.'

Mary King nodded, eager to show her understanding even though Astrid would have laid good money that she had none.

Astrid had been the shadow to Rose's light for millennia and she had wanted a change. They had *both* wanted a change. Being an unbroken circle of creation and destruction was all very well, but the chance to walk amongst the flesh and blood for a few days, just to experience it, had seemed interesting. To see what it was like to feel air on skin, and muscles contract and flex. It was only supposed to be a short-term arrangement. A bit of fun. They couldn't be contained in one human form, though, so they split into two. Their essence was just energy and it was divided neatly into two, ready to take two separate human forms. Astrid had been clever, and in the moment of splitting, Astrid had given the energy which had become Rose MacLeod a little nudge. Or, more accurately, thrown the power of an exploding star in Rose's direction and crossed her fingers. Rather than becoming one human form, Rose's essence had splintered further, her power dissipated and scattered across the earth.

Astrid had assumed that they'd disappeared into the vastness of the universe. She had imagined them floating out there in the beautiful blackness of space, waiting for Astrid and Rose to go home and scoop them up. Now Astrid realised that each splinter had moulded into a girl, more human than they ought to be, while she had held on tight, bearing the pain as she formed a single being, more god than human. Astrid held the knowledge and some of the power of her original existence, plus she had a cute little human form to run around in for a few days.

But she had discovered sex and booze and hot chocolate, and the more she had of those, the more she wanted. It simply wasn't possible to cram enough into just a week or two. And so the days had become weeks and then months. Rose was easy to keep happy. Just a little time loop, living the life of a young student. Before Astrid had known it, twenty years had flown by; time on this little planet bound in the lives of barely sentient apes had been more engaging than she had expected. Or, perhaps, the experience had changed her little by little, the human form she had chosen to wear squeezing like a tight suit. Whatever the truth, she wasn't ready to give it up. Not yet.

'You may look for the other girls,' Astrid said. 'But do not harm them. Keep them for me.' She would need all the juice she could get to put Rose back in her box. Perhaps if she was the one to kill them, the fragments would slip into her instead of Rose.

Mary King seemed to hesitate so Astrid lifted her into the air. It wasn't so much a case of levitating the body, but more of shifting the air around her. Astrid could see the gravity that was holding Mary King to the ground, along with the furniture, but it was a piddling little force.

She spun the woman once, slowly, and then again, a little faster, just for the fun of it, and then placed Mary King gently back onto the floor. Her mouth was opening and shutting with no sound coming out, the skirt of her suit wrinkled and climbing way above her knees, exposing a run in her stocking.

Mary King found her voice. 'Of course,' she said.

Astrid trusted her as far as she could throw her. Which was, she realised with a smile, quite far indeed. But Mary King was a survivor and she knew how to lean with the prevailing wind. She hadn't lived this long without being able to recognise superior power.

She tugged her skirt back into place and retreated to behind her desk, but she tilted her chin upwards, showing a vestige of her old steel. 'I hope that concludes our meeting.'

Astrid paused just long enough to make Mary King sweat before nodding. 'For now.'

Mal was lost. He knew he wasn't going to complete the job for Pringle and that he was a dead man walking. He tried not to think about the consequences for Euan, as he knew he had no choice. He could no more hurt Rose than he could stab his own brother through the heart. He didn't know if it was a charm or divine intervention or romantic love, Cupid's arrow piercing his side and rendering him incapable of rational thought. He just knew that he would do anything to protect the woman who was sleeping on the big double bed, one arm thrown up behind her head.

The travelling hadn't felt as bad this time and they had arrived on Princes Street, outside the entrance to the Caledonian Hotel. Rose hadn't seemed affected at all, and she had walked past the doorman and demanded a castle-view room in the time it had taken Mal to kick the sand from his shoes.

The room was nothing like his usual accommodation. There was endless thick carpet and three sets of drapes at the windows and not a dodgy stain in sight. Wooden panelling along one wall toned with the expensive-looking furniture, but the room was dominated by a gigantic bed dressed in shades of taupe and dark rose, with more pillows than Mal had ever seen in one place. Rose stirred from her position on the bed, sat up and stretched.

'How did you check us in to this place? Did you use a credit card?' Mal was thinking about a possible trail.

'I need to wash.'

'Okay,' he said. 'You've got time. I don't think anybody will find us here soon.' He didn't add his next thought, which was that Rose seemed to be radiating more power than before. She seemed brighter, somehow. Stronger.

She didn't answer, just walked into the ensuite bathroom. Mal had used it earlier, while she was sleeping. It had two sinks side by side, marble counters and tiles, and underfloor heating. He had peeled back the bandage from his side and checked that the wound was healing cleanly.

Now he sat on one of the winged armchairs, facing a wooden cabinet which he assumed hid a television from the delicate eyes of people who would pay for a room this fancy. He heard the water running and then the door to the bathroom opened. 'Come inside,' Rose said.

Her voice sounded different too, more melodious and lower than before.

Mal turned to ask what she meant and found himself looking at a naked figure. She was a human woman. Beautiful, shapely, with pale, pale skin and a triangle of black hair that was the most erotic sight Mal had ever encountered, but definitely human. The skin was real, with variation of tone, and the breasts were slightly asymmetrical. But despite all that human imperfection, she was glowing. Not in a way he could describe with words, but he was certain of it nonetheless.

He was certain of one other thing. He wanted her. He wanted to climb inside her and never leave. He wanted to fall to the floor and worship at her feet. He couldn't think about anything else and knew himself to be utterly powerless in her glow.

Then she smiled and said, 'Scrub my back?' And the feeling of joyous paralysis released, just enough, so that he was able to stand, shed his clothes and follow her into the steam-filled bathroom.

Rose stretched, feeling the delicious sensation of muscle movement and satisfaction through every part of her body. Now she knew what Astrid had been talking about and what had led her to spend time with so many people. Bodies together, blood pounding, nerves alive and jangling, the mind filled with chemical euphoria.

She knew she was a killer. She knew that, somehow, she had just been in a city of dust and heat, taking the life of another girl. Hannah Weston. She used Mal's phone to look up the news story. They weren't dreams and she was a monster. And she didn't quite care. There was something else tugging at the edges of her mind; a memory of a vast black space filled with spiralling clouds.

Mal was stretched out on the bed next to her, fast asleep. She turned onto her side so that she could watch him for a moment. A wave of satisfaction rolled over her body and, without intending to, she closed her own eyes. She thought perhaps she would sleep for a little while, too, but it wasn't sleep that came. It was the realisation that she needed to see Astrid. She was a killer but she had the strongest feeling that Astrid already knew. Which begged many questions, and it was time they were answered. Without knowing why, she spoke out loud. 'I wish to see Astrid here and now.' It was the same tone she had used to request a room in the hotel reception, and the pleasant company of Mal, and she felt, deep in her bones, that Astrid was on her way.

She rose from the bed and dressed, then went to the window to wait. After a few minutes, she clicked her fingers to wake Mal up so that he could join her. She didn't want to be alone, and that longing for company felt like a weakness that frightened her. After pulling on his jeans, Mal padded to the window in his bare feet and put his arms around her from behind. It was so similar to the way he had held her in the street before he put a knife to her throat, but as Rose leaned against his bulk, she reflected on how different it felt. It was so strange how almost identical physical mechanics could have such different meanings. It was confusing and not at all orderly. She realised that she liked orderly.

He kissed the nape of her neck and she felt the sensation run through her body. It was very pleasant and she thought about leading him back to the shower, to embrace without clothes underneath the hot water. But a blaring of car horns broke the moment and she looked out of the window to the street below. More car horns joined in as cars weaved around each other, and a particularly impatient driver bumped up onto the pavement and drove along it for a while, scattering pedestrians before re-joining the road. Even from this high up, the sound of screams, angry shouting and the screeching of brakes was loud. It was utter chaos.

'That's not good,' Mal said, squeezing her more tightly.

'It's interesting,' Rose said. She had wanted Astrid and now here she was, walking along the street, her blonde curls unmistakable. Behind her a car slammed on its brakes and the driver got out, abandoning his vehicle in the middle of the road. A cacophony of horns blared behind it, but the driver didn't even turn around – he was following Astrid.

'Jesus,' Mal said. 'That's some serious road rage.'

'It's chaos,' Rose said, watching Astrid. The driver had caught up to her now, and seemed to be shouting at her. She didn't turn around, didn't break stride. Then the man sat on the ground abruptly and burst into tears.

'It reminds me of something Dad said,' Mal was saying. 'About Mum's accident.'

'Accident?'

'She drove a van. For her work. And it was madness on the roads that day, Dad didn't really talk about it, not that I can remember, but he must have done at one time because I remember him saying 'madness'. Like it was a really bad word. It was on the Newcraighall junction and nobody paid attention to the lights. Not just one eejit, speeding through, but everyone. Every single driver rammed at once and there was a massive pile-up. Cars in the traffic behind shunted into the ones in front. It made the papers around the world, it was so big.'

Rose pulled her gaze from the street below to look at him. 'When was this?'

'Twenty years ago,' he said. 'I was six.'

'And your mum died?'

He nodded. 'I don't remember much about the time before, just snapshots, but after Mum had gone, that was when Dad started training us. He had hunted before but he really threw himself into it.' He paused, remembering. 'Threw us into it too.'

'I would have thought he'd have got more protective, not less,' Rose said.

He glanced at her, surprised. 'He said everything was getting worse and we had to be able to protect ourselves. Besides...' He shrugged. 'We might just as easily die crossing the road. Mum had just proved that.'

'Twenty years,' Rose said, turning over a thought in her mind. She was twenty years old. Or had thought she was twenty years old. 'Had things got worse. Suddenly, I mean?'

He shook his head. 'I have no idea. I was only a kid.'

'What did he say? Your dad?'

'I'd forgotten about it until now,' Mal said, indicating the traffic below. More vehicles were randomly stopping, people getting out. Some of them were engaged in heated arguments and one man was gripping another man who seemed to be trying to get away. He head-butted him in the face and blood spurted down his shirt. 'Dad said that it was like they had all gone mad at once. Just like this.'

'I don't know if they've gone mad, exactly,' Rose said. 'I think it's more like a temporary loss of control.'

Astrid had mounted the steps to the hotel and was no longer visible. The doorman had abandoned his post and was sitting on the bottom step, still in his full high-land regalia, but he had removed his hat and was throwing it up in the air and catching it. As Rose watched, he missed a catch. The hat fell to the pavement, but the doorman pulled his ceremonial sgian dubh from his sock and plunged it into his own stomach. He twisted the knife and blood cascaded over his kilted lap, bright gleaming red in the midday sun.

'Fuck. We should help him,' Mal said, his voice uncertain. He had started towards the door, but he stopped. Turned back. 'Shouldn't we?'

'Too late,' Rose said, as the body tumbled forward.

'Jesus Christ,' Mal muttered. Rose looked at him and saw how pale he was. It reminded her that she ought to feel horrified by the violence and death, not merely irri-tated. A cold shiver ran down her entire length as she realised how much she had changed. The person called 'Rose' was compressed into a tiny corner, commenting and noticing, but soon, she felt that it would be squeezed out utterly. Stars were spinning through the dark, calling her home, and the room she was standing in, the scene outside, Mal's concerned face – none of it seemed real or substantial.

'It's Astrid, isn't it?' Mal was speaking and Rose forced herself back into the present moment. 'Should we go and meet her? Stop her from hurting anybody?'

'No need,' Rose said, and as she expected the door swung open to reveal the tiny figure of Astrid. 'Hello, stranger,' Rose said.

Mal stepped forward, pushing Rose behind him.

'Well, this is perfectly horrible,' Astrid said, ignoring the half-naked man and looking, instead, at the suite. 'I fucking hate taupe.'

Rose patted Mal's shoulder and moved around him to drink in the sight of Astrid. He moved to the side of the bed and reached down for his t-shirt, but when he straightened up he was holding a gun.

'We need to talk,' Rose said, keeping her eyes on Astrid. 'I would be fascinated to hear what you've been doing.'

'Keeping you safe,' Astrid said, her hands on her hips. To Mal she said, 'You can stand down, soldier. I've come to an agreement with your boss.'

'Pringle?' Rose and Mal said at the same time.

Astrid's eyes narrowed. 'What's going on with you two?'

'Nothing,' Rose said.

Mal lifted the gun, pointed it at Astrid. 'How did you find us?'

'It's okay.' Rose held up her hand.

'Where have you been hiding my girl?' Astrid asked him. 'It's been most inconvenient.'

'Do you see the gun?' His arm was steady but his eyes were wide with shock, anger and something else that Rose couldn't identify. 'You'll be answering questions, not asking them. Did Pringle mention my brother?'

Astrid gave him a dazzling smile, one which Rose had seen render students mute and dribbling. 'You're not going to shoot me, sweetie.' To Rose she said, 'We should go somewhere hot, have a holiday.'

'I don't want to go on holiday. And I've just been to Egypt.'

'What happened to your hair?' Astrid's smile slipped for the first time. She turned to Mal. 'Was that you?'

'I did it,' Rose said.

Astrid looked surprised. 'You changed something?'

'I'm so glad to see you.' And it was true. Rose drank in the sight of her friend, gorged herself. Then she remembered. 'Where did you go?'

'Around,' Astrid said. She was frowning at Mal. 'What have you done to her? Did you wake her up?'

'I thought something was killing girls like me.' Rose spoke very quietly. 'Like us. But I was doing it. I remember now.'

'Ah.' Astrid sat on the bed. Her brow furrowed for a moment and then she said, 'That makes sense, actually. You've always made things difficult.'

'I killed someone called Hannah Weston in Alexandria. She was a teacher and I killed her like it was nothing.'. Rose didn't look at Mal, frightened of what she might read written on his face.

'She wasn't real,' Astrid said.

'You're not a killer,' Mal said. His voice was pain mixed with hope and Rose felt it like a pinprick to her skin.

'It felt real,' she said. 'But I didn't care. Explain.'

'Oh, it was real. But she wasn't. She wasn't a real girl. Just like you aren't one either, Rose MacLeod.'

There was something about her name being said out loud in that voice that pulled at Rose. She watched Astrid's slow smile and wanted to be closer to her. She forced her feet not to move.

'Laura Moffat was real. She left a corpse.' Mal's voice helped to focus Rose.

'I killed Hannah Weston. I killed a person.'

'No,' Mal said, reaching for Rose's hand. 'It's a trick. Don't listen to her.'

'Do you really care?' Astrid raised her eyebrows at Rose. 'Or is this a performance for your boyfriend?'

'I thought I was dreaming about girls being killed. I felt them die as if I was dying. I felt the knife on my own skin. I felt the fear like it was my own. I don't understand...' Rose forced herself to stop speaking and turned away from Mal. She knew things had altered, that there was something wrong with her and she wasn't reacting the way she ought, but she still didn't want to see his face as she said the words. 'I killed her. I did it.'

'You released her spirit from confinement.' Astrid waved a hand.

'Same thing,' Rose said, the disappointment hitting her in the chest. She felt her knees buckle and realised that she had been hoping Astrid would have a different answer. That it had been a hallucination. That she was, actually, insane.

There was a wave of something rolling off Astrid. It was familiar and calming and Rose had to force herself to fight it.

'Breathe, sweetie.' Astrid's voice was melodious and beautiful. 'It's going to be okay. We're together and I will look after you. Keep you safe.'

Rose sank onto the bed next to Astrid. It would be a relief to stop pretending. To stop trying to be horrified. She had killed those girls with her bare hands and she felt nothing.

Astrid put a hand onto her arm and looked into her eyes. 'Everything is okay, Rose.'

Rose remembered her parents, her bedroom with the posters on the walls and her pile of textbooks in the corner. If she relaxed she could go back to that safe place. Astrid was here and Astrid was her friend.

'Leave her alone.' It was a man's voice. It was familiar and Rose wondered where she knew it from. Mal. The man was called Mal. He was scary and then he was nice. Then she remembered; he had rescued her. From the Sluagh, but again, before that. The world shifted and Rose suddenly knew where she had met Mal before, why she had known his name.

She was in a small room with bare white walls. She was sitting on a single bed and when a buzzer sounded she knew that her day had begun. Then she was out of that small room and in a much larger space. There were several tables with wipe-clean surfaces and lots of chairs. People were sitting in the chairs and they were familiar.

She couldn't think of their names, but she knew that she knew them.

She was sitting here, too, and she looked down at her hands resting on her lap. She was wearing loose jogging trousers, navy. She didn't like them. There was something wrong with her hands, they looked different to usual. The fingernails were bitten down and Rose didn't bite her nails. She was sure of it.

'Aislinn, honey.' A soft voice was surprisingly near and it made Rose jump. She pushed up her sleeve to check her rose tattoo but there was nothing on the skin, no hint of the image at all. This was bad – she had lost so much time that it had healed completely. This had never happened, not in all the time she had been using the inkless tattoo as a check. She could feel the panic rising, clouding her thoughts.

'Aislinn, it's time for your pill.' The voice was louder, now. There was a firm edge to it and Rose looked around to see who was speaking.

A woman in a uniform was holding out a small plastic cup with a couple of tablets inside and another cup half-filled with water. It was familiar and wrong all at once. 'Am I Aislinn?' Her voice was also wrong. It was lighter than usual and it hurt a little coming from her throat, as if she hadn't spoken in a long while.

'Pill time, honey,' the woman said, and Rose reached out the hand that didn't really belong to her and took the cup. She put the pills into her mouth and felt the smooth plastic capsules on her tongue. The water next. She knew that she could tuck the pills, or one of them at least, into her cheek or she could swallow them both like a good girl.

'They will make you feel better,' the nurse said. Encouraging. Kind.

Rose took the cup of water and swallowed her medicine. As the pills travelled down her throat, Rose remembered. And then, as easy as falling asleep, she knew exactly what she had to do.

CHAPTER NINETEEN

Rose had sat next to Astrid and then fallen back, suddenly fast asleep. Mal lowered his gun and went to her, checking her pulse. Her chest rose and fell in time, with deep and even breaths.

'This happened before. She must be sick. We should take her to hospital.' He began pulling on the rest of his clothes.

Astrid was twirling a curl of hair around her fingers. 'She's gone.'

'What do you mean? Did you do something to her?'

Astrid shrugged. 'Just calmed her down a little. Gives us a chance to chat.'

'But it's happened before,' he said. 'I really think she's sick.'

'I wouldn't worry,' Astrid said. 'She probably just popped off.'

'Popped off where?'

'If I knew that, it would make things much easier. She's never been one for convenience, though.'

Mal looked at Astrid more closely. There had been bitterness in her voice.

'She has always made things difficult,' Astrid said and then shrugged, her voice suddenly bright. 'Good thing I love her!'

'What are you?' Mal said, taking a step back.

Astrid gazed up at him with a calculating look. 'I thought it was you killing them. You killed that girl in the bar.'

Mal thought of Laura Moffat. 'I did not.'

'Well, you didn't keep her safe. She slashed her wrists and you left her to die on the floor of one of the oldest bars in Europe.'

Mal felt the stab of pain, guilt, but he knew Astrid was baiting him. She reminded him of Pringle, when he was having fun. Right before the pain began. 'How do you know about Aislinn?'

'She had the sight,' Astrid said. 'I know that much. And when you decided to use her for your craptitudious little sting operation, you as good as killed her.'

'I was going to let her go,' he said.

'Oh, sweetie.' Astrid shook her head sadly. 'That poor girl had been seeing bad stuff her whole life and she didn't have anybody to hold her hand, to tell her it was okay, or that she wasn't crazy. Then you came along and used her. You picked her up like she was a wrench or a hacksaw and you used her to take a peek at Rose.' Astrid smiled widely. 'Problem is, Aislinn wasn't a saw. She was a magnifying glass and you held her up to the sun. You killed her.'

Mal swallowed. He didn't trust himself to speak and he didn't know what he would say anyway.

'The question is, did it do you any good? Did it give you a little jolt? Have you worked out what Rose is yet?'

'Laura Moffat had psychic ability too,' he said. 'What do you know about her? I know she was killed.'

'Her and many others,' Astrid said.

'You fit the profile,' Mal said. 'You could be in danger. Rose thinks she's responsible but I don't believe that. She's confused. She's ill.'

'You shouldn't worry about me.' The cute blonde smiled in a way that made the skin on the back of his neck attempt to slink away. 'I'm in the business, so to speak.'

'The business?'

'Death, sweetie. I'm in the death business.'

It had been a very long and difficult day and Mal's hand went back to his gun. He straightened his shoulders. 'I'm sorry about Aislinn, I am. But I didn't know she was going to do that.'

'It's all right,' Astrid said. 'If she hadn't topped herself, Rose would have got to her eventually.' She looked at Rose fondly, brushing a lock of hair away from her face. 'You've been at it since the beginning, haven't you, pet? I thought we were having such a lovely holiday, but you've been trying to go home all along.' She made a 'tsch' sound with her tongue and then moved away from the bed, exploring the room.

Mal took the opportunity to finish dressing. He

shoved his feet into his boots and laced them. He had to get Rose out of here, get some medical attention. Then check on Euan. Find out what was going on with Pringle and what the new arrangement with Astrid involved. His chest ached as he pictured his brother.

Astrid climbed up onto the desk by the window and looked out at the view. The castle was lit in the dusk and it cast white sodium through the murk. She was striking a pose with one hand on her narrow waist, as if well aware of Mal's gaze. In that moment, the big window and the desk and the heavy hotel drapes disappeared, and Mal could see a huge vaulted tent, the dark reaches impossible to see or judge. In a sparkling circus outfit, a pretty girl on a tightrope put one foot carefully in front of the other. He could hear the crowds inside the big tent and smell greasepaint mixed with horseshit. He blinked and the blonde in jeans and a hoodie stepped lightly off the desk and winked at him. 'Let's talk about you for a while. I hear you have a brother.'

He shook his head, dislodging the glamour or whatever it was the girl was throwing at him. He had been trained for this, and although Astrid's pull was strong, equal even to Mary King's, he set his jaw and endured the waves of pain and confusion, letting them flow over his mind and body and drain away. The trick was to become as smooth as a polished stone, not giving the power a place to snag and burrow inside. During practice drills, his father had made him imagine the exact stone, and now Mal could conjure it up easily. He was a lump of labradorite, roughly oval in shape and just the right size to sit comfortably in the palm of his hand. He knew how it felt, had bought the piece from the fossil shop in the Grassmarket when he was fifteen. It was dark green, almost black, and iridescent in places. The surface was crazed with fine lines which could almost be capillaries or nerve endings, making it look alive. The whole thing had come from a volcano millions of years ago. It had survived this long and it would help Mal survive now. When he could think clearly again, he said, 'I'd rather hear all about you, *sweetie.*'

The blonde narrowed her eyes. 'That's a good trick for a human.' She moved forwards, closing the gap between them. 'What else can you do?'

'I'd rather talk about you,' Mal said. He forced himself not to take a step backwards. 'What are you? Really. And what is Rose?'

'I'm Astrid. And Rose is Rose. Together we are the closest thing to a god you are ever likely to meet.'

Mal didn't say anything. He could feel something pacing outside his mind, looking for a crack, a way in. After a moment, Astrid sighed and opened the fridge. She selected a bar of chocolate and ripped open the foil packet with her small white teeth. After the first bite of chocolate, she said, ' I prefer Death, but that's just me.'

'Death. Tall dude with a skull for a face and a scythe for—'

'Harvesting the souls of the dead. Yes. Him.'

'You're a—' Mal began, but Astrid rolled over him before he could finish.

'Girl. Chick. Dudette. Female. Yes.' Those impossibly big eyes narrowed again. 'Are you being this dense on purpose?'

'I'm sorry,' Mal said. 'I'm just adjusting. I knew about ghosts. The Sluagh. Demons. I didn't know about gods.'

'Demigods at most.' Astrid lowered her eyes modestly. 'The full-fat variety are long gone.'

'Where?'

'How the fuck should I know?' she said. 'Mars, maybe. Or further still. It's a big fucking universe. And there are millions of them.'

'Gods?'

'Universes.'

'Ah, the multiverse.' Mal was proud of how well he was holding up. Even his father might have been impressed.

Astrid smiled. 'I apologise for calling you dense. You are quite bright for an ape.'

'Thanks,' he said.

'You still pissed me off, though. It's not fair.'

He fought the urge to apologise again. 'What's not fair?'

'That death got painted as a dude. Who do you think has the greater connection with death – men or women?'

'Well, men traditionally held the jobs that encountered it,' Mal said. If he could keep Astrid talking, he could buy enough time to work out how to get Rose out of the room. He wouldn't shoot Astrid, she had been right about that. More worrying, though, was the fear that it wouldn't make any difference. He was so out of his depth it was terrifying.

'You mean soldiers?'

'And priests performing last rites or doctors battling

or pronouncing death. I'm not saying that was right,' he added hurriedly. 'Gender inequality. Very bad.'

'Pronouncing it is right. Not always accurately, I might add. As for battling death...' Astrid paused, seeming to be at a momentary loss for words. She settled on a sound like 'pfft' and a violent head shake.

'You're very cynical,' he said, wondering if she was sufficiently distracted for him to make a move. Attack or flee. Something.

'I'm old. It goes with the territory.' She grinned. 'I'm also starving.' She removed a bag of nuts from the fridge and tore the packet open. Through a mouthful she said, 'I was making a point about death's partner. It's not doctors, not priests, not men at all in fact. Who's there when the body breaks down and there's piss and shit and blood and vomit everywhere? Women. Who traditionally washes the dead and dresses it in a clean sheet after the idiot with the holy book has buggered off back to the tea table? Women.'

Mal thought about the death he had seen, his father plunging a dagger into the femoral artery of some creature and then digging a grave for it after. He wasn't exactly normal, though. Not a poster child for the average.

Astrid tilted her head, her expression saying that she was about to deliver her final blow. 'And who creates life?'

'Surely that's the opposite?'

'Two sides of the same coin. Like me and sleeping beauty here.'

'Fine,' Mal said. 'Let's say I believe you. Which I

don't. What do you want? Why are you wandering around Edinburgh looking like—' He broke off, gesturing instead to the tiny form of Astrid and her corkscrew curls and very human face.

'Holiday.' Astrid waved a hand and Mal saw a wall of white. It filled his vision until there was nothing else.

Mary King picked her way along the street toward the Caledonian Hotel. She had no problem in following Astrid's footsteps, as she had left a trail of destruction and chaos in her wake. There was a small crowd of people on the steps in front of the brass-and-glass revolving doors of the hotel, almost hiding a prone and bloodied figure. She heard an argument starting, raised hysterical voices which sounded endearingly out of control. The humans had never seemed more like little children. They were oblivious and vulnerable and Pringle was gone; Mary King wanted to hug herself in delight. The Sluagh would have fallen with him, which left her victorious. About bleeding time.

Inside, the reception desk was empty apart from a lithe and beautiful young woman who was talking animatedly on her mobile phone with tears running down her face. Mary King swept by and entered the lift. It was decorated in tartan and smoked glass and there was a broken wine bottle on the floor in a puddle of dark red. She pressed all of the buttons so that the lift would stop at each floor. When the doors opened she leaned out, trying to sense Astrid.

On the fifth floor, she saw a burst of light before the

doors had even fully opened. She stepped out into the empty corridor, blinking to regain her vision. The air was electric and it made her teeth ache. One door was ajar and she heard voices. She moved softly and peered through the gap. She could see the end of a large bed and a desk. It was an executive suite which had probably not advertised the inclusion of a small blonde demon. Astrid was cross-legged on top of the desk, speaking animatedly to an unseen person. Mary King shifted as quietly as she could until she could see more of the bed. The hunter was sitting on the edge and, next to him, a girl was sleeping. Mary King could see very dark hair and pale skin. She slid her favourite knife from its sheath and weighed her next move. Astrid was talking but was she distracted enough?

She summoned every piece of cursework she knew, every scrap of shine. She only needed to buy a few seconds. Long enough to cut Astrid's throat. Then she would do the same to her sleepyhead friend and eat her fill.

She hesitated. She was not used to indecision. Living on so little for so long had made her tough and quick. There was a banquet laid out on the bed and she could almost feel the knife slipping in, how easy it would work, and the shine that would fill her up. Shine she could live on for another hundred years.

There was a new voice speaking. The girl on the bed was awake. Mary King peeked around the door, sharpening her senses to see through whatever glamour or cursework was being used.

She never got that far. All was blinding white light

and a ringing sound which Mary King would have felt in her soul, had she possessed such a thing.

Rose felt the pills as they went down her throat and she knew it wasn't a dream or a vision. It was a memory. She knew that she had been Aislinn at one point. Or part of her had been Aislinn. When Aislinn had died, and Rose suddenly knew that she had, that part had come home. It was lodged, now, inside Rose. Part of her had been Melody, too, and Hannah and Françoise and Eve. She remembered killing each of them and how the white light inside her had got a little brighter each time.

She blinked and sat up. No longer asleep, no longer filled with the calm that Astrid had poured into her. Astrid was sitting on the end of the bed, tipping a bag of salted cashew nuts into her mouth. Rose looked around, but Mal had gone. She couldn't see a body, so she hoped that meant Astrid had sent him away or locked him in a cupboard. The small part of her that was still Rose MacLeod hoped he wasn't dead.

'Isn't salt the best?' Astrid licked her fingers.

Half of Rose was still with Aislinn in the hospital and she felt the pull of sleep. 'You lied to me,' she said.

'Not lied. Held back some truth.' Astrid smiled. 'I had to, for your own safety.'

'I've been killing people and you're worried about my safety? Does that sound even remotely likely?' Rose knew she couldn't reveal what she suddenly knew, that all the girls were part of her. Every death she had dealt had been a blessed release and, with each one, she had got closer to her true form. She hadn't been killing lost girls, she had been bringing the flock safely home. No. She had to string Astrid along for a while until she worked out what Astrid knew, what Astrid wanted.

'You haven't killed anyone.' Astrid waved a hand, like she swatting away a fly. 'Not really.'

'I woke up covered in blood.' Rose could remember the iron smell of the blood, thick and choking. She had a memory of drawing a knife across a throat, a clean, fast cut that felt merciful but couldn't possibly be so. 'I used a knife. I cut—'

'That was just a soul case. A shell. You released the spirit.'

'That's just a fancy way of saying 'killed'. Melody was a real person.' Rose swallowed, trying to keep herself from retching. Part of her felt sick but another, larger part felt utterly calm. The calm part was terrifying. She could feel it encroaching, wiping away the Rose MacLeod she had been building in her mind. 'So was Laura Moffat. She had a job, a family, a life.'

Astrid shook her head. 'Set dressing.'

Rose wanted it to be true. Wanted an explanation for her monstrous actions, her lack of emotion. If they hadn't been real then she hadn't murdered anyone, hadn't really taken lives. 'Why should I believe you? You've lied to me over and over again. For years. For—' Rose stopped. 'For how long? How long have I been in Edinburgh?'

'At the uni? About twenty years.' Astrid crumpled the foil packet and opened another one.

Rose sat back on the edge of the bed. 'I've done my degree over and over?'

'No, you've done your first year over and over. New intake each time, new students, means you just blend in with all the other newbies.'

'No one's noticed?'

'Humans are very focused on their own needs. You'd be amazed at what they don't notice. You could fill a continent with things they don't notice. In fact, take a bit of land, call it foreign and they'll never see it at all.'

'I'm not looking for a sociology lecture.'

'Psychology, but whatever. Perhaps you need another twenty years?'

'Is this funny to you?' Rose had an emotion then: anger. It burst across her skin like fire. 'Are you feeling amused at this moment?'

Astrid smiled a little wider. 'A little. I'm sorry. It just feels so good to be able to talk properly.' She stretched her arms above her head. 'It's been so constrained. I've been in a tiny little box and I'm finally out.'

Somehow, that didn't sound like good news. The girl Rose had known as Astrid wasn't the same as this creature in front of her now. She looked the same, her voice was the same, her syntax was even the same, but it was all a costume. 'I need the bathroom,' Rose said, getting up. She walked to the ensuite and locked the door. She made bathroom-style noises, flushing the toilet and running the taps at the basin. She didn't know if Mal had escaped or if Astrid had disposed of him. The wet towels from earlier were still on the floor, reminding

Rose of how happy and free she had felt for those minutes.

Back in the suite, Astrid was flicking through the channels on the flat screen.

'So. What happens next?'

'I missed *A Place in the Sun*,' Astrid said. 'I love that show.'

'It's on all the time,' Rose said, just for something to say. 'Change channels.'

'No.' Astrid clicked off the screen and turned away. 'I checked. It's on again at five.'

Rose looked out of the window, hoping to catch sight of Mal on his way along the street. Safe and alive. He had tried to help her.

Astrid had liberated a cola from the mini bar and was watching Rose over the rim of the can. 'You're unhappy,' she said. 'Have some pop. The bubbles are cheerful.'

'I'm a murderer, I don't think bubbles are going to do the trick.'

'Are you still upset about that?'

'Yes,' Rose said, stifling the urge to shout or stamp her foot or punch something. 'It's still on my mind.'

Astrid sighed. 'Would it help if I talked about nature and survival of the fittest? Or mayflies and how they only live for a day?'

'I don't think so. No.'

'We could get drunk. That's often pleasant.'

'No.' Rose went to the other window this time, tried to look as if she was just checking out the view.

'He's not out there,' Astrid said.

Rose looked around. Astrid's heart-shaped face, wide blue eyes and blonde corkscrews no longer hid her power. She pulsed with it and Rose was afraid.

'He's not important,' she said lightly.

Astrid gave her a stern look. 'Don't play games. Not with me.'

Rose tried to swallow the sudden lump in her throat.

'I told him he wasn't needed. He stood down.' She giggled. 'He's a good little soldier. What we do next, is visit Mary King. She's got the juice.' Astrid stopped speaking, her head cocked as if listening. 'I think the lovely Mary King has saved us the walk. How nice.'

'Juice?' Rose said, but Astrid was skipping to the door and opening it wide to reveal a woman slumped in the hallway.

'To restore you to your former glory,' Astrid said over her shoulder. She reached out and touched the woman. 'Damn it!'

The body was stiff and pale with unnaturally red cheeks and a multitude of piercings in her nose, ears, lips, and brows. She was like an empty shell or mannequin, not a real person. 'Is that Mary King?' Rose asked. 'What's wrong with her?'

'It'll have to do,' Astrid said. She squeezed the woman's head between her hands for a moment, before turning back to the room. Her face was flushed and her eyes even brighter than usual. Astrid had always been attractive but now she looked like a Hollywood starlet.

Rose took a step back. 'If I'm back the way I was, what will you do?'

'Worship you, of course. Worship. Serve. Obey. Protect.'

It was clear that Astrid was lying, but Rose forced herself to smile. 'Well, when you put it like that.'

Astrid grinned, looking like her old self. The friend Rose had relied on for so long, the friend she had loved. She felt as if her insides were coming apart but she knew she couldn't show it. She couldn't let Astrid see that she knew the truth. That her eyes were finally wide open. She had to find the last missing pieces of herself and release them quickly. Regain her full strength before Astrid succeeded in putting her back to sleep.

Rose kept her expression carefully neutral while she concentrated. The feeling that she'd had when she jumped to Paris had been unexpected, not under her control. It had been born of fear and desperation and adrenaline but she could remember the taste of it, the texture, and she recalled it now, gathering it like a cloak and wrapping it tightly around herself.

She slipped a hand into her pocket and felt the pebble Mal had picked up on the beach. He'd given it to her and she'd felt happy. She concentrated on that feeling, let it fill every corner of her body and mind until she could feel the sun on her face, the salt-filled breeze on her lips, her skin. Her hair, in its new bob length, shifted in the air current, strands straying into her eyes. Astrid's eyes widened and, for a moment, Rose thought that she was being too slow, that Astrid would have time to react and stop her. And then she was gone. No longer in the hotel room with her traitorous friend, no longer in Edinburgh. The sun was hot on her face and Rose knew with utter certainty that she was exactly where she needed to be.

Astrid stared with deep annoyance at the empty air Rose had just vacated. If she had known how quickly Rose could snap out of her trance state, she would have been far more careful to keep her as a clueless student. Of course, she was still weak. Astrid would put her back under. Just as soon as she located her. She snapped her fingers and the covering charm which had concealed Mal from Rose fell away. He was still bound and gagged, although he'd managed to wriggle over to the edge of the bed, perhaps hoping to make his escape despite the overwhelming odds against him. There was something endearing about the human capacity for optimism.

Astrid took a knife from her boot and sliced the gag away from the boy's mouth. 'Where has she gone?'

'How should I know?' he said.

Still. There was a time for optimism and there was a time to know when you were beaten. Astrid touched the point of the knife to her finger and watched the blood well up. It was a good sharp blade and would help her to educate this boy in the difference.

CHAPTER TWENTY

Mal licked his dry lips. The blade in Astrid's hand was long and wickedly sharp and he wondered how long he would manage to hold out. His father had taught him to go inside himself, far away from physical pain, and he knew he could take a beating. Torture, though. That was something different, however much he wanted to be brave.

'She will have gone somewhere she felt safe and happy,' Astrid said. 'That doesn't leave many options.'

Astrid appeared satisfied with this notion, and it turned Mal's stomach. He pressed his lips together.

'I'm waiting.' She leaned over and looked into Mal's face.

He held her gaze with enormous effort. 'If there aren't many on your list, why don't you check them all? I'll just wait here.'

She smiled. 'You are doing a wonderful job of pretending you are not frightened but it doesn't fool me,

I'm afraid. I'm very well acquainted with fear and you reek of it.'

He didn't reply.

'This doesn't have to be unpleasant,' she said. 'You tell me all the places you and Rose spent time together. Alone.'

'What makes you think she'll—'

Astrid snapped her fingers. 'Stop playing for time. It doesn't matter. There is no urgency. I have all the time I need, but I'm bored and I want to finish this.'

Mal closed his eyes. 'Why would I help you to destroy her?'

'Because I'll save your brother, of course. One snap of my fingers and that sleepyhead will wake right up.'

Mal licked his lips. They were sore from the gag but his heart was aching in a more visceral way. 'That's impossible.'

Astrid laughed, and he wondered how he'd ever mistaken her for human. She twirled a finger in the air, leaving a spiral of smoke that hung for a moment before disappearing.

'How?'

'I'd just pay him a little visit. The Royal Infirmary isn't far from my booth, after all.' She paused to let the breadth of her knowledge sink in, the knowledge that she could visit Euan at any time – for good or for ill. 'And I'd lean down and whisper into his ear. And he'd open his eyes and sit up.'

'He needs a machine to breathe,' Mal said, despair warring with hope.

'Not after I whisper the magic words.'

'What will it cost?'

'Just the information I've asked for. It's a very good deal.'

'What will it cost Euan?'

Astrid shook her head. 'Not a damn thing.' She spread her hands. 'I would say that I'm in a generous mood but you'd know that's a lie. I just really want the information and generosity seems like the quickest and easiest way to get it. Come on, Mal. I've got nothing against you personally. You or your brother. I don't care about you one way or another, and I mean that in the nicest possible way.'

'And if I don't?'

'That would be very silly, given the circumstances.'

'I agree,' he said, 'but just for the sake of argument. I'm assuming something bad will happen to me.'

'I'd pull your insides out through your eye sockets, one piece at a time.' Astrid smiled widely. 'And then I'd wake up your brother and do the same thing to him.'

'Good to know,' Mal said, willing his voice to stay steady. 'We have a deal. I'd spit into my palm and offer to shake hands but I'm a little bit tied up here. I could spit on the bed?'

'No spitting required,' Astrid said. 'I'm so over all that pagan shit.' She crossed the room and sat on the bed. She placed one hand gently on his cheek and said, 'Tell me.'

'How do I know you won't just kill me anyway?'

She sighed quickly. 'I'll show you.' She leaned down and kissed him. Her lips were soft and she smelled of cinnamon and freshly cut grass and baked bread and clean mountain air. He knew she was death and that her smell was a lie. He also knew he didn't have a choice.

When she sat up, she looked pleased. 'Now, tell me.'

'Once Euan is awake,' Mal said. He steeled himself for her anger, but she surprised him by smiling.

'I can see why Rose took to you, little soldier. As you wish.'

Afia was daydreaming as she walked through Makola Market. She was carrying a big steel pot from her auntie's shop for a customer who had just spent a good amount of money. The customer still had some shopping to do so Afia would follow them back through the market and carry their other purchases until they had finished. Then she would pass the pot and the sugar cane and pineapples and kente fabric and whatever else this rich lady wanted to the driver man and be free to walk back to her auntie. There would be a slice of time when her auntie would not know that she was not working and she could wander a little, maybe treat herself to some maasa. Afia had never been able to resist the sweet-fried cakes and her stomach rumbled at the thought.

Afia picked her way through the crowds of people and the confusion of parasols and piled goods, keeping an easy eye on her customer. The noise of the market was as familiar as a lullaby, so it was an unpleasant shock to see something out of place. Not something, someone. A skinny white girl with black hair.

The girl from her dreams. Afia had only made the mistake of telling Auntie about her dream-girl once and auntie had drawn back, crossing herself. Although she was a good Christian woman, Auntie remembered the old ways, and she said that a white girl in a dream was a witch.

Afia did not want a witch in her dream. No matter how forward-thinking the Ghanaian, and Afia considered herself very modern indeed, the idea of a witch, just the word, even, was enough to make one shiver. But whether Afia wanted the girl or not, she appeared when she closed her eyes at night.

After many years, Afia had decided to accept this affliction. She never spoke of it. Sometimes, the elderly would talk about children being born cursed, and Afia would dig her fingernails into her palms and close her ears. Maybe her mother had whispered to a snake or seen something ugly when she had been carrying Afia, but there was nothing Afia could do about that. She had always tried to be a good child, hoping that the witch would leave her dreams, but after many years, she grew used to her presence. She even wondered if the elders were wrong. Maybe dreaming of a white person did not always mean something bad. She was never afraid in her dreams and she found, to her surprise, that she wasn't afraid now.

The market people flowed around the girl. A woman with a tin bath on her head barged her from one side, while a running boy clipped her from the other. Anybody with any sense knew that you couldn't stand still in the middle of the street, but her body hardly moved. She looked like a twig that should be spun by the current and taken downstream, but she remained rooted to her chosen spot.

Afia did not think the girl would be able to do that for long. Somebody would shove her properly sooner or later. It was not the done thing to stand so still in the middle of the passageway. If you wanted to dawdle, you had to go close to the stores, or down one of the many little alleys which cut through them. There were back-alleys too, which ran behind the main activity of the market, and where you could hardly see the sky for the towering piles of jars and handbags and tools and only-God-knew, but not all of those were wise. Some of the hidden paths were good shortcuts and some were not.

And some were not even real passages, and Afia took one of these. It was just a narrow strip between a man selling guava and another selling giant snails. The snail man shouted as she went past, but Afia did not stop. She was not afraid of the witch from her dreams, but she was not a stupid girl, either. There was something wrong and she wasn't going to stand out in the middle of the street waiting for it to find her.

She took a sharp right-hand turn down an even narrower passage and then, after a bit of a squeeze past a woman carrying three giant cardboard boxes, she turned onto one of the back-way paths. She knew the boy who ran a stall down here – they had been at school together. His name was Kofi, because, like her, he had been born on a Friday, and she had always felt he was a kindred spirit, ever since she had spotted him reading a manga comic. Now she identified Kofi by his bright yellow t-shirt and felt a rush of relief. He would let her stand behind his plaintain stall for a few minutes and then, when the white girl had gone, she would go and get that maasa.

She was only a few feet from Kofi and was already opening her mouth to greet him, when she felt a hand grip her upper arm. She was spun around so quickly she almost lost her balance. It was the witch.

'Afia Magdelene Nana Sika Owusu.'

Afia was so shocked to hear her full five names spoken with such confidence and clarity by this strange white girl that she simply let her mouth drop open.

'Well?' the girl said. Her voice was friendly but there was urgency in it, too.

Then the voice registered and Afia closed her eyes. She knew that voice. She had been hearing that voice her whole life, always wanting to hear more, but it was always just out of reach. She would lie at night with her head turned and her best-hearing ear lifted to the air, hoping to catch a note or two, while her brothers and sisters slept soundly.

'It's you,' she said, no longer aware of the market around them, the sounds of hawkers and customers and the blare of the radios fading.

The girl smiled. 'Don't be afraid,' she said. She was so pale she seemed to gleam, and the closer Afia looked, the more it seemed that she reflected back the little light available in the shaded passageway. The light was getting brighter by the second, and all at once it was almost too painful for Afia to keep her eyes open. She wanted to keep looking, though, wanted to see the girl for as long as possible. The girl had a flower on her arm and she was the most beautiful thing that Afia had ever seen. More beautiful, even, than she had appeared in her dreams. Afia wasn't afraid. 'I have been waiting for you,' she said, her voice barely a whisper.

The dark-haired girl smiled and opened her arms. The light was brighter still, and Afia's eyes were streaming, the image of the girl blurring and dissolving. Afia stepped willingly into her embrace and the world went pure white.

Rose felt herself rise up. The white light surrounded her and Afia until they were both made from the light and there was no form left. It was like the old days. Rose thought about Iona and the way the sky had kept changing. It went from bright blue to silver to dark pearl and then back again, like a light show just for her. The sea changed with it, two halves of the same whole, one affecting, reflecting the other. They needed each other, the sky and the sea. They were bound.

Iona wasn't just dark water and white sand, though. A name came back to her. Mal. She could taste the salt on her lips and feel him stood with her. She went there, just for a moment, and relived it. Mal's deep voice reverberating through her body as he said 'I won't let anything hurt you' and the heady, hormonal pull which had made her want to join their physical forms. He had said that she could always choose to be the Rose MacLeod who was standing there on that beach, but she wasn't sure she could. The salt air was already disappearing. The wind that had been whipping her skin died away and was replaced with stillness. Warmth.

Rose was back in the form that had eyes which could

be closed. She could sense Astrid but she also smelled antiseptic and knew that they were no longer in the hotel room. She opened her eyes and found that it was a much smaller room, with plain white walls and medical equipment next to a metal bed with raised sides.

Astrid was leaning over a figure on the bed. Mal was there too, hovering behind Astrid. He was frowning. Rose was disturbed to realise that she couldn't decode the expression. She didn't know if it was physical pain or something emotional, and both of those possibilities felt alien. Remote. Like something she had read about in a book long ago. She hesitated and then settled on a simple, 'Hi.'

Astrid's attention switched away from the young man lying in the bed. 'You came back,' Astrid said.

'Leave him be,' Rose said, waving a hand, and Astrid stood up automatically. She looked cross about it.

'Why?' Astrid said. She was frowning, irritated. 'Why did you come back? I was just going to find you, this boy was going to tell me where to look. But now you've just come back. You're always doing that, stealing my fucking thunder.'

'I realised something,' Rose said. She felt calm. She could still feel the sea breeze on her face, taste the ocean. And the humid heat of Ghana and, behind it, the dust of Alexandria and a hundred thousand other impressions. She could feel the sky stretching out and she knew that this room, this building was just a blip. It hadn't been here before and, in a few short years, it would crumble to dust. She felt very old. 'We're meant to be together.'

Mal had moved closer to the bed, to the figure lying there. His brother, Rose realised. Euan.

He appeared oblivious to anything else in the room and Rose recognised something in Mal's expression as he looked at his brother. They were bound together. Just as Rose and Astrid were two sides of the same coin.

Astrid was looking cautiously hopeful. 'We are meant to be together. We're a team.'

It was at that moment that Rose realised something else: the room was shaking.

'What are you doing?'

'Stop resisting me, Rose,' Astrid said, coming closer. 'I showed you what would happen if you resisted.'

'What do you mean?'

'Your vision in the lecture hall? Those children dying all around you, spilling blood across their cute little desks.'

Rose understood, suddenly, that Astrid had been feeding her more than just the safe little world of student life. She had been keeping her in line with thinly veiled threats, keeping her off balance and afraid, clouding her mind with whatever means necessary. It was inventive, and Rose felt admiration along with the inevitable anger. 'People are dying, anyway,' Rose said. 'Look out there.' She indicated the window. 'You have been causing chaos for the last twenty years and now that I'm awake it's only got worse.'

'So go back to sleep, make it better for your precious apes.'

Rose felt the temptation of this. If she let Astrid put her back to sleep, shatter her power and scatter the pieces, she would become Rose MacLeod again. She felt a flutter in her chest at the thought of being with Mal, living a human life. The shaking was worse, now, and a crack appeared in the wall underneath the window. The sound cut through Rose's daydream. She could live a kind of human life but it would be a lie. And her presence in this world was bringing death and chaos.

'No,' she said.

Dismay flashed across Astrid's beautiful face. 'But I like it here.'

'I know,' Rose said.

'Hot chocolate,' Astrid said plaintively. The ground underneath the hospital shuddered as if in pain. The bed frame rattled and the sound of beeping alarms, running footsteps and shouts came from the corridor.

'It's not built for us,' Rose said. 'We're just breaking it.'

'Rose.' Mal was cradling his brother's head, his body curved over to protect him from the debris that was now falling from a crack in the ceiling. He looked at her with pleading in his eyes, begging her to do something. 'It's a hospital,' he said.

'Exactly.' Astrid snapped her fingers. 'This lot only need the tiniest of nudges.'

At that moment the lights went out and the machine next to Euan became silent.

'No, no, no,' Mal said. He looked at the screen, which was blank and no longer emitting a regular 'beep' sound. 'There must be a backup generator.' He looked around wildly. 'Help.'

'It was just a little holiday,' Astrid said. The window

was shaking in its frame so violently that the glass cracked.

Rose felt the power surging, could hear the ocean crashing and, beyond it, the beautiful silence of the stars. The creature that had been Rose and Eve and Françoise and Hannah and Laura and Melody and Aislinn and Afia was almost home. She touched Astrid's face. 'Please,' she said.

'But you will cease to exist,' Astrid said, confusion and hurt on her face. 'So will I.'

'You know that's not true,' Rose said. 'And we will be together. Forever.'

Astrid gestured to Mal, who had linked his fingers and was executing chest compressions on Euan, tears pouring down his face. 'They are ants. What difference does it make?'

Rose didn't know what to say. She felt the pebble in her pocket and held it out to Astrid in lieu of words.

After a pause which seemed to hang in time, while the screams and shouts got louder and the sound of breaking masonry and glass mixed with the wailing of sirens, Astrid blew a curl of hair away from her face. 'Fine,' she said. 'You always spoil things, you know?'

'I know,' Rose said, and opened her arms.

Astrid stepped into them and white light filled the room.

'Where did she go?' Mal was blinking in the light which still remained. He was pale and sweating, with dark shadows under his eyes like crescents of soot. Humans were so fragile.

The shaking had stopped abruptly and, somewhere in the basement of the hospital, an emergency generator sprang into life, feeding the intensive care unit and the respirators. Throughout the building, humans began to breathe again. She could feel them. All the little sparks.

'What happened?' Mal checked the machine, which was once again keeping his brother alive, and then looked searchingly at Rose. 'What did you do?'

The thing that had been Rose MacLeod shrugged and the boy took a step back, stumbling slightly. She could feel all the memories rushing together, clicking into place. Aislinn, Melody, Hannah, Françoise... all the lost girls were found. Astrid had been the last. The trickiest.

'Where is Astrid?'

'She's right here, sweetie,' Rose said. She was stretching out, pushing the limits of her form. She would escape it soon, let the soul case wither and blow away. She could feel the vast reaches of the sky calling her home.

The boy looked worried. No, frightened.

She watched his skin crease as the small muscles contracted to form the expression of concern, and wondered how Rose MacLeod had felt anything for this creature. She could remember how Melody had felt about her bully of a father and how Laura had loved Freya and how sad and lonely and afraid Aislinn had been, but it was just knowledge. She couldn't feel those things anymore. They had been her, inside, but they had been wrapped in human form. They had been living as little sparks on this funny wet rock, but now all of them were back where they belonged.

'It was just meant to be a holiday,' she said. 'It got a little out of hand.'

'But where's Astrid gone?'

'Don't worry about her.'

'I do.' Mal took a step forward, clearly uncertain, but still forging ahead. Human spirit. Stupid, but admirable in its own way.

'What if she tries to hurt you again?'

Rose wanted to laugh at his incomprehension, the way his mind was battling the truths he had been given, but there was still something inside her which made her voice gentle. 'She told you what I am?'

'Yes,' he said.

'So you know what she is too. We are two sides of the same coin. Creation and destruction. Birth and death.' Rose clicked her fingers. 'The complete package.'

'So you're safe now?'

'We were supposed to just be two, but Astrid split one side into many pieces. She hid little bits in many different cases and scattered them as far as she could. Twenty years ago she did this, but we're all back together now.'

The being that had been Rose and Astrid, Afia, Eve, Françoise, Melody, Laura, Hannah and Aislinn was surprised to feel something smooth and alien in her hand. She lifted it to her face, the word 'pebble' floating across her mind as she studied the green-white surface of sea-polished rock and tried to remember why it had seemed important.

A beeping split the air. Euan's machine was throwing a fit and Mal didn't know if it was an after-effect of the power cut or a malfunction. Euan's chest was no longer rising and falling and he felt the panic back in full force, his brain short-circuiting in an attempt to process everything that had happened.

The woman who had once been Rose MacLeod was standing stock still, studying the pebble he had given her on Iona as if she had never seen a piece of rock before. She still looked like his Rose, a little at least, but she was taller. Much taller and much more... real. Looking at her hurt. It was as if she was the only true thing in a faded cardboard cut-out scene.

He knew that he needed to call a nurse, get somebody in to help his brother, but the noise had become louder. The alarm from the machine had been joined with another sound. It was piercing, so high-pitched that he held his ears to try to block it, and soon he couldn't think about anything except making it stop.

Tears leaked from his eyes and he scrambled back, his head hitting the wall in his effort to put some distance between himself and the noise, which seemed to be coming from Rose.

He heard his own voice say 'Stop! My head!', but he wasn't sure if it had been out loud or in his own mind.

'Hush, now. Why don't you have a rest?' Not-Rose gestured to the padded chair next to Euan's bed. The chair in which he had spent hours of his life, wishing for a great power to fix his brother. 'You look tired,' she said. She patted his arm and the pain in his head receded.

'I've got to help him,' Mal said. 'He needs a nurse.'

Not-Rose smiled and, although she wasn't Rose, Mal felt a little better. She leaned over his brother and cupped his clean-shaven cheek. Her other hand reached out and slipped into Mal's. He felt her pass him the pebble and calm washed over him in a wave. He sank onto the chair.

He was tired. That was the problem. He was just tired. If he had a little rest he'd be able to cope with the weirdness, the vastness of it all. His mind caught on that thought, snagged on it, and his heart began hammering again. He felt the edges of his mind grow dark, his thoughts slow.

Rose was Not-Rose. Euan had been about to die. No, that wasn't right. Rose was right here with him. She wasn't quite a girl and someone had wanted to use her. Someone with a funny name. He had been running away. They had been running.

Rose was a good friend, he thought as he laid his head against the smooth back of the chair. A bit unusual but she had a good heart. He had felt it, held it. He was sure. A memory leaped up and it was of Rose naked, her skin shining. He felt the pull of desire deep in his stomach and remembered touching her, joining with her, and the feeling of being both excited and at peace. He had been alone for so long, but then there had been Rose. She stroked his cheek and he closed his eyes. It had been bliss. He had held Rose in his arms and felt true bliss.

The being that had been Rose MacLeod for a couple of decades, a time span which had no meaning now that they were in their true form, was spinning away from the funny little building with its machines and tubes and wires and sickly mammals. The being that had once been divided into so many tiny pieces, each making sense of itself with a human form, could feel the wide sky above beckoning, beckoning. They gratefully stretched up to meet it.

The sea was like the sky. The being didn't know where that thought had come from but it paused their ascent. Back in the cramped space of the hospital room with the bad stinging smells and the sound of animal fear, the being heard an echo of something which it couldn't name. And then it could. The word came tumbling back along with the sensation. A feeling. It was remembering feeling, and with that memory came knowledge. They saw the boy in the chair and rememembered his pain. They remembered his yearning for a different life. They saw the broken boy in the bed and knew they could fix it. Outside this room, and this building with its ailing lifeforms, there were thousands of different creatures. Some were soulless and hungry, some calm, some crackling with energy and desire. Thousands of sparks of light, like the stars in the cosmos, but crying out in pain. What difference did one make? They couldn't remember why it had mattered. The stars were calling them home. Back to peace and beauty. They stretched, ready to leave the filthy rock. But first...

Mal wasn't sure if he was asleep or awake. The plasticised surface of the hospital chair changed. He felt a rougher texture, more like material against his skin, and now he was lying down horizontally, not sat up in a chair. He felt a weight across his legs and reached down to find a blanket folded there. He pulled it over himself, like a child home from school with the chickenpox. He'd never had the chickenpox. Euan had got it, and Dad had said he would get it, too, but he never did. He'd watched Euan get hundreds of itchy red spots and he'd wanted them too. He hadn't cared that Euan was sick and that he complained incessantly about the rash and the scratching. He'd wanted them. Always wanted to be just like Euan.

When Mal opened his eyes, the room had grown dark. He was in the living room of his flat and, for a moment, he didn't understand why that was strange. Had he been somewhere else?

He must have been unconscious for a long time, he knew that. His neck was stiff from the way he had been lying. It had been a deep and dreamless sleep, and he was on the sofa. He cursed himself for falling asleep there when his bedroom was only a few feet away. He swung his feet off the sofa and stood up, not noticing when a green and white pebble fell from the cushions onto the floor. He kicked it under the sofa with his foot as he walked to the window. It was early evening but fully dark and he paused at the window for a moment, looking at the orange glow of the street lights and the bright yellow of the car headlights moving down the road outside. He pulled the thin curtains shut and then went to check that his front door was locked, although, after he had done so, he wasn't sure why.

He rubbed a hand over his stubbled chin, trying to shake the weird dream-feeling. He went into the kitchen and flipped the switch on the kettle. Then he put the grill on to make some cheese on toast. It was gone seven in the evening but he couldn't remember what he had been doing before he had fallen asleep. He sliced cheese and got out a plate. He was following a routine, a normal night in, but something felt odd. It wasn't the blanket on the sofa, although he didn't remember having one before. Maybe it was the smell in the air, like burnt matches and ozone, like sea air on a warm, blowy day. He closed his eyes for a few moments and then looked around, trying to see the room afresh, to put his finger on what had changed. Had there been someone here? Before he fell asleep? He had the feeling he hadn't been alone. There had been a girl, he was almost sure.

The smell of burning came from the kitchen and he rescued the bread he'd put under the grill and scraped the charcoal into the sink. He put cheese on the non-burned side and put it back under the heat. His phone rang. It was Euan's number on the caller display and he spoke as soon as Mal picked up. 'Pub?'

Euan's voice was strong and familiar. It was so good to hear, and it chased away the last of the strange feeling.

Mal smiled as he asked, 'I thought you weren't going to drink on week nights anymore?'

'Aye,' Euan said. 'But it's Thursday. That's nearly the weekend.'

'Okay. Half an hour?'

'Magic,' Euan said. 'See you in the Hart.'

For a moment Mal thought there was a reason he shouldn't go to the Grassmarket, but then the feeling passed. He ate his cheese on toast with brown sauce drizzled over the top. He drank a pint of water. Got his wallet and his keys and zipped up a hoodie. A strange thought crossed his mind: it was amazing that Euan was up and about. It was a miracle. They had to celebrate. He stopped dead, his keys in his hand. What a weird thought. What the hell was wrong with him? And then he remembered; he'd been dreaming about when they were kids and Euan had had the chickenpox. Euan had been really poorly with it, been off school for weeks. He shook his head, laughing at himself. That had been fifteen years ago. Euan was the strongest, healthiest person he knew.

As he opened the door, the birds that had been circling the ceiling flew through the gap and down the stairs. Mal didn't notice.

The End

YOUR NEXT READ?

Enjoyed The Lost Girls? You might like Sarah Painter's exciting new paranormal mystery series, Crow Investigations. The first book, The Night Raven, is out now.

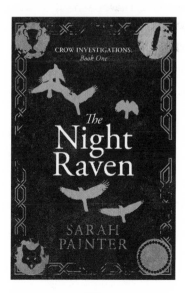

ACKNOWLEDGMENTS

Books are always a team effort and, as ever, The Lost Girls would not exist without the support of my family, friends and fabulous agent.

Huge thanks to Sallyanne Sweeney, and Holly and David Painter for reading early drafts and encouraging me to keep going with this strange tale.

Thank you to the listeners of The Worried Writer podcast and my writing friends for keeping me (mostly!) sane, especially Clodagh, Keris, and Nadine. Extra hugs to Sally Calder for the wine and nibbles!

Thank you to Serena Clarke for the fabulous copy-editing and Stuart Bache for the perfect cover design. You are both brilliant!

I am deeply grateful for my wonderful ARC team who gave me invaluable encouragement, spotted mistakes, and asked brilliant questions. In particular, thanks to: Matthew Dashper-Hughes, Beth Farrar,

Karen Heenan, Jenni Gudgeon, Ali Cowieson, Tricia Singleton, Paula Searle and Dave Wood.

Also, thanks to Mel MacLeod for the French advice and surname inspiration.

Finally, my eternal love and gratitude to Holly, James and Dave. I couldn't do this without you.

ABOUT THE AUTHOR

Before writing books, Sarah Painter worked as a free-lance magazine journalist, blogger and editor, combining this 'career' with amateur child-wrangling (AKA motherhood).

Sarah lives in rural Scotland with her children and husband. She drinks too much tea, loves the work of Joss Whedon, and is the proud owner of a writing shed.

Head to the website below to sign-up to the Sarah Painter Books VIP group. It's absolutely free and you'll get book release news, giveaways and exclusive FREE stuff!

geni.us/SarahPainterBooks